"Powe   wind ey
throug   want me you
want to reach for a flak jacket and glance over your shoulder for
surveillance, even as you're marvelling at its abiding humanity."

Dan Fesperman, author of *Lie in the Dark*

"One rarely finds Iraqis in American fiction except as Orientalist
stereotypes or objects of political desires and fantasies. *Baghdad
Central* is unique in this respect. Its Iraqis are subjects with agency
and humanity. Colla knows the cultural and political topography
very well. The chaos and cacophony of the American occupation
are captured vividly. The narrative is smart and smooth. This is an
intense and well-written novel. A pleasure to read."

**Sinan Antoon, author of *The Baghdad Blues*
and *The Corpse Washer***

"A gripping tale of mystery and intrigue in the claustrophobic,
morally treacherous world of post-invasion Baghdad, an environ-
ment where relationships can detonate as readily as car bombs.
This is a compelling noir crime novel told from inside Iraqi society
that lays bare the easy slide from personal to political treachery,
where every crime is also a national wound. A great read!"

**Jenny White, author of *The Winter Thief*
and others in the Kamil Pasha series**

"Just when you think that nothing in the overcrowded crime field
can surprise you any more, along comes a writer like Elliott Colla
who takes the genre by the throat and shakes it vigorously. *Baghdad
Central* is a rich and allusive piece of writing, informed by the
writer's experience in both the Middle East and Washington. Its
authenticity is matched by a masterly command of the mechanics
of suspense."

Barry Forshaw, *Crime Time*

Elliott Colla divides his time between Washington DC and the Middle East. He teaches Arabic literature at Georgetown University. This is his first novel.

BAGHDAD CENTRAL

Elliott Colla

BITTER LEMON PRESS
LONDON

BITTER LEMON PRESS

First published in the United Kingdom in 2014 by
Bitter Lemon Press, 37 Arundel Gardens,
London W11 2LW

www.bitterlemonpress.com

A CIP record for this book is available from the
British Library

ISBN 978–1–908524–25-6
EBook ISBN 978–1–908524–26-3

Typeset by Tetragon, London
Printed and bound in Great Britain
by CPI Group (UK) Ltd, Croydon, CR0 4YY

To Umm Mrouj, as ever.

Heroism does not always mean going on the offensive. It can just as well entail patience or staying put. Bravery does not always mean raising a fist at the enemy before you. More often than not, it entails confronting the enemy within. A true hero fights against his own despair and love of comfort.

MICHEL AFLAQ

April 2003

In the chaos of retreat, a few stand and fight. Some fall back, some take the fight to another time and place. Some remain at their stations to wait and listen.

We sip tea. We watch television. We check our weapons again. Then we change clothes and go home. Entire crowds of men vanish. Some will slip across lines, others across borders.

After days of battering, an eerie quiet begins to hold. They will arrive tomorrow at the latest. They are already here in the suburbs. There is fighting in al-Dora by now. Some say it has reached Firdos and Jihad.

No one is surprised by the men in trucks or by the order to evacuate. Everyone knew they would be coming on a day like today. The instructions are easy to follow. The men in the records office finished their job a week ago and never came back. These men begin unloading boxes from trucks, then drag them into the building. Only a handful of us are left, bewildered. We hang around outside. Then one by one we start to walk away, down the sidewalks and under the arcades on Khulafa Street until we disappear for good.

Behind thick concrete walls, the first explosions sound like thunder. There is a crack of glass as windows splinter in the morning sun. Then silence. Eventually, the silence retreats, though only softly at first. It grows into a roar. Fires burning deep, somewhere out of sight. Scorching winds whipping through empty hallways and offices, corridors and closets. Then from the empty windows, a storm of burning files, folders, and forms erupting into the sky. The flames eventually burn themselves out.

When the first American missiles hit, Baghdad Central Police Station is already an empty shell.

RED ZONE

...Full members of the Baath Party holding the ranks of Regional Command Member, Branch Member, Section Member and Group Member are hereby removed from their positions and banned from future employment in the public sector. These senior Party members shall be evaluated for criminal conduct or threat to the security of the Coalition. Those suspected of criminal conduct shall be investigated and, if deemed a threat to security or a flight risk, detained or placed under house arrest. Displays in government buildings or public spaces of the image or likeness of Saddam Hussein or other readily identifiable members of the former regime or of symbols of the Baath Party or the former regime are hereby prohibited. Rewards shall be made available for information leading to the capture of senior members of the Baath Party and individuals complicit in the crimes of the former regime. The Administrator of the Coalition Provisional Authority or his designees may grant exceptions to the above guidance on a case by case basis...

COALITION PROVISIONAL
AUTHORITY ORDER NO. 1
16 MAY 2003

Sunday Evening
23 November 2003

"I'd like to, but I can't. I'm not a detective."

Nidal stares at his brother-in-law as if he's never seen him before. "So what are you?"

"You know as well as anybody."

"You work for the police and they call you Inspector – what else am I supposed to think?"

"Worked. Past tense. And it wasn't like that. I sat at a desk. I did paperwork and filing. I read reports about investigations. Then I read the informers' reports they were based on. Then I wrote my own reports and filed them alongside all the other reports."

"Do I have to draft a report for you?"

"Look, sorry. Let me think about it."

Nidal looks down into his teacup, then across the room at the place on the wall where the picture of the Great Leader used to hang. Muhsin Khadr al-Khafaji waves the *chaichi* over and orders another tea. Around them, pairs of men sit at low wooden tables, sipping tea, smoking, and staying up late like they'd do on any other Ramadan night. Some roll dice and slap backgammon pieces back and forth. In one corner, old men play cards. Their faces show no emotion, just intensity. Small piles of bills sit in the middle of one table.

Nidal watches the men playing their game. Khafaji watches Nidal's stiff profile until the man begins to sob and heave. Khafaji claps a hand on his massive shoulder. After a while, Nidal leans back in his chair and wipes his eyes with a thick peasant hand. Only now does Khafaji notice that Nidal isn't wearing his gold cross. They used to tease him about it all the time. Now it was gone. Khafaji was going to cry too if they didn't change the subject.

"OK. I'll help you. But tell me again from the beginning."

"One night last week Sawsan didn't come back from work, and now Maha sits at home and cries all the time. She's going out of her mind. You hear stories and you imagine the worst. After everything that's happened, we were thinking we would leave. But now we can't."

"Why didn't you tell me when it happened?"

"Because we don't know what happened and we still don't. She just hasn't come home is all we know."

"When was this?"

"Thursday."

"Anyone call?"

"…?"

"Anyone call asking for money? Telling you to meet them somewhere? Did you contact anyone else?"

Nidal grabs Khafaji's arm and raises his voice. "Brother, who the hell are we going to call? You're the only police we know."

"I quit. And anyway, there's no police now."

"You're the one with all the connections in the Party."

"That was years ago. And there's no Party now."

"So all we're left with is you, I guess."

Khafaji struggles to look optimistic. He mumbles, "I can

try to help." He clears his throat and starts over. "Tell me the rest again."

The third time he tells it, Nidal's story is still threadbare. A few broken strands tied in a knot. Sawsan graduated in August from Mustansiriyya University. Institute of Management and Administration. Wanted to study programing but ended up studying finance. The family had met a few of her friends from the university but didn't know much about who they were, or how to contact them. After graduation, Sawsan started working. As a consultant, she said. Helped out with the household expenses, especially since Nidal's job vanished. She worked for a professor at the university.

"It is a good job. Sawsan even had a driver to pick her up every morning and drop her every evening."

"Write down any of the names you know. Classmates. Teachers. Anything. I'll see what I can find."

Nidal pulls out a piece of paper and starts to write.

An argument erupts at the card table in the back. The entire café goes silent. Cups are spilled. Glass splinters on the ground. Hands and fists lunge out at piles of bills. A scrappy old man with a week's beard grabs the edge of his *dishdasha* and hobbles off toward the door, yelling something about mothers and cunts. The rest of the men call after him, taunting him and laughing at the mess. A waiter arrives with a broom and wet rag. Nidal and Khafaji look at one another again.

"How are things in the new apartment?" Khafaji asks. Like so many Palestinians, they'd been driven from their homes during the first weeks of the invasion.

"Baladiyat was our home. Our friends were there. Our life was there. Thank God we had Mikhail and the rest of the family. But Saadun will never be home."

"You're managing?"

"You'll see how we're managing Tuesday when you and Mrouj come over. We're crammed – nine of us in two rooms. It's bad enough when there's water and electricity. But when there isn't…" Nidal's voice trails off. "But that's not the issue any more," he says. "It's the attacks. They're not random. They know who to go after and when. We're lucky we left when we did. Remember the Jabrawis? They tried to stay on. The rest of us got the message."

For a moment, Nidal tries to smile. Then his face collapses.

"Look, Muhsin. We lost everything and thought we could adapt. But this is different. As soon as Sawsan comes back, we're leaving. Have you heard about what's happening at the stadium? There are thousands of people living in tents there. Most of our building is there, I think. And then there are tens of thousands of others stuck on the border now. We're getting out before that happens to us."

He pauses and sips his tea. His eyes remain locked on Khafaji's. "We're eligible for a Canadian visa, but we have to apply in Jordan. We're going to stay with cousins in Amman while we wait."

"Amman? Really?"

Nidal knocks Khafaji's shoulder playfully. "Lighten up, Muhsin. We're Palestinians. We're good at getting expelled." Khafaji sees his wife's emerald eyes again in the eyes of her brother. And also Suheir's kindness and beauty.

Nidal is a man whose entire life has been spent here in this city. Suddenly a foreign army invades and he becomes a foreigner. This city belongs to him more than it does to me, Khafaji thinks. Suheir and Nidal's parents were driven out of Jaffa. When they arrived in Baghdad in 1949, they decided to raise their children as if they had always lived here. Typical cosmopolitans, making a good life out of catastrophes. And as the years went by, Baghdad really was home. Over time they came to realize it mostly belonged to the clans from Tikrit. But still, those Tikritis were kind enough to leave scraps for everyone else. And they could never fence in all of the river. Maybe that's why people never left.

When Suheir died, Khafaji told Nidal to get out while they could. The sanctions were just beginning to hurt, but most people figured out how to adapt and survive. It didn't occur to Khafaji to leave until it was too late. He would have left with Suheir if he had known how sick she was. Like everyone else, he thought that things couldn't get any worse. "Patience and strength," everyone said. "Steadfastness and resistance." Like most slogans, they taste bitter when you put them back in your mouth later.

Ten years ago they could have gone. Khafaji could have left with Suheir and Mrouj and started over, maybe in Sweden. But somehow they believed that oranges and carrot juice could cure cancer. They needed real medicine, but there was no chance of getting that.

Khafaji looks up and tries to sound strong. "Nidal, we all should have left long ago."

They order another round and sit in silence. The men in the room continue drinking tea, talking to one another, reading papers, and rolling dice.

When Khafaji looks up, he sees Nidal pulling out crisp 1,000-dinar notes to pay the *chaichi*. Khafaji starts to argue about paying the bill, but it's too late.

Khafaji continues to protest until Nidal hugs him. "Next one's on you, brother. We'll see you Tuesday for lunch? Maha's already started cooking. Come as early as you can and spend the whole day with us. Thanks for agreeing to help."

"It might just be me for Eid."

Nidal pauses. "How's Mrouj?"

"Still the same. No better, no worse."

"God protect her."

"What's God got to do with it?"

"It's just how we speak, Muhsin. You know that."

Khafaji scowls as he looks at the scrap of paper in his hand. He sees only one name.

"Zubeida Rashid? Who's this?"

Nidal shrugs. "Sawsan's professor. The one she works for."

"A picture of Sawsan might help jog people's memory."

Nidal reaches into his wallet. "I've got one from graduation."

He hands Khafaji a photograph of Sawsan in black robes, holding roses and a diploma. Khafaji stares at it. A beautiful girl of twenty-two. Olive-skinned, with a long, straight nose, raven-black hair and stone-green eyes. A conspicuous beauty mark to the right of her mouth.

The spitting image of her aunt Suheir when she was that age.

May 2003

The morning air was already hot when he burst in the door. He threw the bundle of clothes and papers on the floor and walked past me without saying a word. I followed him upstairs into the bedroom and watched him rifle through the wardrobe. He never said a word. He pulled out every bit of clothing he could find. Shirts. Ties. Slacks. Jackets. Caps. His jaw was clenched so hard I thought his teeth might break.

Finally, he turned to look at me like he just noticed I was there. "I'm sorry. I'm in a hurry."

"Can I help?"

"Check through the pockets and make sure there's nothing in them."

"What are you doing?"

He grimaced. "We need to get rid of it all."

For the next hour, we collected everything. Tie clips, medals, belts and shoes. Then we went through desks and cabinets, collecting scraps of paper. Identity cards. Passports. Birth certificates. Diplomas. Commendations. We heaped everything onto the bed.

He told me to get a suitcase and as many bags as I could find. When I came back, I saw that he had made two piles. He put one into the suitcase. He stuffed the other into plastic bags. He went to the kitchen and got the kerosene.

"I'll be right back," is all he said when he went out. He looked so strange with all those bags.

When he came back later, he did not look at all relieved. He walked past me again and went upstairs. When I walked into the room, I saw him staring at the fire. Thick plumes of acrid smoke flew up in the wind. I thought the little date palm might catch fire, but the flames died as quickly as they had started. Finally, he turned toward me and tried to smile for the first time that day.

"What's happening?" I asked.

"I don't know."

"What are we going to do?"

"I don't know."

"We can wait."

"Yes. We'll stay put until things become clearer."

I had never seen him cry before.

Monday
24 November 2003

Khafaji wakes up and walks down the hall to Mrouj's room. He quietly opens the door. She hasn't moved at all from where she was when he peeked in on her late last night.

He puts the kettle on, and goes searching for cigarettes.

Khafaji never fasted during Ramadan, and this year was no exception. He never wanted to be counted among those who fasted in order to feast. And he certainly never wanted to be someone who fasted because a book or old men told him to.

Ramadan meant a month of drinking morning tea in complete silence. A month of swallowing the smoke of his first cigarette and hoping his neighbors didn't notice. A month of stealing through the kitchen so that no one would hear. Only a fast-breaker knows the racket a pot of tea can make during daylight hours. The whole building can hear you if you don't do it right. You rest the kettle gently on the stove and cringe when the gas flame begins to hiss. You wince every time the spoon clinks against the glass as you stir the sugar. And still, no one's ever fooled. The neighbors never say anything, but they know.

All Khafaji can find is an empty pack of Royales, and a stale old pack of Sumer 100s. He lights a cigarette and waits.

With the teapot, cups and sugar bowl on a tray, he shuffles through the sitting room and over to the balcony as he does every morning.

As he does every morning, he stares at the disaster, at the charred mess of the balcony. And he remembers the August morning when the whole block shook. Windows shattered up and down the entire side of the building. Even the paint on the walls seemed to catch fire. As he does every morning, Khafaji imagines what would have happened if he had been sitting on the balcony drinking tea on that morning.

The villa across the street bore the brunt of the attack. It is now nothing but a concrete shell. Its gardens, buried under piles of debris, are a local garbage dump. Cement dust turned every tree on the street snowy white. The green won't return again until the first rains. Things are quieter now. Since that day, the windows have been shuttered with cardboard and tape and wood. Since that day, the balcony has been abandoned.

Khafaji puts down the tray in the sitting room, lights a cigarette and has his first sip of tea for the day. He picks up the photograph Nidal gave him. Khafaji is looking at Sawsan's picture, but remembering another girl. Another time. Suheir at the university. Final exams. Holding all those books. Not textbooks, but books. Old books. Books she insisted on buying from dusty shops on Mutanabbi Street. She waves her hands wildly whenever she talks, and the books teeter back and forth. *I am listening to her words but looking at the books, hanging in the air. I am looking at the skin on her arms. Her bare shoulders. I can't help staring. She notices me and stops speaking. She smiles, then runs over to her friends. Time stops. Suheir stops. She turns back to look at me. Smiling with her whole body.*

Khafaji lights another cigarette and looks at the photograph one more time. It is always so difficult to remain in the present. Now more than ever. He looks at his niece and tries not to see Suheir. He looks at the present and tries not to see the past. Eventually he succeeds.

When he finishes the pot, he puts it back inside and spends a couple minutes cleaning up boards and sticks. Last week, he cleaned up most of the broken glass. At this rate, the balcony might be ready for rehabitation by the time the American occupation comes to an end. Whenever that will be.

Khafaji starts to wash his face in the sink just as the water goes out. He dresses slowly, then cleans the kitchen slowly, hoping that if he takes long enough Mrouj will wake up. Eventually, he gives up and goes outside. Before he leaves, he rifles through the drawers in the back of his wardrobe. He picks up his Glock 19 and checks the clip, then thinks again. He picks up his badge and puts it in his jacket pocket. Less trouble. He smokes one last cigarette before going out the door, knowing it'll be his last until he gets home.

Khafaji listens to his neighbors as he climbs down the stairs. In May, the building emptied out. Everyone else left. But now, somehow, it is full again. A complete change of residents. Terrifying, the process was also slow and surprisingly orderly.

Khafaji was at home the day they tried the lock. They were almost in before he stopped them. He never saw their faces. He only talked to them through the thick door. What he said made them go away, but probably not forever. It was enough to make him want to stay at home all the time, which was something he wanted to do anyway these days. There were so few reasons for leaving the house, and so many for staying.

Khafaji walks over to Kahramana Square to catch a taxi. As he waits, he studies the bronze statue of the heroine pouring boiling oil over the forty thieves. In this new version, he thinks, it's the oil that the thieves came for. So how will you rescue us now, Kahramana?

A taxi stops and he gets in. Khafaji tells the driver to take him to the main gates of Mustansiriyya University. Khafaji takes the paper from his coat pocket and studies the name Nidal handed him. Zubeida Rashid. It sounds familiar. He thinks back to his years in the General Security Directorate. But there's so little to remember if there's no desire to remember.

Khafaji looks at his watch, and thinks about last night's story. A fool's errand, with checkpoints.

He looks out the window. At the first checkpoint, the traffic is not too bad. Hidden behind concrete blocks, bulletproof vests and thick helmets, American soldiers wave them through.

The streets are more crowded than before these days. More traffic. There are the old Brazilian Jettas, the Mercedes, the Audis and Peugeots. But there are new ones too. The driver sees the expression on Khafaji's face and guesses. "That's an Opel."

"They have other names, don't they?"

"Of course. That's a Jimsy." He points to a huge GMC. "Bikab, you know. There's a Monika. A Duck. That was an Alligator that just passed by."

"Too many to count."

"They flooded the country with them. Lucky for us, we get to name them however we want."

As they sit in traffic, the driver continues with his list: Hyundais. Land Rovers. Explorers. Suburbans. Khafaji remembers another time when Baghdad was flooded with new cars that were used cars. It was late August 1990, when suddenly American sedans began to appear everywhere. Their license plates were stripped, but everyone knew they were from Kuwait. Those cars didn't last long.

At each petrol station, massive queues turn roads inside out. Khafaji looks at his watch again.

The driver adjusts the mirror and says, "God willing, we'll be there in an hour." The driver decides to put an end to the conversation with a tape of Quranic recitation. At first Khalil al-Husari's voice is faint. Khafaji cannot make out what they are listening to. The driver turns up the volume. The Sura of the Merciful fills their ears. And eyes, to Khafaji's annoyance.

"Quite a stereo."

"A sound system," the driver smiles back.

Dashboard lights flash and dance with each verse, with each change of pitch. Khafaji closes his eyes and tries to forget the visuals. *Which is it, of the favors of your Lord, that ye deny?*

The third checkpoint delays them twenty minutes, and the interpreter makes both Khafaji and the driver get out of the car before they can go.

At the front gates of the university, Khafaji pays the driver and hands him two cigarettes as a tip. The man nods and puts them in the glove compartment for after sunset.

At first, the guardhouse looks empty. As Khafaji walks through, a voice from inside calls out, "Where are you going?"

Khafaji walks over and flashes his badge. The other man turns around without saying another word. Khafaji looks around at the courtyard inside. What he sees makes him wonder whether he wasted his time. Not a campus, but a grove of burnt eucalyptus trees, a field of dead grass and acres of broken tile and concrete. As he walks inside, he spies a group of workmen filling sacks with dirt and bricks. Khafaji walks over and asks, "Excuse me, where is the Institute of Management and Administration?"

Only one man appears to have heard him. He looks up at Khafaji's knees and shakes his head. Then, with his pickaxe, he points at a small path. Khafaji thanks him and walks until he finds himself along a row of identical concrete buildings, each suffering an acute case of .50 caliber acne. On one building, marked "Fine Arts", each empty window is framed by black and gray smudges. Five floors that, one day, went up in flames. The building looks like a monumental composition, a giant, conceptualist sculpture.

Khafaji walks over and steps inside. He looks up, through a web of broken concrete and twisted rebar. A sheet of frozen plastic spills out from somewhere above. Like a cascade of iridescent lava. Not a window remains, not a door – only shell guts. Khafaji looks down to see a floor cracked and cratered.

Beyond a long reflecting pool, Khafaji sees another building that might be the one he is looking for. The dead date palms and the abandoned pickup in the water suggest the pond is not ornamental. Khafaji walks around the water toward the building. By the main entrance, water gushes from a broken pipe. White froth rushes over broken marble steps, across the walkway, and into the dirty pond. Khafaji tries to step over the water and curses when his leather shoes get soaked.

With its ordinary concrete walls, the Institute does not stand out from other buildings. On the outside, it's pockmarked like everything else.

But when Khafaji walks inside, he sees a different world. Freshly mopped marble floors. People coming in and out, even though classes are not in session. Some clutching folders. Others briefcases. And everyone with a cellphone. The sight of pressed suits makes him hesitate. He stares at shiny shoes. He stares at the workers in boiler suits and plastic sandals. At coils of wire unspooled. He stares at the busyness. He stares too long.

Khafaji feels a heavy hand on his arm. "Excuse me, Uncle. Can I help you?"

Khafaji turns to see a tall man dressed in a familiar way. Wearing the usual cheap suit. The usual scowl. The usual thick neck and bad tie. Regimes change, but plain clothes never do.

Somehow, Khafaji manages to smile down while looking up at the man. "This is the Institute of Management and Administration, isn't it?"

The man's hand is a heavy iron shovel and now it's digging into Khafaji's shoulder.

"That's right, Uncle. This is a place of business. I'm going to have to ask you to come outside. Go to the front gate if you need directions."

"I don't think you understand," Khafaji says, flashing the badge in his pocket.

The man attempts to grab it, but Khafaji pulls it away. "You can look. But you're going to have to wash your hands if you want to touch it."

Years ago, it had taken Khafaji months to figure out what exactly a cop's authority could be in a police state. Compared to Military Intelligence, General Security had been second-class. But compared to both, civilian police were much lower. The only way to make up for this, Khafaji learned, was never to let on you were merely civilian. And it wasn't that hard to fool thick-necked country boys from the north.

Khafaji looks up, and sees the man staring in disbelief. Or anger.

Khafaji wastes no time. "I'm here to see Professor Zubeida Rashid."

"Then you should make an appointment, Uncle."

"Appointment, sir."

"Don't overdo it, old man. I don't know who you are, but I know your better days are behind you. You should check the expiration date on that badge before you try to use it again."

Khafaji doesn't move. The man goes on. "Prof. Zubeida is a busy woman. Call her secretary. Maybe she'll make time to see you, but I doubt it." Before he finishes his sentence, the man's already signaled to other guards to come over and help him.

"Listen, she'll want to see me. It's about someone who works for her. A girl."

The man laughs. "It's always about a girl, isn't it? Tell me something I don't know, old man."

"Her name's Sawsan Faraj. It won't take much time."

The grin on the man's face turns sour. "Wait outside on the steps."

The guard at the door pretends not to watch Khafaji. The man returns minutes later. He makes Khafaji go first as they climb the marble staircase. Each individual step has been carefully mopped.

A young secretary opens the office door and Khafaji finds himself alone on an overstuffed couch. Half an hour goes by, but no one comes. Khafaji wishes he had brought his cigarettes, then thinks again. A buzzer sounds and the secretary takes Khafaji into a luxury office. This might be the only room in Iraq with no trace of concrete. Everything is wood and silk and glass. The walls, the desk, and even the floor and ceiling are oak, the edges softened by silk curtains and carpets. Crystal trinkets decorate a coffee table in the middle of the room.

A raspy voice calls out from behind the desk, "Yes?"

"I'm here to see Professor Zubeida Rashid."

"Yes, that's me. Who are you?" A laugh sits on her lips in the shape of a smirk.

"I'm… It's about…" Khafaji stumbles. "Is there something funny?"

Her smile begins to crack around the edges. "You look like someone I know. Or used to know. I'm sorry."

"My name's Muhsin Khafaji. As I told the fellow at the entrance, I am here regarding someone who works for you. My niece, Sawsan."

"Sawsan…?"

"Sawsan Faraj. I think she was a student of yours at the Institute. She has been working for you since…"

"Of, course. Sawsan is your niece? She's like a daughter to me. What would you like to know?"

"Well, anything really. Her family is worried. They haven't seen her in a number of days. She hasn't called. I was hoping I would walk in here and find her."

Her fingers tremble as they reach for a pack of cigarettes. "It upsets me to hear this. I didn't know. I don't know…" Her eyes catch Khafaji's again, then flicker away.

"You're Hassan's brother, aren't you?"

Now it's Khafaji's fingers that tremble. "You know Hassan?"

They spent so much of their lives apart that Khafaji is always surprised to remember he has a brother. Not so much an actual brother, but a memory usually buried deep. Until someone else digs it up again, like this woman right now. Khafaji stares absently at the crystal figurines on the table in front of him. A ballerina. An elephant. A lion. A horse. A poodle. A giraffe. A clown holding balloons. A whole crystal circus. Ready to break.

Khafaji looks up again. When he catches her eye, he wishes he hadn't. Golden eyes, like almonds. Arched eyebrows and long dark lashes. Dark skin and wine-red lips. She smiles and pearls flash in coral settings. A minute goes by as they sit looking at each other.

The professor finally lights her cigarette. She inhales and turns toward the window.

"People have always told us that we look alike…" Khafaji's voice trails off.

She puts down her cigarette. She reaches into her purse and takes out a handkerchief. She wipes her nose so gracefully that Khafaji wishes she'd do it again.

Khafaji looks at the ceiling, then the walls of the office. For the first time since he set foot in the room, he notices the portrait of Abd al-Karim Qasim. "Mercy on him," he murmurs to himself.

She squints at Khafaji for a moment, then leans forward. "Would you like a cup of tea, Muhsin? You're not fasting, are you? You don't look hungry."

Without waiting, she is speaking into an intercom. They wait silently until the secretary enters with a porcelain tea service. Not a word. She hands a cup of tea to Khafaji and points to the sugar bowl.

"I met Hassan at Exeter. I was just a grad student in civil engineering. He was the famous professor in the English department. The great Iraqi genius. The brilliant scholar of T.S. Eliot. He had an English wife, but it was me he was in love with. When his first son was born, he said he would leave her. But then he changed his mind. 'We have to be modern about these things,' is how he used to put it. 'We have to be modern.' Being modern with him dragged on for years. I only began to wake up to how awful it was much later. He wasn't going to leave his wife. At least, not for me. By that time, I wasn't the only other woman in his life. He rather enjoyed being modern with everyone around him. But I didn't. Being modern hurt too much."

Khafaji looks down at his old clothes and wishes he'd worn something nicer.

"I finished my degree and left England for good. I would have stayed. I wanted to. But I didn't want to live anywhere near him. I didn't want to run into him. I didn't want to hear about him from friends. So I came home. To the one place where I could be certain I'd never see him."

She lights another cigarette and looks at Khafaji. She tosses the pack onto her desk, and the lighter beside it.

"Go ahead, you've already broken your fast for today."

Khafaji laughs. "You'd have to meet me earlier in the day if you want to help me break my fast."

She raises an eyebrow. "You know, Hassan used to talk about you, 'my brother Muhsin'. You and I should have met long ago. You were the person I wanted to see most when I first came back. I don't know why, since I didn't know you. Still, I wanted to see for myself if Hassan really had a brother. The poet, right?"

Khafaji turns red. "Failed poet. It's been years since I wrote anything that rhymed."

"I'm glad you found me, Mr Muhsin. So, you're here. And now finally we meet. You do look like him."

Her smile evaporates in another cloud of smoke and she looks out the window.

"About my niece. Sawsan. She's not here, is she?"

"No. Suzy is usually working somewhere else."

"Suzy?"

"Sawsan. Sometimes days go by without us meeting in person. We talk all the time on the phone, so I don't even think about it."

"When was the last time you saw her?"

She thinks for a minute before answering, "Last week. Thursday maybe."

"Have you spoken since?"

"I'm not sure. No."

"Do you know where Sawsan is right now?"

"On any given day, the work might take her anywhere. Just because I don't know where she is doesn't mean anything."

"Her family's worried, though. She has been gone for days, Professor. Could you tell me what Sawsan does for you?"

"Mr Muhsin, I would like to tell you everything. Her university studies made her particularly valuable. But for security reasons, I can't tell you any more than that."

Khafaji nods, though he doesn't like the way this is going. "It might help the family relax if they knew what she was doing for you."

"I don't need to tell you how dangerous it is. Every day, things are getting worse. And right now scholars and teachers are especially at risk."

"Is that because you're so smart?"

She squints at Khafaji before smiling again. "No. It's because we are the conscience of the nation, Muhsin. I don't say that to brag. I'm just repeating what our enemies say. If they can get rid of intellectuals, then they can wipe the slate of history clean. They can't build their Iraq until we're out of the way."

She lights another cigarette and takes a long drag. She throws the pack on the desk again.

Khafaji leans forward and asks, "Professor, I am not sure I understand what this has to do —"

The professor interrupts him: "Should we just give our country to the exiles? Like hell. We're the ones who stayed and suffered. Damn if I'm going to let them sell our country to foreign oil companies. And damn if I'm going to let the ayatollahs take our country away from us either." She sees the look in Khafaji's eyes. "Here, have another."

She slides the pack over to Khafaji. He fumbles for a cigarette. "So, how will we defend ourselves? We have to find allies. Which means, we have to create allies. Old enemies might become new friends. Old friends might become new enemies."

She exhales and another cloud of smoke fills the room. "Relationships might become complicated. Does that make someone like me a collaborator, Muhsin?"

Khafaji nods, then corrects himself. "Of course not." His tone is too emphatic.

She shakes her head and puts out her cigarette. "You've seen the security outside. We don't hire guns because we're VIPs. No. We hire them because we have to. Because there are people who know that for every intellectual they murder, ten others will leave of their own accord. Half of them think that when they get rid of us, Iraq will magically become a mosque. The other half think it will turn into a gas station or a minimart. They're both right, actually. Without us, this country doesn't have a chance."

"Professor Zubeida, is there anything you can tell me about Sawsan that might help me find her? You provide a driver for her, right? Can I talk to him?"

When she looks at Khafaji again, he imagines that she is speaking to someone else, probably Hassan. "Suzy is like my own daughter. I'll call the driver and put you in touch with him. Please convey my greetings and concern to her family."

She takes a fountain pen from her desk and asks, "What's your cellphone number?"

"Take down my landline."

As he rattles off the numbers, Khafaji looks down at the empty porcelain teacup in his hand. The professor frowns as she copies them. Minutes go by as he wonders what will happen next. Nothing does. Eventually, he sets his cup on the tray and stands up.

"Thanks for your time."

As he walks out the door, she calls out, "We will be in touch soon, Hassan." Khafaji doesn't correct her. He doesn't even mind.

June 2003

They came in the middle of the night. It was hot. The electricity was out, so we had our windows wide open. I heard them when they pulled up in their pickup trucks. You could almost see them through the shutters. I tried to get a better look through the peephole, while waving the children to go back to sleep.

We were expecting it, it just took them longer to get to us.

Why are we here? We had nowhere else to go.

Those who could, left. Years ago.

Three men stayed downstairs at the entrance. The drivers turned off the engines and lights; you could barely make out the pickups. Two of them walked to one end of the street, a few more walked to the other end, then disappeared behind the heaps. With all their clicking and chirping, their radios sounded like little birds. There weren't any patrols in our district. Not that night. Not any night.

It was pitch dark. And their faces were covered. But still, you could see right through the masks they wore. I don't need to tell you who they were. A group of them climbed up, floor by floor. One of them stayed behind on each landing. Their flashlights went on and then off again. We held our breath as one of them knocked on doors with the butt of his rifle. No one opened. No one said a word.

Five men went up all the way to the third floor. Outside, you could hear the portable generators humming and coughing. Then there were a couple shots from down the street. I remember hearing a car's engine, another shot, and then silence. A long silence. It was like we suddenly remembered how hot it was, and we went back to fanning ourselves while we waited in that silence.

When they shouted, "Ibrahim Jabrawi, come out!" none of us was surprised. What surprised us was that he opened the door. Then a scuffle, cries and sobs. I wasn't close enough to hear what happened next, but the man next door heard everything. Ibrahim told them he would come with them. He asked them to leave his family in peace. Then all you could hear was the sound of bone and flesh on concrete.

You know how time stops when you get a shock? Well, that's what we felt as we sat there waiting in the darkness. For minutes. The whole building could feel the silence. It was like getting a shock. That silence was an electric wire lying on the ground.

They told me later that some revolvers are louder than rifles. But what would I know?

The children on the fourth floor began to cry right after the first shot. No one saw a thing, but that did not prevent us from seeing everything. Even those who kept their eyes closed tight saw it all. Those kids kept crying until the last shot, then the building went quiet.

As soon as we heard the pickups roar off, we lit lanterns and rushed over. We told the women to get towels and buckets of water. Not because it would do any good, but because we didn't want them to see five bodies swimming in a pool of blood. Two were so young that the blast severed their heads.

By the next afternoon, we all left and came here to the stadium. They say people moved into our apartments on the day we left. I don't know who's living there now and I don't care.

Monday Evening
24 November 2003

Eid Mubarak. There is much to be thankful for at this special Eid for Iraq. This Eid, Saddam the dictator has become Saddam the fugitive. This Eid, there is no Mukhaberat. This Eid, Iraqi schoolteachers earn enough to put food on the table. This Eid, for the first time ever, you know you are going to have a democracy – and you know exactly when you will have it.

ADDRESS OF L. PAUL BREMER
TO THE IRAQI PEOPLE

The electricity goes out just as he opens the door.

In the dark, Mrouj calls out, "Is that you, Baba? I'm getting the lamp."

Khafaji puts down his shopping bags and pauses.

"I got some cucumbers and yogurt, Mrouji."

The lights flicker on again and his daughter's silhouette floats into view. With unsteady hands, she holds onto the door frame.

"How do you feel?"

She hobbles across the floor, reaching for a chair, then a table. As she approaches, he sees the familiar smile on her face. Teeth like pearls. Eyes flashing like moonlight on the river.

"Still the same. I got up because I had to. I was getting sick of sitting in bed anyway."

"And?"

"A little blood, but not as much as before."

She is young, though her face doesn't give it away. He reaches out for her hand. Girl's hands, still soft. Outside, the call to prayers goes up from the mosque on the main street.

"Are you hungry, Baba? I can make dinner."

"Only if you eat with me."

"I'll try, Baba."

"Let's see what there is." Mrouj leans against her father, and the two of them shuffle across the rug then onto the cold tiles of the kitchen floor. They know the refrigerator is empty; they unplugged it finally last month. They look anyway. They open cupboards, pretending surprise when they find nothing but cans, cartons, packets and jars. Nothing that needed refrigeration, nothing that would spoil. Mackerel, tuna and sardines. Chickpeas and condensed milk. Tea and crackers and juice. Rice, sugar and powdered milk. Dried apricots, prunes and sour cherries. Thyme and sesame, cardamom and saffron. Dates, dried limes, apricots, almonds and walnuts. Pickled turnips, carrots, cauliflower and cucumbers. Briny white cheese and lemons. Pomegranate syrup and olive oil.

When Suheir was alive, the family ate well every day. No matter how bad things were, they always ate their late lunch together. But that was years ago. When Mrouj began to lose her appetite, Khafaji stopped eating too. Neither of them ever cooked anything more elaborate than a pot of tea or rice.

When they sit down to eat, Mrouj looks at the calendar and says, "Happy Eid, Baba. I can't believe it's here already."

"Happy Eid, Mrouj. I saw your uncle today. They're expecting us tomorrow."

"I wish I could. You go, Baba – for both of us."

"Did Sawsan ever talk to you about her work?"

"When, Baba? I haven't seen her since summer. Why do you ask?"

"I was just wondering."

"Invite them over, Baba. They could come on Friday. Tell Sawsan to come over in the morning. She can help me cook."

"I'll ask. It's been a long time since you made *fasanjan*. Would you make it?"

"Of course, Baba. Tell me something you like about Eid."

"I like that day at last goes back to being day and night to night. Everyone can finally go back to their routines. And this absurd cycle of abstaining and gorging ends."

When he sees the expression on Mrouj's face, Khafaji apologizes. "I also love seeing the children in their new clothes. That's something I'll never stop loving. Your mother always spent so much time buying just the right Eid clothes for you. We loved watching you parade around the neighborhood in them. You and Uday were so proud of your fancy new clothes."

Mrouj looks away. "Baba, can I take your plate?"

Mrouj's voice brings him back to the present. He looks down and sees the fork in his hand. He sees that his plate is now empty.

"No, I'll wait until you finish, Mrouj. Try to eat a little more."

She puts another cucumber into her mouth, but chews without enthusiasm. She drinks the rest of her yogurt, then wipes the smoky flavor from her lips. He looks outside to see the night drinking up shadows. He looks again at his watch as if it had something to tell him.

Mrouj insists on washing the dishes. Khafaji stands beside her and dries. Together, they listen to the neighbors talking and laughing. Families end their fasts so solemnly and quietly at first. But with each bite, the table becomes a feast, then a carnival. As he dries the last of the dishes, Khafaji listens to the cackles coming from across the way and the floor below, and then to the sound of televisions being turned on one by one in the neighboring apartments. Somewhere, behind the televised noise, Khafaji can hear another call to prayer. As he stacks plates and bowls in the cupboard, he listens also to a parade on the stairwell. Only when he is folding the dish towel does he notice that Mrouj is sitting at the kitchen table, her head in her hands.

"What's wrong, my love? Can I help you get up?"

"Baba, will you read to me?"

"Of course, my love. Let's get you to bed."

Khafaji helps his daughter to the bathroom and closes the door gently behind her. He waits down the hall for minutes as she tries to urinate. Mrouj washes her face, then opens the door. He looks at her, and she shakes her head. Together they shuffle down the dark hall. She lies down. He reaches over to turn on the light.

"Mrouji, what would you like to hear?"

"Something you like, Baba."

Khafaji walks back to the living room and takes a worn book from the shelf. When Mrouj sees the book in his hands, a puzzled look interrupts her grin. She closes her eyes as her father begins to read. Words go by, then stanzas.

Immortality, they said
And I found it in a shadow
That emerges from the shriveling of life
And flings itself in a leisurely way
On the graveyards
I found it in a word
That lingered on the lips of those

Who mourned their past
As they denied it.
They sang for immortality
As they passed. Alas!
They spoke of immortality
And I found all that is
Would not last.

The poetry of Nazik al-Malaika always takes Khafaji back to his childhood. Poetry was everything in the house where he grew up.

"Wine, pure wine!" their father would call out whenever he heard a good line of poetry. It was the only bottle he ever drank from. Poetry was the glass he poured each night when he came home from work. When the brothers were old enough to memorize, Khafaji's father let them drink it too. He taught them the best lines, and then made them pour the poetry back to him while he stretched out on the old sofa. Eyes closed, he corrected his sons until they knew how to pull every pearl to be found in the dusty old books on his shelves. When the aunts visited on Friday, their father would send them into the kitchen to recite the kind of poetry that made women blush. They would shoo the boys back into the men's quarters, but not before stuffing cardamom sugar cookies in their mouths.

"Baba, you're reciting, not reading. I want you to read to me."

Khafaji opens his eyes and sees his daughter staring at him. He looks at the faint smile on her face and picks up the book from his lap.

"I was reading, my love."

"No you weren't, Baba. You were reciting from memory. I need you to read, not recite."

He smiles as he turns page after page to find his place. One day, when he and his brother were still young, their sister Rahma came home from the university clutching a small book of poetry, *Splinters and Ashes*. Their father looked at it that night and shrugged, "That's not poetry." But the boys raced to memorize whole poems, not just lines. Nazik's poetry took over. New grapes in an old vineyard. Long before Khafaji could grasp what Nazik was talking about, she had become everything.

"Baba, what are you thinking about?"

"I'm just looking to see where I was. You wanted me to read it, right?"

"Yes, Baba. You can start wherever you are. Just read."

An hour later, when he stops reading, she says, "Thanks, Baba. Which one was Mother's favorite?"

"She loved every line Nazik composed."

Only when Suheir appeared in his life did Nazik's poetry become living, breathing flesh. Her images taught Khafaji what to desire. Her language became a mother tongue. With Suheir, he began to hear the sadness in Nazik's language, then its anger. As he grew older, he continued to learn from her. How to accept compromises, how to suffer defeats. How to be middle-aged, how to grow old.

In 1995, Suheir died. They packed their books and moved out of the villa. Khafaji continued reading Nazik, but there was no longer any comfort or consolation in her words. Just the opposite. Each line would summon another time gone forever, another past lost for good. He would read Nazik, and for a brief moment Suheir would appear before his eyes. And then, just as fast, she would disappear across a shoreless ocean and leave him stranded again in the past.

"It's different when you read, Baba, isn't it? When the words are in your head, they always say the same thing. But when they're on the page, they begin to live their own lives."

Khafaji looks at his daughter and smiles, surprised. Her hand rests on his sleeve, the two of them sit still for minutes.

"I'm going to go to sleep now, Baba. Could you turn off the light?"

As the room goes dark, Khafaji whispers from the doorway, *"Eid – in what state have you come, Eid? Have you gone and taken something with you, or do you bring something new? / A desert lies between me and my loved ones while I am with you: how I wish there were deserts..."*

His silhouette fades as the last word trails off.

From the bed, Mrouj's voice is faint. "That's easy. Mutanabbi, 'and deserts between us'. *A desert lies between me and my loved ones while I am with you. How I wish there were deserts and deserts between us!* What a sad line to choose, Baba! Goodnight."

Khafaji tucks the book under his arm as he walks out. In the living room, he sets it down softly, then goes to the sideboard. Reaching behind vases and porcelain figurines, his fingers find a bottle of Scotch.

There's a knocking at the front door and he puts the bottle back in its place without making a sound. Looking through the peephole, he sees nothing but the gloom of an empty stairwell. A light crashes on, and the boy from next door comes into view. "Who is it?" he calls out as he opens the door.

"Blessed Eid to you! My father and mother want to know if you and Mrouj would like to watch TV with us. The dish is working again and we're going to watch the last episode of the Syrian soap opera right now."

"Good evening, Jaafar. Could we do it tomorrow night?"

"On my life, I will not accept it!" a voice booms out. For a moment Khafaji can't tell who the speaker is. "Not tonight, Mr Muhsin! Tonight is the start of Eid, and you're our neighbor! Please come and at least have some sweets. Umm Ali made *kleitcheh* this afternoon. You can't refuse."

Jaafar's father appears on the landing, and the two men shake hands and smile. Abu Ali is a slight man, not much larger than his skinny kid. His thick glasses make his bulging eyes even bigger than they are already.

"God bless you, Abu Ali! I wouldn't want to impose on you and your family tonight of all nights! Tomorrow, I swear."

Now, another voice calls out, "No – that won't do. We've already laid out the sweets and heated the kettle for you and Mrouj."

"Bless you! Mrouj has gone to sleep." Abu Ali smiles until Khafaji relents.

Khafaji puts his thumb between his fingers and asks Abu Ali to be patient. He goes back inside to check on Mrouj and then comes out, gently closing the door behind him. Jaafar takes Khafaji by the hand and walks him next door.

Khafaji spends more than an hour pretending to enjoy the platter of sweets. He sips syrupy cardamom tea and praises the hand that made it. He watches the soap opera and feigns interest in its twists and turns.

Jaafar cocks up his voice like a television broadcaster. "Tonight is the last episode, all will be revealed!" He is the only one who notices that Khafaji has no idea of what the plot is or who the characters are. When he catches Khafaji's eye, he winks.

Another night of avoiding questions. The neighbors are recent comers. What they know about the building is the only thing squatters ever really know: there are vacancies.

But they must also know from experience that people can step from one life into another. That an entire building can leave in one night. They might even know that those who stay behind have their reasons too. Abu Ali knows not to ask questions, and so does Khafaji.

When Abu Ali curses Saddam, Khafaji nods, but not too much. When they make fun of the cowardice of the generals and officers, Khafaji joins in, his laughter sincere. When they talk about the Republican Guards shot yesterday at the checkpoint on Jamia Street, Khafaji just shakes his head, "Everyone gets what they deserve, don't they?"

From the outset, they accepted Khafaji for who he said he was. A retired librarian living with his daughter. A widower, whose daughter was not always an only child. An old man who preferred the company of books.

When the electricity goes out, Khafaji breathes a sigh of relief. Now he is free to go. Back inside, he lights a candle and finds the bottle of Black Label. The first shot goes down quickly and he pours another. Warm now, he sits in his reading chair and listens to the celebrations outside. Children laugh and call out to each other in the street. The racket of whacking sticks and metal wheels rolling in the broken road. The clanking of gas canisters and the distant calls of fruit sellers, the stomping of feet up and down stairs. Every so often, the crackle and pop of fireworks and gunfire like a hundred weddings across the city. Or another outbreak of fighting.

Khafaji finds the photograph of his niece in his hands. He looks at it again, but regrets it. Once again he finds himself looking at Suheir. The present is never thick enough.

Khafaji puts the image down on the table and rubs his eyes. He strokes his moustache, looks at his hands. In the twilight, the creases of his palms grow sharper and deeper. Across the darkening room, the shapes of the furniture lengthen and swim. Khafaji sits in a small pool of warm light. Nazik's poems rest on his lap, the book untended, but the words alive in the air. While his eyes stare off into the shadows of the bookcases, a voice reads on:

I will hear your voice every evening
When light dozes off
And worries take refuge in dreams,
When desires and passions slumber, when ambition sleeps
When Life sleeps, and Time remains
Awake, sleepless
Like your voice.
In the drowsy dusk resounds your wakeful voice,
In my deep yearning
Your eternal voice that never sleeps
Remains awake with me.

Khafaji falls asleep the way he does every night – letters into words, words into sounds, into images, into dreams and then, nothing.

There is a crash outside, and something like an explosion down below. The electricity is on again. Suddenly, the apartment is naked, exposed. Everything is still in its place, but to Khafaji's startled eye, it seems that every object has just come alive. As if everything in the apartment has been dancing while he slept then jumped back into its place as he woke up.

Heaving himself out of his seat, Khafaji puts the bottle back in its hiding place. The cabinet door shuts like a punctuation mark, and now he can make out the sound of sobbing somewhere nearby. Khafaji closes his eyes and listens.

Suddenly, the lights go out and the front door comes crashing in. Men and flashlights and guns pour in. Khafaji tries to count them, but they seem to fill the living room and hallway and spill out onto the landing and beyond. Lights stab at his eyes, everything becomes a blur. Hands grab at Khafaji and twist his arms. He is on the ground. His cheek presses against the icy marble tiles. His arms cock backwards until his shoulders begin to scream. There are shouts. Guns click and clank, flashlight beams swing around in the blackness. He closes his eyes and imagines the whole street filled with these men. He imagines a line of them stretching down to the river.

Khafaji remembers his sleeping daughter, opens his eyes and shouts her name, "Mrouj!" Boots kick at him, but he looks for eyes. When he finds them, he sees nothing but fear. The man in the black mask orders Khafaji to stay on the ground. Someone pulls plastic zip-ties around his wrists and ankles and his fingers go numb.

Before Khafaji passes out, he thinks, *An old man like you has no business fighting them.*

July 2003

MEMORANDUM FOR:

    Deputy Commander, USASOC HQ

    Commander, U.S. Army 75th Regiment

    Commander, 10th Special Forces Group

SUBJECT: Operation Report, 10 July 2003

Acting on intel (INSCOM 02-003Z2) concerning High-Ranking Target (King of Clubs: Izzat Ibrahim), 75R unit surrounded villa in Tishrin area at 0200. Process of securing perimeter entailed taking possession of adjacent residences. In main domicile, possible explosive materials discovered.

Ibrahim determined not present, whereabouts unknown. Female inhabitants appeared withdrawn. Male residents displayed threatening behavior. Three resisted restraint efforts. Cable ties and hoods employed. Acting on threat, unit called for support at 0225. At 0300 10th SFG unit arrives. 75R unit proceeded to search surrounding residences. At 0315, two male Persons Under Control attempt escape. Despite repeated efforts by members of 75R to constrain their movement, PUCs managed to leave premises. 10th SFG unit posted to building exterior issues warning for suspects to halt upon exit. Multiple warnings ignored. Suspects counteracted by force of weapons. Medics attempt resuscitation, suspects declared dead at 0330. Melee with family members as bodies secured in transport. Quelled at 0415, number of civilian injuries unknown.

Preliminary review determines residence used as workshop for portable-generator repair. Incident compromised primary objective of operation. HUMINT assets damaged. Advisement requested.

Tuesday–Wednesday
25–26 November 2003

"Confirmed. Three of Diamonds!" A voice cuts through the throbbing in Khafaji's head. He's lying on his back, his arms tied, his legs tied. He can hear, but he can't see. There's a soft ache where his eyes used to be, and his sinuses feel like someone set them on fire. His head is wrapped in a wet sack. His clothes are drenched. Hours go by. Every now and then, his body begins to shiver uncontrollably. Sometimes there is nothing to listen to but his heaving breath and pounding pulse. Sometimes there is loud thumping music. Then it starts again. He hears them come in without saying a word. He feels their fingers, but cannot stop them. They tip his feet up. They tip his head down. Slowly, carefully. Suddenly, he is in the Tigris. Suddenly, he is drowning. Water floods his sinuses and fingers probe his stomach and chest. And then he is drowning again. And drowning again. Each time he comes up, he is not sure if he is inhaling or exhaling or even breathing at all. The hood comes off, and it goes back on. He can feel the pain in his head, but he cannot see a thing. Darkness falls.

Hours later, Khafaji wakes to another voice. He is on his side now. On concrete. "We got him, sir. Not a face card, but a high target. We got the right intel and the right luck. Yes, sir. Thank you, sir." More people come and go. Another voice when he drifts off, another voice when he comes to. American voices. He goes to sleep, but the pain never does.

"What's the reward on this bitch? What? Get on it, Sergeant." It is not the shouting, but the shivering that wakes him up. The floor beneath Khafaji is ice. His clothes are gone, his skin feels warm, even hot. Between his ears, a knife slices through his mind.

"Good morning, you fuck. We know who you are. Mr Chairman, right? I'm gonna call you Chairman Fuckin' PUC, since it's easier to say than your hajji name. You may not be America's Most Wanted. But you're in the deck, Bitch. You belong to us!"

Khafaji feels a shoe by his ear. He feels someone breathing. A hand pulls at the cloth over his eyes. A new voice. "What the hell happened to this PUC's face?" A long pause. The man hums for a moment then shouts to someone else, "Something's not right." Khafaji listens to the sound of boots crossing the room.

"You don't understand a word I'm saying to you, do you? I'm gonna smoke your PUC ass." A sudden kick to the kidneys, and Khafaji falls into another dark dream.

At some point, the blindfold comes off, and cold water slaps his face. Only now, gasping for air, does Khafaji feel the tape over his mouth. His screams come out in mute heaves. *There's not enough air in this room to fill my lungs.*

His naked body shakes like it belongs to someone else. His skin twitches each time it remembers the frozen concrete. He tries to control his sobbing, but he can't. Gradually, his tears just stop and things begin to loom out of the fog. A bare room. A metal door. Walls of paint peeling from cracked concrete.

A standard-issue metal desk. Two standard-issue metal chairs and a wooden one. Fluorescent lights that blink and pop at random. Missing ceiling tiles. All somewhat familiar. Even an office man like Khafaji knows this kind of room. He's just never seen it from this angle before.

An American walks up sideways. Like a crab, his arms a pair of ragged claws. He reaches out and snaps something. Khafaji's legs spring free. Then they begin to throb and ache. He unbinds Khafaji's hands then fastens them again in front. When Khafaji begins to roll his shoulders, the blood pours in. A thousand sharp needles turn muscle and skin into meat. Even so, his fingertips are numb. Khafaji looks closely at the man in front of him. A face like a dish that was broken and glued back together again. The American unfastens the gag and smiles intimately. Like they've met before. Khafaji knows the look. Two other men walk up and grab Khafaji by the shoulders. They heave him onto the wooden chair. Beneath his weight, it creaks and settles. Someone throws a dirty blanket over his shoulders, and Khafaji manages to pull it around his body.

Only when Khafaji hears the voice offering him a cigarette does he realize there's someone else in the room. An Iraqi.

"Happy Eid, you son of a whore. You like American cigarettes? Virginia tobacco? I know you do. You say you hate those Americans, but you love their cigarettes more than anything else in the world." Someone lights a cigarette and sets it on Khafaji's lips. He takes a drag. When the smoke hits his gut, he coughs. The nicotine begins to set in, though not soon enough. The pain, now dulling, recedes to the background.

The voice is familiar, but there's something off. Khafaji can barely make out the short bald man in the corner. From Mosul, by his accent. Italian suit. Spotless shoes. The man must never have to walk on our streets. A leather smell. Cologne. His face is almost famous.

But there's something puzzling. *Why is he showing his face?* Then it sinks in. *He doesn't care.* To take his mind off the pain, Khafaji studies the man's face. Pink flesh. Hairless, except for eyebrows. Loud blue eyes. Minutes go by before he realizes the Mosuli is talking to him.

"...and this is just the start, you piece of shit. When we find your brother, we'll bring him in. And the rest of your family too. Want to know how we'll treat them? You'll get to see. You'll get to watch."

"Where's my daughter, you cunt?"

From behind, someone slams Khafaji's face into the desk and shouts, "You need to be more respectful." Hands tear the blanket off and throw it on the ground.

Khafaji coughs and gags. A plastic cup of water appears on the table in front of Khafaji, and he swallows it in one gulp.

"I will." When Khafaji speaks, the sound of his own voice stuns him. Weak and distant. Floating in mid-air, like it came from somewhere else. Like a child shouting from a locked room. Suddenly he wants to look at himself in the mirror.

The American nods at the Mosuli, and the two men leave. Khafaji sits alone with his thoughts again. The blanket just beyond his toes.

Nazik appears behind him and whispers in his ear:

There is no Mutassim I can call
And there is no Saladin among us.
We sleep at night, and wake at dawn wounded,
Stabbed, killed.
How do we make peace with tyranny?
How do we shake hands with Satan?

For some reason, it's the Mosuli's face that makes Khafaji think of these lines.

The American comes back in, followed by a man in a black hood. They sit down in the metal chairs opposite Khafaji. Someone places the blanket on his shoulders again, and Khafaji pulls it around his body as tightly as he can.

As the American opens a file, Khafaji stares at the hood. The man will only look at the ceiling.

The American turns to the hood and asks in English, "Is he Muhsin Khadr al-Khafaji?"

The voice inside the hood asks, "Inta Muhsin Khadr al-Khafaji?"

"Naam."

The American asks in English, "Can he confirm that he serves as Party chairman and commander in the Qadasiya militia?"

The interpreter begins, "Mino ygool…?"

Khafaji interrupts. "What? No. Police. Not military."

The American and the interpreter look at one another. Khafaji interrupts them again. First in English. Then again in Arabic: "You're looking for someone else, aren't you?"

They get up and leave in a hurry. When the door cracks open again, Khafaji sees the Mosuli looking in. Standing next to him is a slight man. Another business suit. Two more perfectly polished shoes. The only thing different about him is that he's wearing a hood. The Mosuli speaks to the man then points. At first the hood nods. Then it shrugs. Khafaji imagines another hairless pink face behind the mask. A hand shuts a door somewhere and Khafaji is alone again. The pain in his sinuses and head is unbearable now. He closes his eyes and tries to disappear.

This wasn't the first time it happened. Once, early on,

there was an official notification about a job promotion. It was addressed to him, Muhsin Khadr al-Khafaji. A huge promotion. A leap over ranks and pay scales. As soon as Khafaji saw the letter, he rushed home to show it to Suheir. They celebrated by going out to dinner at one of the new restaurants on the river. Suheir's brother Nidal and his wife Maha joined them and they all drank too much arak. That was on 16 July. He could never forget it. Late the next morning, Suheir woke him up and together they listened to the news of the coup. Arif on a plane to London. Ahmed Hassan al-Bakr, the new president. As he straightened his tie in the mirror that morning, he realized that the whole world had changed while they were sleeping.

But that letter was meant for someone else, another Muhsin Khadr al-Khafaji. Long after the mistake was corrected, Suheir loved to tease him about how much money they spent on their celebration. For his birthday the next year, Suheir had framed a photograph taken of the four of them at dinner, embossed with the words "Congratulations on your success!" It was one of the few photos from that period Khafaji still possessed. That evening, and that mistake, became one of the brightest moments of their life together.

The second time it happened was just after Kuwait. A boy in a uniform appeared at the door. When Khafaji opened it, the boy rushed to shake his hand and embrace him with genuine tears and compassion. Khafaji was too stunned to interrupt. The boy said little at first, just vague praise for martyrs. Over tea, he launched into a long story about his friendship with Khafaji's son. They were more like brothers than friends. He talked about how their entire unit sent its regrets. By this time, Khafaji was so confused he did not know what to say. Three years before, when Uday was executed, there had been no visit and no condolences. No body recovered. No burial. No funeral. The news delivered late one night, a rumor passed on by an acquaintance. The only official recognition of Uday's death they ever received was his punishment – the abrupt fall to civilian police.

In 1991, Khafaji knew from the outset what the visit from the soldier was about. It just took him a while to figure out why it was happening. After an hour, they cleared up the misunderstanding. The messenger was supposed to visit another Muhsin Khadr al-Khafaji. Still, the scene replayed in his mind for days after. Khafaji allowed himself to imagine that the death of the other man's son meant that somehow his own son had survived. That somehow Uday had managed to eke out a few more years of life somewhere. As if that would have taken away some of the pain.

At that moment, Suheir's doctors had just discovered that her cancer had metastasized. That misaddressed report of someone else's death was news neither of them could stomach. They never talked about it again.

When the other Muhsin Khadr al-Khafaji first appeared in his life, it was farce. When he returned a second time, it was tragedy. And now? Khafaji clenches his jaw and tries to ignore the pain.

Minutes later, the American and the Mosuli walk back into the room, brisk and serious. In their hand, a thick Manila folder. This is the only script he knows, so he recognizes it immediately. *File and Dossier.* They don't bother to sit. And now Khafaji recognizes the man. Of course. His picture used to appear in the papers and on the television. Spokesman for the exiles. Anyone would know the face. But it was his Arabic that was so confusing. Until today, Khafaji had never heard the man speak anything but English. It never occurred to him that the man even spoke Arabic, let alone like an Iraqi.

The man's dream of retribution was now coming true. Now, purity would sit in judgment over corruption; those who left would judge those who remained behind. It's not for nothing they call exile the cheapest form of patriotism.

The man looks at a file in front of him, but directs his words at Khafaji. "You claim you're not Muhsin Khadr al-Khafaji?"

"That's my name, but you have the wrong person."

"You are not Muhsin Khadr al-Khafaji of the Qadasiya?"

"That's someone else." Khafaji hears the words coming out and is once again surprised at how remote his voice sounds. Like a wounded bird.

"You're an officer in the IPS?"

"I am Muhsin Khadr Ali al-Khafaji. Born Karbala, June 6, 1942. Chief Inspector. Iraqi State Police at Baghdad."

"Party rank?"

"Section Member."

"Says here you were a Branch Member."

"No." Khafaji pauses. "I didn't have much of a choice. It was the same rank anyone else in that position would have. Just look at my file."

The two men stare at Khafaji, but say nothing. The American scribbles something in his notebook.

"Where is my daughter?" Khafaji asks abruptly.

"Hmm?" The American makes another note. "We'll come back to that later."

He picks up a photograph and holds it in the air. He squints at it, then at Khafaji, and then at the photograph again. He makes a note. The Mosuli leans over the desk, and gestures for Khafaji to look into his eyes. The light reflecting from his bald head is distracting.

The American takes more notes, then whispers to the Mosuli, "They look enough alike." Turning to Khafaji, he asks, "How can you prove who you are?"

"You can ask anyone. Look at my file."

"You burned them."

"We never burn archives. They were stored away. I'm sure you have them by now."

The Mosuli grabs Khafaji's right hand before he can pull it away. He studies the palm and fingers. When he speaks, formulas roll off his tongue. "Start with fingerprints. And investigative detention. Custody recommended until we can ascertain his identity."

Khafaji tries to pull his hand back, but can't. The Mosuli's grip is rougher and stronger than it appears. He squeezes the hand until Khafaji winces. "You've got blood on your hands, cunt – but whose?"

The Mosuli turns to the American. "Let's save him for the IGC tribunal. Keep him apart from the others, at least until we know who he is. No – better idea. Put him in with the jihadis."

Khafaji holds his throbbing hand and studies the man's clean-shaven face. The sculpted eyebrows. The neatly turning lips with more than just a touch of redness. And skin so smooth, like it's never seen a razor. A boy. A pink rat.

Suddenly, his voice begins to speak again: "*They say that the Minister of Oil has a tail that he keeps hidden! / They say that the Minister of Oil has a tail that he keeps hidden in an American pocket / In an American pocket!*"

The Mosuli's fist is thick and fast. It knocks Khafaji to the ground. "Learn some respect, you cunt! Learn who you're talking to. You lost. We won. Smell that shit smell around you? Welcome to your new home. The dung heap of history."

By now, he has Khafaji's skull in his hands. Khafaji's head hits the concrete. Once, twice, and then he loses track.

The little man's shiny face is up against Khafaji's, whispering, "It doesn't matter who you turn out to be. You Baathist cunt. You're going pay for what you've done." Khafaji stares at the man's perfectly shaped eyebrows. He imagines the man plucking them in front of a mirror.

Then it dawns on Khafaji that they know nothing about him at all. The strange voice in his throat begins to laugh. He begins to sing with his whole body, though the words are Muzaffar al-Nawwab's.

While the party of castrati pursue me
While the party of castrati hound me
O seeker, search for another door
You had better search another door
While the party of castrati hound me...

The Mosuli lets go of him and takes one step back. Khafaji's song is still hanging in the air as the Italian shoes begin to work.

"You're a dead man and your poetry is shit." After the first few kicks, Khafaji's eyes close and he feels sleep approaching. He hears shouting, then feels hands putting the hood over his head. He feels hands tying his legs. He feels hands dragging him for miles.

At some point, Khafaji becomes conscious of the fact that he's in a room with many other people. His arms are now tied in front, and he manages to roll onto his back. His body jostles others in the process. The ground beneath is cold and wet. Other naked limbs nestle against his legs and arms. It doesn't matter. He surrenders to rest and sleep. In the muffled darkness, he remembers the hood on his head.

He listens and it feels as if he's floating on a gentle sea of human voices. Every current is distinct as they swirl around his ears. Someone on the left is Egyptian. One on the right is from Yemen. The man behind is Sudanese. Like switching from station to station on a radio of the entire Arab world. Khafaji hears snippets from the far west, from Morocco. From Tunis and many from Libya. Others closer to home, someone from Aleppo and someone else from the Hejaz. They are young. Khafaji smiles to himself when sleep finally takes him by the hand.

August 2003

We were just finishing dinner when my husband heard the knock at the door. Yezid got up from the table to answer it. He was out of his seat and racing down the hall as if he was expecting someone. He was wearing socks and skated halfway down the hall like he always did. We all heard the door open. And we all heard Yezid talking with someone. His sister says she heard at least two other voices. The conversation was friendly. Yezid's sister is sure that he knew the boys who came to the door.

When we heard the door close, we thought nothing of it. Yezid used to disappear after dinner all the time. In summer, he was always in a hurry to go outside for another game of soccer. Or to go play video games. What was it he liked – Grand Auto? It could have been any of his friends from upstairs. He never even put his shoes on.

We never received a note or a ransom demand. No one ever found his body. None of his friends ever came forward to tell us anything. No one here would ever talk to us about it. It took us a long time before we connected it to what was happening at the university. I stopped going to work. Yezid's father began to pray for the first time in his life. He's probably praying right now! When the internet is working I check email. I've been writing to people in Europe to see if there are any university positions in clinical psychiatry. Do you know of any?

Thursday
27 November 2003

When Khafaji wakes up, the hood is off, but his head is pounding. He rubs his temples and neck for a minute before it registers that the cuffs are also gone. He blinks and coughs, and then sees a motley group of young men. Most are wearing nothing more than filthy pants. He looks down at his own nakedness and shudders. He tries to cover his penis with his hands. Someone hands him a dirty towel. With numb fingers, he wraps it around his waist as best he can.

Khafaji sits up and someone offers him a tin cup of water. Not water, but a tepid liquid stinking of sulfur. He drinks it quickly, though it does not go down easily. The throbbing in his head begins again, then the spinning. He lies down again. Hands pick up his body then set him down gently on a cold metal bench.

"Thanks," he mutters. His old voice has returned, frayed around the edges.

"The brother is Iraqi. We're honored by your presence."

"The honor is mine." His right hand touches his heart.

Khafaji lifts his head slightly to see the faces of his helpers. In an instant, the stench of twenty men shitting and pissing into buckets hits him. He covers his face with filthy hands and fingers. He's smelt it before, but never from this side of the door. He looks down at his wet legs, uncomfortable and now even more ashamed.

Khafaji closes his eyes. He was right – they are young. Half are boys. A couple aren't even old enough to shave. They talk. They tell stories. About families at home. About brothers. About famous men. Two make a point of talking about how much it cost to come. To liberate Muslim Iraq. Khafaji guesses that of the twenty, maybe one was trained to do something more dangerous than picking beans.

The day passes in winding conversation, interrupted at random by loud music that suddenly blasts into the cell for minutes, and that, just as suddenly, disappears again. The light turns on and off without warning, without pattern. When the cell is dark, Khafaji feels at his head and face. He is stunned to find his hair cut, along with half of his moustache. His fingers travel up to his face to feel the patches of bare skin. No sooner does he manage to forget this than his fingers are there again, prodding at the skin on his scalp and his lip. The more his head throbs, the more his fingers dig into his temples.

The lights come on again. The older ones are more than curious to know what an old man is doing in their cell. Khafaji tells them his name is Omar. He says his wife's family comes from Tikrit. He hints that he was captured while leading a unit in Salaheddine province. A string of lies, but Khafaji isn't entirely insincere. A couple of the boys pepper him with questions, others tune out.

The lights go off and they ask Khafaji about the fate of the world. Why were Iraqis so slow to take up arms? Who built this prison? Did Shiites collaborate with Americans because they hate Islam so much? Why did the Kurds love Israel so much? Khafaji says as little as possible. Nothing to encourage or dampen hopes. Nothing specific. Nothing verifiable. After a few hours, Khafaji pieces together that they were all picked up around al-Ramadi. Most within days of arriving in the country. Some within hours. If they ever returned home, this cell would be the only Iraq they knew.

The weeping is so faint that it takes Khafaji a long time to realize what it is. When the light comes on again, he sees the boy in the corner. Crying. He's been crying for hours. Khafaji watches him urinate on himself more than once. The others around him try to comfort him, but they also move away from the puddle he sits in. His body never stops shaking.

The first time they prepare to pray, they ask Khafaji to lead. He wonders, *Do you remember how?* He apologizes, and his sorry state excuses him. The next time, they don't even ask. After they pray four times in a matter of what seems like a few hours, he realizes: they don't know what time it is any better than him. It could be day or night. A boy complains about the light, and someone else answers, "At least it keeps the bugs away."

And then there's the sound. Only now does he begin to hear it. There is no sound at all. Or rather, there seems to be no sound except a distant, white roar. From somewhere in the building itself, a distant hissing sound floods the air. No other noise. No sound coming from other cells. No sound from the outside. A seashell's whisper, soft, almost imperceptible. Except that when you wake up to it, it's a deafening roar.

Never once does the power go out here.

One by one, the others fall asleep. At one point, the only other person still awake is the sobbing boy in the corner. Khafaji nods to him.

"Tired?"

"Yes. I haven't slept since I've been here."

"In this prison?"

"No. In Iraq."

"Really?"

"Yes. Longer than that, actually. Not since I left home."

"Egypt? How long's that been?"

"Three or four months, I think. I don't know. Forever."

"Does your family know you're here?" Khafaji studies his face. The long nose, round cheeks, and soft lashes might have been copied from an ancient temple wall. A Pharaonic scribe with sleepless eyes.

"Only my brother and cousin. They helped me buy my ticket. No one else. If my father knew, I'd be dead."

"But he'd also brag about how brave you were."

"Maybe. But it would only bring trouble. He'd kill me."

"He must be a good man to have raised a strong young man."

"Until they made me a girl."

"What?" Khafaji immediately regrets asking.

"They did that to me. Right outside in the hallway. They made us all take off our clothes. They said I was a girl, and then they made me one. Then they did it over and over. Everyone saw it." The boy begins to cry.

Khafaji doesn't know what to say. He reaches out his fingers and rests them on the boy's shoulder. The boy leans onto Khafaji's shoulder as he sobs. Onto the warmth of his skin. Khafaji still does not know what to say. The minutes go by as they sit side by side in silence. When the lights suddenly shut off again, the boy stops crying. Khafaji moves away to another corner of the cell.

"Do you ever dream?" the boy asks.

"Of course."

"I mean, while you're awake? Do you ever see dreams like

they're real? And they are real. But then, later, you realize they were in your mind?"

"Everyone does. When you're sick enough. Sleep is the cure. Sleep, son. Sleep and forget your dreams."

"Do these dreams come from God, or from the Devil?"

Khafaji shakes his head in the darkness. He wants to laugh, but it's too late. Like laughter, grief is also infectious. Khafaji's breath slows and slows until his body finally gives way.

It is hours before the door opens. Two Americans walk in and look around the room. When one of them speaks, they realize she's a woman. She throws a pile of what appears to be women's underwear on the ground and laughs. The boys in the room go bolt rigid. Alert and on guard. The Iraqi guard accompanying them orders a thin Yemeni boy to take the buckets down the hall. The buckets are full, almost too heavy to lift. He carries each one with both hands. The liquid splashes out over his toes, and leaves a spattered trail across the concrete floor. A minute later, the boy is back and retrieves the next one. As he goes back and forth, his plastic sandals slip and slide. By the time he's done with all of them, a large puddle of mess covers half the room. The door closes. In an instant, a line of boys forms, their faces turned away from the others already emptying their bowels.

Khafaji rummages through the pile of underwear and finds something he can put on. Then he dozes off. Khafaji dreams that the Tigris has become a lake, its waters swelling green and stagnant with garbage and human waste, sweating oil and tar. He stares at the heavens and the sky opens. Rain begins to pour down. He smiles to himself. It has been months since it rained in this city. Violent storms sweep across the sky. Clouds fly and loosen like purple turbans unfurling themselves. Sheets of rain crash against the window. Water gushes down minarets in frothy cascades. The alleys and streets fill with puddles. The crater outside becomes a dancing pool. Streams surge across sidewalks and avenues. A flood sweeps down every street, washing away all the debris and litter. Small cars get caught in the deluge, then trucks, buses, troop carriers and helicopters. The streets are now torrents, spilling everything down to the Tigris. Khafaji and Suheir are eating *masgouf* at their favorite restaurant. He is chewing slowly, picking bones out of his mouth as he watches the gathering destruction. Something sticks in his throat and he begins to gag. Soon he is choking and spitting. As he begins to vomit, a huge carp leaps from of his mouth into the river. He reaches for a glass of water, but the table, the restaurant, and now Suheir are floating off, beyond his reach. He is in the Tigris now, drifting with its current. It is no longer a lake, but a strong, swift river. Slowly, the currents begin to gather speed, and he is carried away. The water is clear and cold and sweet on his lips. He drinks and drinks then gazes into the blue-gray depths below. The whole city, clean and still, drifting hundreds of feet beneath his floating body. Baghdad Atlantis. Suddenly, small dots begin to rise up from the streets and buildings beneath. First in ones and pairs like loose balloons, then like flocks of geese, they float up from below. They grow in size until he can see them clearly: crowds of bloated corpses, gathering speed as they ascend. With a whoosh and splash, each one breaks the surface. Soon, Khafaji is surrounded by a thicket of lifeless bodies, so swollen with air that their shiny bellies look like fleshy spring-onion bulbs. The body next to him turns over, and Mrouj's lifeless eyes gaze up at his.

Terrified, Khafaji wakes up. He stares up at the fluorescent bulbs until the floating sensation becomes a dull throbbing again. He rolls over and feels the vomit on his face and chest. His stomach is a wolf gnawing at the rest of his body. He can't remember the last time he ate. The others tell him that food arrived while he was sleeping and they saved him some. They see his face and tell him to eat. He crawls over and sits in front of the food. He drags a piece of dry bread through cold, viscous soup, and puts it in his mouth. Bite by bite, he finishes the plate.

As soon as he finishes the last bite, his body seizes up. In a second, he is heaving and convulsing, and everything comes out again. The more he vomits, the clearer his head feels.

He can't stop the tears when they begin to well up. He turns his shaking body to face the wall, and tries to do what he has always done whenever he is sick or tired or sad. He tries to escape into the music he knows by heart. Poetry, the same liquor that his father poured whenever he wanted to drink himself into oblivion. Khafaji wants to drink it too. He wants to drink until he can't see straight any more. His father used to say that Arabs called poetic meters "seas" because you could sail on them, and because you could drown in them.

Khafaji tries to recall lines from the book he was reading to Mrouj yesterday. *Where is Mrouj?* he wonders. *Was it yesterday?* No. He thinks about the poems, hoping that something might float up from his memory. A line or fragment. These are poems he's known his whole life. They are who he is.

But, tonight, nothing. As if someone had erased the diwan of his life. For the first time in years, there's not even a poem to keep him company. He cries hot torrents of tears, but they're not enough to wash away the dirt and blood on his cheeks.

At some point, he finds a hand gently resting on his arm and looks up to see the young Egyptian boy sitting next to him. They look at each other until, suddenly, the lights turn off again.

September 2003

My boy, Munadil! God protect him! Here is his picture. Look, here is his identification card. Here is his certificate of citizenship. I have all his papers. I have all of them.

Last year, they told me he might be in Abu Ghraib. But he didn't come home when Saddam released everybody, so I don't think he was. That's why I'm here, that's why I come every day. I'm hoping that God willing – God willing – the Americans will help me find him. Who else is going to help us, if not the Americans?

He was a good boy. He didn't mean any harm. He made a mistake, but God forbid, my boy was not a criminal. He did not steal, he did not kill. Since when does changing money hurt someone? Since when is it a crime? Where in the Quran does it say that the punishment for changing money is chopping off a hand? Where?

You want to know what is criminal? Hunger. Poverty. Murder. Those things are criminal. If Saddam really wanted to fight crime, he would have locked up those things, not my Munadil.

Can you help me? Do you know anyone inside? I know that the Americans are here to help. And I know that if they heard my son's story, they would help.

Tell me – where else can I go? If they don't let me in to meet with someone today, I'll come back again tomorrow morning. I'll keep coming back until I find my son.

Friday
28 November 2003

Some time, the metal door opens and someone calls out, "Mossen El Koffeggie!"

Khafaji comes to the door and two American soldiers, one short and white, the other tall and copper-skinned, take him by the arms. With their haircuts, they could pass for Ottoman janissaries. Without speaking, they walk him down long wordless corridors. Eventually they come to a large, cold, concrete bathroom. They close the door and let him go.

Khafaji walks over to a mirror. Through a film of grime, defeat stares back at Khafaji. He fingers the ugly patch of moustache left by his captors. He rubs his palms over his head, feeling the tufts of hair on the back of his skull. The white soldier stands next to Khafaji as he studies the plastic razor and bar of soap. For the first time in forty years, Khafaji's moustache comes off in a series of sharp, painful tugs. He scrapes at his lips until they are clean and smooth, then rinses the blade under the cold water. He shaves his chin and cheeks and looks at himself. The cheap blade is dull; it has left thin red threads of blood across his neck. He washes his face and his head, and looks again. He wipes at the mirror for a minute, but the image he sees still belongs to someone else. Something else.

Khafaji asks for a toothbrush and the white soldier shakes his head. Khafaji turns toward the wall as he removes the underwear. The copper-skinned soldier looks away as he showers. After Khafaji towels off, he hands him a bag with a suit and underclothes. Khafaji puts on the jacket. It's two sizes too large, and still smells like the last man who wore it, and the one before him too. Khafaji finds a pair of plastic sandals in the corner of the shower and puts them on.

They walk down another concrete hallway, and then open a pair of doors to step outside. The noon sun is blinding. Khafaji tries to shield his eyes. The world blazes in then fades away into fog. When Khafaji's legs give out, the two soldiers carry him by the arms across a yard to a cluster of bright white trailers. They walk beneath a snapping sound, and Khafaji looks up to see an American flag. A metal door opens then springs shut with a flimsy smack. Khafaji finds himself inside a wood-paneled room filled with file cabinets and wooden desks. The hum of air-conditioners fills the air. Even so, it is stuffy and warm.

An American voice booms, "That's all for now, gentlemen. You can wait outside." A huge man in crisp military fatigues rises to his feet. His face is a piece of dough, his smile, honey on cream.

"Good morning, Mr Khadr. I'm sorry for all this. It looks like you've had time to shower, so I hope you feel better. Please sit down. I want to speak with you."

The man smiles sugar. His gaze never lifts from Khafaji's. He waves toward an empty chair. When Khafaji sits, the man starts to shuffle through a pile of paper on his desk. A minute later, he begins to speak. His words come out very slowly. He enunciates each syllable very carefully. "You understand some English, huh? Very good, Mr Khadr. Would you like something to drink while we talk? I drink coffee. Would you like coffee? Or would you prefer tea?"

At first, Khafaji doesn't mean anything by his silence. A minute goes by with Khafaji looking around the office and then at the man. The smile finally fades from the American's face. "You do speak English, don't you, Mr Khadr? It is very important that we speak. I would like us to communicate with one another."

"..."

"Pardon?"

Another minute goes by before Khafaji breaks down. When the words come out, it's that distant voice again. "Sorry. I speak English. I would like tea."

The man speaks into a phone and orders tea and biscuits. Khafaji looks around the room again. The man said his name too quickly, but Khafaji does not ask him to repeat it. There is a forest of pictures on the desk. The frames are tilted the other way, but Khafaji imagines a woman and children. On the wall, a large, familiar picture of an American city skyline. Underneath, a screaming eagle and words. Khafaji sounds out "Never Forget" twice before he stops himself. The only other decoration in the room is a floating cluster of metallic balloons, covered with festive pictures of confetti and flowers and the words "Happy birthday".

The man wipes his brow as he begins speaking. "Let's get straight to business. We know who you are. We know your rank and where you work. This isn't a whole lot, but it's enough for us to get started. You see, we need you right now. This country needs its police. We need you to go back to work."

Khafaji shrugs. "Too late. I retired."

"That's not what this says," the American says. He looks again at a paper on his desk, and says, "Nothing here about you retiring. According to this, you are still on the force. No flashing sirens, just lots of experience. Says you managed the archives."

Khafaji leans back and says nothing.

"Look, I understand there may be some confusion, so let me clear something up. We dissolved the Army, but there was apparently some misunderstanding about how that was going to be applied to the police. Of course, the decision was meant to apply to the Military Police. And the National Police. But it wasn't meant for the Iraqi Police Service. Except at the highest levels, and I don't think that fits in your case. There are obviously some gray areas, but..."

He pauses, and wipes his mouth with a tissue.

"The IPS disappeared when the country was liberated. Where'd they go? I don't need to ask you – you know better than I do where they went. Just as your country began to need you for the first time, you guys vanished. That was a mistake. And now we're all paying for it."

Khafaji looks at the man and vaguely nods. He goes on. "Let me tell you how I see it. The original message probably wasn't clear enough for people in your situation. And then there's the Interim Governing Council with all their talk of settling scores. You were right to wonder what was going to happen. If I were you, I would have disappeared too."

He pauses and wipes his brow. "How does that sound? Sounds reasonable to me. But you don't have that luxury any more, do you?"

He looks intensely at Khafaji and pauses again. Khafaji looks down at the paper cup in his hand. He swallows the warm tea in a single gulp. The sugary taste dissolves, leaving behind a film of cotton in his mouth.

"Would you like another?" Before Khafaji says a word, the man is on the phone asking for two more cups of tea. Khafaji stares at the balloons, puzzled. *Do Americans really decorate their offices with balloons?* The man's voice brings them back to the moment.

"We are aware of the sensitivities of the situation, Mr Khadr. But we also have our security needs. And these are growing, not shrinking. Iraq has no army. No police. No order. And that means chaos."

The man wipes his brow and leans forward across the desk. "And so, we're forced to make some difficult decisions. Don't get me wrong. No one has any interest in turning back the clock. At the same time, we did not liberate Iraq, Mr Khadr, to watch it fall into ruin. And that means we've got to march forward and see this through."

Khafaji nods and wonders where all this is going.

"Mr Khadr, I studied history in college. And that inclines me to look at this situation in its proper historical light. This is what I see. I see a group of thugs that took a whole country hostage. I see a few men with blood on their hands. And the rest terrorized into submission. Did any of you really believe that Baathist crap?"

He rubs his temples with thick thumbs, then goes on. "We came here to swat at ghosts and phantoms, it turns out. We came to stamp out an ideology that doesn't really exist. I look at you, and I don't see a ghost.

"Your file describes a real person, Mr Khadr. Reading it, I see someone who had very few choices. A solid career in the General Security Directorate. Regular promotions. Up and up – until one day in 1988, you're out. That particular memo is missing from your file, for some reason. After years of loyal service, you're sent down to civilian police. What did you do? Who did you piss off? Then you spend your last years running around after thieves and smugglers and rounding up beggars. I see here you play a role in an anti-drug campaign, then a stint in vice. Then you're shunted over to the records office. Says you're the archivist."

Only Khafaji's hand moves. His numb fingers reach for his upper lip as if drawn there. The skin is soft, like a woman's.

"You didn't have many real options, Khadr, did you? It must be next to impossible to pursue a career in law enforcement in this part of the world."

The American laughs again. "This is where you're supposed to talk."

Khafaji shrugs and disappears into the folds of his suit.

"Let me put it differently then. We're in a hurry here. I'm not trying to be your friend. And I don't want to hear your life story. All I want is for you to go back to work."

Two minutes go by as Khafaji stares at the desk. A man enters with a tray of paper teacups. Khafaji's shaking fingers rip at tiny packets of white sugar. Finally, the American interrupts the silence. "Maybe you weren't the one they were looking for. But that doesn't matter much any more. You made a big impression with someone in the IGC. Normally they couldn't be bothered with the details of a case like yours. But now they're coming to look into the files. You can appreciate that, can't you? They have everything. The North Iraq Archives, for starters. The HRW reports. You and your friends in the Central Security Directorate took lots of notes and drafted lots of memos. If you spent any time up there, they know about it."

The American pauses, unsure whether he has Khafaji's attention.

"If they get their hands on you, they won't have any time to hear all about your difficult life choices. You'll be lucky if your case falls through the cracks. But even then, you're not going free, you know."

When Khafaji looks up, the man's smile is long gone. Khafaji's eyes begin to swim in the tea. The paper cup rips in his trembling hands. Warm liquid spills onto his crotch, but he says nothing.

"We can't undo the past, Mr Khadr. But, once in a while, we're given the chance to decide which parts of it are relevant, and which are not. So tell me, are you a good cop? Or do you want to be a bad cop?"

"I am not…" Khafaji's voice is barely audible.

Trickles of sweat roll down the man's temple, and he ignores them. "Pardon?"

"I am not going to work for you."

The American smiles and says nothing. He looks down at his papers and acts as if Khafaji isn't there. The two soldiers walk in. With a single heave, they throw Khafaji's arms behind his back and tie his wrists together. This time when he's paraded outside, there's nothing to shield him from the blazing light.

October 2003

When her shift ends, the translator changes back into street clothes. She wipes the paint from her lips and eyelids and carefully covers her hair with a different hijab. She leaves the base by a side gate and catches the first bus. It doesn't matter which bus, only that it is never the same one as the day before. Just as the bus is about to leave at the fourth or fifth stop she jumps off and finds a taxi that will take her downtown. She is polite, but never talkative. She walks the last block to another bus. This one cuts back on part of the same route she took before delivering her to the neighborhood where she lives.

"I work at the university," she was told to say. Even if her parents and brothers do not believe her, they do not ask.

Today, just two blocks from home, a young man speaks her name and smiles. "Zeinab?" When she smiles back, he hands her a note and disappears.

In the name of God, the Compassionate, the Merciful.
We wronged them not – but it was they who wronged themselves.

To: Zeinab Hussein al-Kadhimi, filthy agent of the American swine!

We have sworn to ourselves and to God and His Prophet to right the wrongs that beset our land. We seek to purify this land that has been stripped bare by collaborators, apostates and criminals. We have discovered that you work as a translator for the enemies of God and humanity, the Americans, the invaders, usurpers and occupiers of our country. You may have kept this fact a secret until now, but the light of truth has come out. Heed this warning and leave Iraq now. If you do not, it will be us, not you, who will be forgiven for what happens. Do not make your mother suffer the loss of her daughter.

Signed: *The Army of the Righteous, Sentencing Committee*
(15 September 2003)

Shaken, Zeinab stays home for a week. When she finally returns to work, she doubles her precautions. She looks over her shoulder with every step. She adds another leg to her winding route. "It'll take another hour, but it's the only way," she murmurs to herself. "They have to help me. Maybe my case for asylum will go through now."

Downtown, Zeinab steps off her first bus of the morning. She is so focused on stopping a taxi that she doesn't notice the young man standing next to her.

Saturday
29 November 2003

Cuffed to a metal table, Khafaji manages to sleep for an hour.
When he wakes up, he finds his headache has returned. He
finds a metal tray that someone set on the table in front of
him. He looks at a plastic bottle of water, a dry cheese sandwich and some pickles or old cucumbers. Khafaji swallows
the food then washes it down with the water. He falls asleep
again without trying. The next time he wakes up, there's a
pack of cigarettes, a book of matches and an ashtray on the
table. Khafaji fumbles for a cigarette and then, somehow,
lights it. Leaning over the table, he attempts to smoke in
peace. He flings the butt to the floor, feeling exhausted but
almost clear-headed.

A few minutes later, he calls out, "I need to use the toilet."
He yells, but no one answers. After some movement in the
hallway, the door flies open.

Khafaji is escorted down the hall by one muscular white
soldier as another stands by the door. The ankle cuffs make
his steps short and jerky. In the bathroom, the man stands
next to Khafaji as he urinates. Khafaji struggles to zip up
his pants, but his shaking fingers fail. He tries to wash
his face in the sink, but the soldier says "No!" and pulls

him away. As they walk back down the corridor, Khafaji notices the back of the wheelchair. Then the back of the girl sitting in it. He doesn't need to see her face to shout, "Mrouj! Mrouj!"

The soldier shoves him into the room.

"Let me see my daughter," he yells, and tries to break free. He trips over and falls. In an instant, the two soldiers are sitting on his arms and legs. A pair of hands grips him by the neck. The voice speaks slowly and loudly. "Don't resist, or you will get hurt." Khafaji feels a knee in his chest. "Stop now, or you will hurt yourself."

It's not Khafaji who stops. It's the pain that stops him. He begins to take slow, deep breaths. A minute goes by, and the soldier on his chest speaks again. "I am now going to release you. If you do that again, we will restrain you and it will hurt."

A knee digs into Khafaji's chest until he nods and says, "Yes." The men stand up, leaving Khafaji on the floor, his legs and arms still cuffed. Khafaji doesn't move. From the smooth, cold concrete, he watches boots walk sideways out the room. Minutes go by before the white soldier walks back in. He stoops over Khafaji and asks, "Better?"

Fingers probe Khafaji's neck and throat. Khafaji flinches and the man heaves him onto the seat. Khafaji begins to fall off the chair, but the man wedges the chair against the table. Khafaji balances there until the door opens again. Another soldier enters the room, pushing the wheelchair.

Khafaji and Mrouj look at each other, but say nothing. Neither seems to notice the soldier when he leaves. Mrouj's eyes are tired and sad. But even so, her smile is un-erased. She looks older but also younger. He reaches to touch her arm, then stops himself before he falls out of his chair. Mrouj pulls herself up and puts her hand on his cheek, then touches his naked lip. She looks at his bloodshot eyes and bruised face. Her smile disappears. When she starts to cry, it comes without tears or sound.

"My God, Baba. What have they done to you?" She begins to cough uncontrollably and falls over. She wipes the spit from her lips, then sits up again.

"I'm here, Mrouji, and I'll be fine."

"Did they hurt you?"

"No. They don't know how to do that. What about you – did they do anything to you?"

"I'm fine, Baba. They came back and told me you wanted to see me. They drove me here."

"Are you OK?"

"I'm not better. And I'm not worse." She coughs twice and shudders.

"You look worse."

"No, Baba. You're the one who looks worse."

Khafaji's silence is heavy, even loud. Louder than the breath in his nostrils.

"Baba, tell me. Are you OK?" She winces and stops herself again.

"I'm fine, Mrouji. They can't hurt me."

"What did they want? What's going on?"

"I don't know. They were looking for someone. Now they want me to work for them."

"Don't do it, Baba."

"Why did they bring you here? Did they tell you?"

"They told me you wanted to see me. They said I could come and see you and that I'd be free to go whenever I want. Don't worry about me. I can manage."

"Don't believe them. I need to think about this some more."

"Really, don't worry about me, Baba." Mrouj begins to cough and doubles over. When she sits up again, her face is frozen in a grimace.

Khafaji looks at her with suspicion in his eyes. "They lied to get you here, Mrouj. They wanted me to see you, and now I have. We need to think about what they're trying to do."

The door opens and a soldier pulls Mrouj's wheelchair backwards. Khafaji screams at the man as he takes her away. He is still shouting her name long after the door closes.

An hour or more goes by before another officer walks into the room. By then Khafaji has made his decision.

"I will do it. But on one condition."

"What is that, Khafaji?"

"My daughter is sick. Her kidneys. She needs to get to a real hospital. You want me to help you? You need to help my daughter. This can't wait."

The man stands up and says, "I'll see what we can do." And then he disappears.

A soldier and another officer enter the room some time later. The soldier cuts the ties on Khafaji's wrists then leaves. The officer puts a file on the table and begins to talk. "Your daughter will be taken to Ibn Sina Hospital. You're being released on probation. Go get your shit in order. You report at the Coalition Provisional Authority tomorrow. You'll be working with Citrone."

He never once looks at Khafaji until he hands him a piece of paper with names and numbers on it, and a couple of stamps. "You want to see your daughter? Bring this with you to Checkpoint Three. They're expecting you at nine."

Khafaji blinks and the man murmurs, "The gate at the Convention Center. You'll see the line when you get there. Go straight to the front with these papers. If you don't follow these directions, it'll be a long time before you see your daughter again."

Suddenly, Khafaji is being escorted out of the complex by yet another short soldier.

He waits in one of the white trailers at the gate while someone bundles papers into cabinets. Every so often, he drinks more warm tea in the same flimsy paper cups. He smiles, and dozes off imagining how good it will feel to sleep in his own bed.

The phone rings and wakes up Khafaji. The receptionist tells him that his transportation has arrived. Khafaji goes outside to a battered Humvee. A boy soldier waves and opens the back door. Khafaji gets in without saying a word to the other three young soldiers inside. The driver says, "Strap yourself in. Where are we taking you?"

Khafaji tells him the name of his street. The boy in the front seat shrugs. "Show me on the map, OK?"

Khafaji looks at a map of Baghdad, only it's not Baghdad. He looks where Jadiriyya should be, and sees the word "Holly-wood". He tries to find Saadun, and sees only a place called "Manhattan". It is Baghdad, only every neighborhood and street is called something else. He points to where he thinks he wants to go, and the soldier looks at his finger, "Great. Chicago. Corner of Madison and Main."

Khafaji forces a smile.

In the back seat, he can see very little through the thick, grimy windows. Everyone else is stiff, alert. The driver speeds up and slows down for no apparent reason. The vehicle swerves back and forth, knocking Khafaji around in his harness. Outside, cars honk and brakes squeal. The chaos of a patrol howling through civilian traffic. More than a few times, Khafaji hears dull thuds and high pings, and imagines things hitting the metal walls around him. For a moment, the vehicle wrenches into something heavy. It makes a grinding noise then disappears. The boy next to him shouts at the window, "Fishdo!"

He turns to Khafaji and whispers, "Fuck it. Shit happens. Drive on!" And the others laugh.

Khafaji drifts off. He suddenly pictures them dropping him off in front of his building. He shouts, "Stop! I want to get out."

The driver laughs and says, "Don't worry, we'll get you there in one piece."

"No. Please. Stop. Let me out."

The boy beside Khafaji is chewing gum. He looks at Khafaji and shakes his head. "Calm down, Hajji. Don't worry. We know how to deal with traffic."

The others start laughing. The driver turns on loud music. They nod their heads back and forth to the beat. The gum chewer pumps his fist in the air and sings along. Khafaji can't hear his own thoughts.

Khafaji unstraps himself and tries to stand up. The car swerves, and he is knocked onto the lap of the gum chewer. Khafaji shouts and pleads, "Stop! Please stop! I need to get out!"

And now the Americans are screaming back at him, "Shut the fuck up, Hajji."

The gum chewer pins Khafaji into his seat, while the driver shouts, "We don't stop on this road, old man. We'll get you to a checkpoint and you can get out and go wherever the hell you like. Until then, we gotta keep moving."

The gum chewer stares at Khafaji, then shakes his head and looks out the window. He blows air through his teeth and asks the driver to turn the music up. Every time something hits the vehicle, his eyes accuse Khafaji.

They drop off Khafaji at a checkpoint on the edge of Karrada. He just walks away and says nothing to the soldiers. For a moment, he stands in the night air and breathes it in. Then he begins to run, putting as much distance behind him as he can. The bright lights of the checkpoint fade. Khafaji jogs through dark streets, half-lit buildings and shadowed balconies. The electricity is off again. On the street, only a few generators can be heard.

As he turns into his street, he finds a gate blocking his path. He starts to walk around it, when voices call out, "Who's there?"

Two young men step out of the shadows on the sidewalk, their guns slung casually at their sides. Now Khafaji can see the chairs they were sitting in.

"I live in that building. Third floor." Khafaji points to his balcony.

"Are you OK, brother? You look…"

"Open it. This is my street." Khafaji stares back at the man holding the gate.

"Go in God's safety." He finally relents and lets Khafaji pass through.

Khafaji enters the foyer of his building and sees chairs lining the wall next to the door. There's new life in the building, somehow. The electric lines are everywhere, following the stairway up to the roof. Lights shine, their brightness almost obscene. The halls reverberate with the echoes of television and conversation. A gentle hum of generators rises from the basement. As he steps in, he thinks he sees Abu Ali's silhouette on the landing above. On the second floor, the lights are on in both apartments for the first time in months. New neighbors. Still in the process of moving in. Their belongings still on the landing. A typical overstuffed couch and well-worn dining-room chairs. The laughter of young children inside makes Khafaji smile. Families.

As he reaches the third floor, Abu Ali's door clicks shut. Khafaji reaches for his keys, only to remember he's still wearing someone else's suit. Someone else's pockets. Then he notices that he doesn't need a key to open his front door. It's not locked. It's not even shut. He steps inside to turn on the light, and feels broken glass crunching beneath his plastic sandals.

Every room except Mrouj's has been ransacked. Some things are merely upside down. Other things are ripped, torn, or strewn across the floor. Others are just gone: the old television, the wedding china, pots and pans, a favorite electric razor. The dining room is empty – someone has taken the table and all the chairs. Now he begins to understand why the furniture on the first floor looked so familiar.

They have thrown books in heaps across the carpet in both rooms. Khafaji picks up one or two, but gives up. Only then does he notice the smooth, smoky odor hanging in the air. A case of Black Label in shards. The carpet is soaked with the stuff. If someone threw a match on the floor, the whole place would go up.

Desperate, he digs through the jumble. To his amazement, he is rewarded. In the debris four bottles have survived. Khafaji goes to take a shower, but there's no water. His second meal in five days consists of stale bread and cracked green olives, washed down with two shots of warm Scotch. By the time he falls into the unmade bed, he has forgotten his headache.

GREEN ZONE

And the kings of the earth, who have committed fornication and lived deliciously with Babylon, shall bewail her, and lament for her, when they shall see the smoke of her burning, standing afar off for the fear of her torment, saying, "Alas, alas that great city Babylon, that mighty city! For in one hour is thy judgment come."

BOOK OF REVELATION 18:9–10

Sunday
30 November 2003

The pounding in Khafaji's head wakes him up. The water is back on, and he soaks his head under the cold tap until it stops hurting. He looks at his face in the mirror. Some of the swelling has gone down, but he looks like someone else. He shaves carefully and slowly until his scalp is as bare as his chin and lip. He takes a quick shower and fills as many bottles as he can find. He fills the tub as well, just in case.

Khafaji walks back to Mrouj's room and quietly, slowly opens the door. When he sees the empty room, it all comes back to him. Including the deal he made. He goes to the kitchen and puts the kettle on. While he waits for the water to boil, he notices the balcony doors wide open. He looks out over the homes around him. Even more satellite dishes have attached themselves to balconies and walls and roofs since last time he looked, each dish bowing toward the same Mecca. The rising sun fills each with the same crescent shadow.

He brings the tea tray into the living room, and looks at the papers the Americans gave him. Checkpoint Three. He decides to clean up the mess instead of going out. For forty-five minutes Khafaji stacks books into piles against the bookcases, then decides to leave the rest for later. He finishes the last cup of tea before going back into the kitchen to get the broom. He brushes splinters and glass off the carpet and then sweeps the floor tiles until everything is relatively neat. He takes the broom and the dustpan back into the kitchen and suddenly realizes he's hungry.

Khafaji hears a knock on the door just as he is spooning olives out of the jar. He wipes his hand, and walks back to the front room. The smell of woody cologne fills his nostrils even before he opens the door. A young man is standing there on the landing. His features are soft, his cheeks are rosy, his forehead is bright, his beard soft and neatly trimmed. His heavy green jacket is the kind they issue during winter, with a *kuffiyyeh* twisted around his shoulders. Khafaji's headache returns, and he can do nothing but grimace. The man's voice is as gentle as his face. "God's grace, brother. Peace be upon you."

"Good morning."

"Brother Muhsin? I'm Ali." Ali extends a hand that is not soft at all.

"Ah!" Khafaji tries to smile. "Welcome, Ali! Welcome. I'm glad you're home safe!"

Somewhere below, Khafaji hears young men talking together in gentle voices. It sounds like Persian.

"Thank you, Brother Muhsin! You have been kind to my family. I am grateful for that. They've told me such nice things about you. Thank God you're home safe too!" But Khafaji notices that Ali's eyes are rock hard. Like pieces of onyx. Khafaji looks into them and sees nothing but his own reflection in black. The pause is heavy, so Khafaji tries to smile some more. Ali's grip turns iron. Khafaji hears the sound of boots on stairs.

"When the Americans came, they told my parents who you were. We don't think it's true what they said."

"No. It's not true. They were looking for —"

Ali interrupts him, "What they said couldn't be true, because here you are, back safe and sound. Still. We can't have any problems. I hope you can understand."

"Understand what?"

"Brother Muhsin, after everything that's happened, you need to leave."

"God's grace! Peace upon you!" a voice sings out from the stairs. Khafaji turns to see two young men with soft beards and army fatigues. Ali calls out, "And upon you peace," and waves at them. They disappear downstairs.

Ali begins to speak again in his gentle voice. "The point is, Brother Muhsin, we don't know who you are. And we can't afford trouble in this building."

"By what right do you —" Khafaji begins, but the throbbing in his head stops him short.

Ali's voice softens. "Just look at yourself. You're a mess, Brother. Anyway, it's not my decision. This is best for all of us."

Khafaji tries to pull his hand away. "How dare you, this is my home! You are the guests here, not me." Ali's hand won't let him go.

"Yes, that may have been true. But look around you. In this country, who can tell hosts and guests apart any more?"

Khafaji tries to look strong, but the pain in his head finally gets the better of him. He clenches his jaw, and stands there for what must be minutes – although he knows he's lost. Before he surrenders, Khafaji remembers that every defeat is a negotiation.

"Could I ask one favor, then?"

"Of course, Brother."

"It would be inhumane to kick me out on the street. I need to find a place. One week."

"We'll give you till Sunday." The answer is so quick that Khafaji realizes that he's up against a plan. Ali continues, "But when you go, you'll leave everything in the apartment as it is."

"Son of a bitch."

"Don't talk like that, Brother Muhsin. My parents say you are a polite man, a cultured man. You can take your clothes, but that's all. Agreed?"

The phone rings, and Khafaji says, "I'm going to get that."

The phone rings again.

"Agreed?" Khafaji feels his fingers begin to crack.

The phone rings again.

"Agreed." Ali finally lets go of Khafaji's hand.

Khafaji hears Nidal's voice on the line just as the door shuts. The first minute of the conversation is devoted to frustration and disappointment. It even gets loud. But then Nidal finally hears what Khafaji has to say.

"They busted down the door and came in. They detained me, and then they realized they made a mistake."

"They just let you go?"

"After giving me a haircut. And destroying the place."

"What?! Are you OK? What about Mrouj?"

"They took her to Ibn Sina."

"Why?"

"For treatment."

"No, I mean, why would they do that?"

Khafaji says nothing.

"Can we visit?"

"No, I don't think so. It's in Tashree. In the American Zone."

"What about you?"

"They gave me a pass so I can go see her. I'm going right now."

"We'll send something to her when we see you. So are you OK?"

"I'll be fine. I've got to shave more often now is all."

"Huh?"

"I'll tell you when I see you. Any word about Sawsan?"

"No."

"By the way, I went to see that professor…"

"And?"

"Nothing. Did Sawsan ever say what she was doing?"

"No."

"I'm supposed to talk to the driver. I haven't found anything. You'll tell me if you hear…"

"Of course. We've decided, you know. Maha's agreed. As soon as…" His voice trails off. "So let's not wait. To see each other, huh?"

"Give me a day to rest."

"Can Maha send you something to eat?"

"I'm fine. I'll call."

He hangs up, and puts his face under the faucet again. Eventually, the cold water dulls the throbbing in his head. He finds the papers they gave him, puts on his shoes, and goes out. In the foyer below, he hears the soft voices again, and wonders again if they're speaking Persian. When he reaches the ground floor, they stop talking.

"God's grace. Peace upon you!" someone calls out in a friendly tone.

"Good morning," Khafaji manages to answer as he finds himself walking through a picket of young men. All in the same uniforms. All with the same neat beards. All sipping from cups of tea. Two sit at the front door, cradling AK-47s in their laps. As he walks past, they get up and almost salute. At the end of his street he nods when the young soldiers greet him at the gate. As Khafaji goes by, he watches them wave back toward the entrance of his building.

He turns the corner and starts to walk faster through garbage. It is everywhere. Piling up in vacant lots. Heaped around gates and entrances and walls. Spilling across streets, filling up alleys. Concrete and broken brick. Plaster, metal, paper and rubbish. Piles of white cement. Dry bread, tin cans, empty bottles, and broken glass. Fish bones and chicken bones. Mounds of soggy stuff, wet matter, rotting meat. Khafaji stumbles over the carcass of a dog. He covers his face with a handkerchief, but the stench cuts through. His toe catches on something, and a thick curtain of flies draws back to reveal more dogs. Khafaji jumps over them and runs as fast as he can. He stops to light a cigarette. The old tobacco smells and tastes like cardboard. He gags for a moment, then forces himself to finish the cigarette.

Khafaji tries to wipe off his shoes with a piece of news-paper. He looks around and decides to give up. The whole city – every street, every heap of trash, every square foot – is covered in a sea of plastic soda bottles. Each filled with two liters of nothing. Thin plastic shopping bags collect around every corner and hang on every tree branch. Khafaji smokes the rest of his cigarette.

Things move heavier than they used to. Lorries move so heavily you can feel them in your feet before they appear. Somewhere downtown helicopters thump over city streets. Whenever he hears the sound of a patrol, Khafaji puts himself behind one of the concrete pillars of the covered sidewalk, or behind a parked car. He continues walking, through one checkpoint, then another, with no apparent direction. Every few yards, he squeezes between cars, some parked, some long abandoned. Once, as he reaches down to remove a plastic bag caught on his shoe, he realizes where his feet are taking him. Home.

Occasionally, Khafaji sees a face he recognizes. Or imagines he recognizes. As he walks across Andalus Square, he imagines he sees more and more. He says hello to old neighbors he sees on the street, but no one replies. No one recognizes him. He turns the last corner and, for the first time in years, he stands in front of the house that once belonged to them.

The house still belongs to them. Khafaji admits that even if they hadn't lived there in years, it is still their home. He buried Suheir and moved away. He locked the doors behind him. But he never sold the place. And it never stopped being their home.

Nothing has changed. It's the same home. The same jagged brown bricks. The same black iron gate leading to the same interior garden. The same tinted glass windows. The same jasmine vines and bougainvillea Uday and Mrouj planted. Khafaji smiles to himself. He avoided it for so long. He never went back because he knew how much of a cliché it would be. Was he really supposed to stand here and cry like the old poets did?

But here he is, on a bright early morning, weeping at the sight of the home he'd once shared with her, weeping at the memory of the life they'd lived together. Why is it so jarring to see your old home just as you left it? Why is it so disturbing to see that nothing has changed after all these years? Because it means you are not necessary, Khafaji thinks. It means that things go on as they were, with you or without. As if you never lived, as if your life never happened.

Khafaji looks at the house and tries to take comfort in the fact that he still knows everything about it. He knows which windows stick. He knows how to find the children when they hide in the crawl space under the stairs. He knows how to keep the bathroom faucet from dripping. He knows how to restart the air conditioners at the circuit breaker.

It takes Khafaji longer to notice the changes. The garlands of razor wire glittering along the tops of the walls and coiled around the front gate. The sandbags in the driveway. The black GMC in the driveway. The men drinking tea at the gate. The camouflage of their clothing. Their matching black boots. Their guns. The man at the window of the master bedroom on the second floor. The man who steps back into the shadows.

At this point, Khafaji knows he shouldn't have come. It's sad when you revisit a place you left behind. It's dangerous to revisit that place when someone else has come along and made it theirs.

Khafaji must have been glaring at the men sitting at the gate, because one by one they stand up and reach for their weapons. Khafaji doesn't wake up really until he hears the clatter of cups and a glass crashing to the ground – only then does he turn and start walking away, like an actor stumbling across the wrong stage. He walks and walks. And with each step, he manages to forget something.

He forgets and forgets until he remembers Mrouj.

Then he remembers his nine o'clock appointment at Checkpoint Three. He sticks his hand out until an old Peugeot station wagon pulls over. Then he walks over and opens the door.

Khafaji looks in skeptically, not sure if this is a taxi at all.

The man's voice booms like a cannon, "Where can I take you?"

He adjusts the mirror and turns to look at Khafaji. Khafaji is surprised to see an unmistakable twinkle in the man's bloodshot eyes. His ragged beard is white, stained brown and yellow around the mouth. A pair of skinny legs and gnarled feet poke out from beneath an old *dishdasha*. A pair of old leather sandals nestles by the clutch.

"Tashree. I can get off at the Convention Center."

"Tashree? The Convention Center. OK. Get in."

The man jams the stick shift on the steering column and they begin to roll forward. He looks at Khafaji again. "I know you, don't I?"

"I don't think so."

They careen down the road for a minute.

"Traffic's all fucked up on Jadariyya Bridge because of something that happened. We'll go the long way and cross on Ahrar. We'll get there faster, just you watch."

Cafés glide by on the right and the river bends off to the left. With the window rolled down, the cool morning wind feels like aftershave. Khafaji sees a heron fishing along the bank. Still as statues, he remembers, they wait to pounce on unlucky fish. They wait for hours, never moving, and then strike so fast no one ever sees it. Not the fish, at least. The epitome of patience and survival. And death.

The man taps Khafaji's arm again, then swerves to miss a car in their lane. He sticks his arm out at the driver.

"Fucking bumpkins. They treat their Mercedes like their donkeys. Back in the village, you know, they fuck tailpipes when their wives are menstruating. Really, swear to God! I've seen it with my own eyes." He laughs at his own joke, licks his lips and slaps the steering wheel.

A minute goes by, and Khafaji doesn't know what to say. The man sticks out his hand. "I'm Karl Abdelghaffar."

Khafaji shakes his hand, but his eyes never leave the road in front of them.

"You don't remember meeting me? Did you ever meet someone else with my name? I know you never have. My father, God rest his soul, loved his teacher. Old Sheikh Marx, he called him. He was a commie back in the day when they existed. God have mercy on them! They were real men."

Karl Abdelghaffar swerves around another car, then adjusts the rear-view mirror again. "My father was the smartest in his class. He could read the future. Knew what was going to happen before it did. I'll give you an example. When it came time for me to go to school, he sent me off to Cairo. Why? I'll tell you. He knew what was going to happen. By the time I graduated, he was arrested."

The man rubs his beard and cries out, "God rest your soul, Father!" Khafaji nods and tries to look serious.

"He also knew that names aren't destiny. If they were, I'd be dead twenty times over by now. God have mercy on the old man. And God protect the Revolution."

He stares so intensely that Khafaji begins to worry. Finally, he shakes his head. "I talk too much, I know. My kids tell me that all the time. If you don't like it, I can drop you off here."

He licks his lips again before Khafaji finally laughs. Then he slaps the steering wheel.

While they move through the traffic, Karl Abdelghaffar goes on. Worked as a driver. Retired after the war. Married. Five children, three boys, two girls. Four grandchildren, all girls, thank God. Pictures taped to the dashboard.

"I took up taxi driving not for the money, but to stay out of the house. Thank God, we're all doing OK. Everyone lives nearby. Thank God. My sons didn't want me to drive. I told them: it's either this, or I take a second wife! And anyway, it's my right to see what's happening with my own eyes. You know what I'm talking about? I've seen some things you won't believe. And they're getting weirder. Now everyone is gearing up for the war that never really happened. Even me. Even you." He taps his chest and looks at Khafaji.

"You think you know me?"

"I used to work at the Directorate. I used to drive you jerks around."

"That was a long time ago. You might be mistaken."

"You're a lot older than you used to be. And balder. But it's you. You and I used to talk about poetry. I wouldn't forget that."

Khafaji rubs his head and looks out the window.

When a military convoy approaches on the other side of the road, Karl Abdelghaffar quickly turns right, then left again down a side street toward the river. Each time they encounter traffic, Karl turns and avoids it. At Rashid Street, near the taxi station, they hit a checkpoint before heading across the bridge. They pass the Mansour Melia, the Television Station, the Museum, the ministries, some wrecked, some intact.

Karl suddenly breaks into verse and Khafaji can't help smiling.

And thou awakest them, they slumber still
If thou arousest them, they sounder sleep
Praised be God, Who fashioned by His will
Mankind like stones, that they may ever keep
Like stones their beds, and drouse until their fill.

It takes no effort for Khafaji to answer with the next stanza:

Begone and depart, Baghdad! Depart from me,
In no way am I of thee, not mine art thou

Yet, though I suffered often and much of thee,
Baghdad, it pains me to behold thee now
Upon the brink of great catastrophe!

Karl slaps the steering wheel and chuckles. "Mashallah! You remember Ma'ruf al-Rusafi – I knew it was you. What a day, and it's not even noon yet!"

The intersection of 14th of July and Damascus is a vast expanse of concrete. Somehow it's comforting to see so much rubble and garbage here too. And hundreds of blue barrels, arranged in rows and clusters. Some abandoned on their side. Some wrapped in coils of razor wire that sparkle in the light. And all wrapped in crowds of people.

"I can't believe you said Tashree when you got in. Who were you trying to fool? It's called the Green Zone now. You work for them, huh? The servants' entrance is over there, if you want to get in line with the other donkeys. Word of advice: get here earlier if you want to get into the barn at all. If it doesn't work out, I'll be at my café across the way. Dijla Café."

Khafaji pulls out his wallet.

Karl pushes his hand back and says, "No. I won't take it. You've already paid, far as I'm concerned."

Khafaji tries to give him money, but Karl insists, "You can owe me a cup of tea. At my café, any time." He reaches into his pocket and finds a tattered piece of paper. Then he scribbles out a phone number. "That's my home number. I don't have a cellular phone."

"Neither do I, old man." Khafaji smiles and they shake hands.

Crossing the road is not so simple. Khafaji picks his way through barrels and wires. He wends around cars and dodges children playing on the abandoned vehicles. Khafaji draws a long arc around the intersection and arrives at a corridor of wire and concrete. And a billboard: STOP HERE! SHOW IDENTIFICATION! TAKE INSTRUCTIONS FROM GUARDS. Unconsciously, Khafaji's hand touches the documents in his pocket. For a moment, he imagines he'd forgotten them. Behind a wall of shimmering razor wire, a line of cars. Soldiers poke out from behind sandbags and concrete blast walls. And every five feet or so on every concrete wall, the Great Leader's monogram. Sad. Haa.

At the end of the corral begins the queue. Or rather, the wedge of men and women between concrete and coils of sharp wire. Shreds of plastic shopping bags flit in the air. Dozens of people crowd at the gate, waving papers and trying to get the attention of the soldiers at the gate. One by one, they turn back or disappear inside. A hundred or more others wait and lean against the wall and sit in the shade. Most hold ragged envelopes and folders in their hands.

Khafaji strides forward, waving his papers in front of him, but the others push him back.

"Excuse me, I'm here for —"

The man next to him pushes him back and shouts, "What do you think we're here for?"

Khafaji sits down against the wall. The stench of urine pushes him back to his feet. The woman next to him won't look anyone in the eye. At some point, she begins to sob softly. Then she begins to sing to herself, "God save us, God save us, God save us." She is clutching two photos, one of a middle-aged man, the other of a teenage boy with faint moustache. The faded images could have been taken yesterday. Or decades ago. You can't tell. Eventually, her weeping becomes a wail. It is only when she begins to beat her breast that other women step in. The sobbing doesn't stop, even as she begins telling stories about a husband and son who disappeared five years ago.

A photographer comes over and begins to take pictures of the woman and the crowd around her. Someone on the wall shouts at him, "Imshi minna! Imshi minna!" He holds up his camera and calls out, "Journalist! Press! It's OK!" He waves a badge hanging on his neck. Khafaji watches him walk off. He stops here and there to take a photograph. Of children playing on old parked cars. Of barbed wire. Of chaos.

When the woman's weeping exhausts everyone, she turns to Khafaji. By now he is sitting on the ground, feet stretched out, and leaning hard into the wall. He pretends to sleep. He keeps his eyes closed as long as he can. He focuses on the rumbling in his stomach. It helps him ignore everything around him. The crowd at the gate begins to thin as one by one people give up.

Khafaji thinks about poetry. He tries to recall a line, any line from Nazik. But he can't. Instead, Rusafi spills out, like it did in the taxi.

> *Though I spoke until I could scarcely express*
> *Scoldings as sharp as the thrusting of swords*
> *Those sleepers never stirred, my words useless*
> *To move a people sleeping like children*
> *Rocked in the cradle of foolishness.*

Like a dull blade in the shaking grip of an old man, the lines slash harmlessly at Khafaji's memory.

1955

"You're not adults, you're children." That's all their father said when they walked in the front door. Muhsin went into the kitchen and asked his mother for a glass of water. She stared at the paint splatters all over his clothes. When he came back, he saw his brother sitting in the chair. Then he heard his father's voice. "You sit down, too, Muhsin."

Muhsin sat there for a minute, afraid to look up.

"I don't need to tell you why I'm angry, do I?"

"No, Baba."

"Which of you wants to tell me what you did wrong?"

Hassan spoke up first. "Everyone at school was…"

"Everyone else was going down to the streets? Demonstrating against the king is not wrong. On the contrary, it's patriotic. You want to try again?"

The two boys said nothing.

"Your turn, Muhsin. Tell me what you did wrong."

"We painted graffiti?"

"No, that's not wrong either." There was a long pause as their father waited.

"OK. Do you want me to tell you what you did wrong?"

"Yes, Baba."

"Look at yourselves. You got paint everywhere. Who saw

you when you came home, huh? Did you walk by the baker, or did you go the other way?"

"By the baker."

"It's too late now, but that was a mistake. Let me tell you what you did wrong: it's not what you were doing, it's how you were doing it. You were doing something adults do, but you were going about it like children. Go wash yourselves off. And give your dirty clothes to your mother."

The doorbell rang while Muhsin and Hassan were in the bathroom. They heard their father's voice talking to someone in the hallway for ten minutes before the door finally closed again.

"Get out here right now, boys."

By now, their sister was home. Muhsin saw the fear in her eyes as they walked into the room. Their father was fuming, his voice quavered. "You want to do what you think is right? At least do it right. Listen to this:

The one thing that is braver each day than I is my sense of self-preservation
It moves not, and stands not, unless it is driven by something important,
I have struggled with dangers until they were left saying:
Has death itself died? And has terror been…"

No one said a word. Muhsin and Hassan looked at each other, and then again at their father.

"Tell me something about these lines."

Hassan went first. "The poet is saying to be brave?"

"No. Muhsin?"

"The poet is saying to be cautious?"

"Are these lines even complete?"

The boys said nothing.

"Why are you telling me what lines mean if you can't even tell whether they're complete? Let your sister try. Rahma?"

"It's the long meter. Acatalectic. There's a missing foot. This line is probably: *Has death itself died? And has terror been terrorized?* That would make sense given the parallelism of the line, and it would also resolve the metrical gap."

Their father smiled at his daughter. "Good. What else?"

"Mutanabbi is probably the one who composed it. At least, I think so. In any case, it would seem to mean that in fighting, your caution must be bold and your boldness cautious – then you will be invincible. That sort of paradox would be typical of the poet."

Muhsin and Hassan looked up at their sister and then their father.

"Well done. Good guess. It's Mutanabbi's panegyric to Ali ibn Ahmad ibn Amer al-Antaki. Hassan and Muhsin, go to your room and think about how foolish you were today. You want to make a statement? Learn to recognize the difference between a complete statement and an incomplete one, then you might be ready."

Sunday
30 November 2003

A boot nudges Khafaji. He rubs his eyes and staggers to his feet. He must have fallen asleep. His headache is back.

The American soldier points with his gun. "Imshi minna."

"Checkpoint Three, right?" Khafaji shouts back. "I'm supposed to report today," he adds as he tucks his shirt in and straightens his collar.

"What for?"

"I'm working for the Americans. Here are my papers."

The soldier squints at the papers in Khafaji's hand. He is maybe eighteen years old. As young as Uday was. He touches the headset on his helmet and speaks. Khafaji can't make out what he says. *With his brown skin, he might even be Iraqi,* Khafaji thinks.

"I'm working for the Coalition Provisional Authority," Khafaji corrects himself.

"Sit here until I get back. Don't move." Then he walks away. Khafaji looks and sees a shadow move on the wall above.

He comes back and tells Khafaji to follow. When they come to the gate, the boy smiles for the first time. "Here you are."

The gate opens enough for Khafaji to squeeze through, then closes again. He finds himself walking along a narrow path between two high blast walls. The only vegetation is a cluster of tall palms. The concrete beneath is covered with dry barhi dates.

"Papers," a voice barks. Khafaji hands his papers over to the man.

"Take off your jacket." Khafaji takes off his jacket and lays it down gently on the floor.

"Pull up your shirt." Khafaji pulls up his shirt, then his undershirt.

"Turn around." Khafaji turns around.

"Put your hands on your head and spread your legs." A soldier pats down his body.

The man nods at Khafaji. "It's routine. We do it to every-body. We're done. Sit down on the bench."

Khafaji stares at the announcement on the wall in front of him. *Attention: If you hold property rights that pre-date the arrival of occupation forces in this zone, you may be eligible for compensation. Bring your ID, a copy of the rental agreement (or deed of ownership), along with any photographs of the property and structures, to the Municipal Council located next to the Abu Ghraib Courthouse.*

And right above that, in molded concrete, the same initials as everywhere. Sad. Haa.

Khafaji watches the man return, then bundle his ID and papers into a clear pouch marked GUEST.

"Wear this around your neck. Until you get your regular identification."

On the other side of the second gate, Khafaji finds a middle-aged American in a civilian suit waiting for him under a cover of camouflage netting. The man smiles and offers an outstretched hand. When he opens his mouth, Arabic comes out. "Peace be upon you, Mr Muhsin. Welcome to Free Iraq."

Formal Arabic, despite the Egyptian accent. His hand feels like a smooth cold stone. The chin of a movie star. And deep-set eyes now studying Khafaji intently. The thin lips may not move, but the jaw never stops moving. Chewing gum.

"Pleased to meet you. Hank Citrone. Liaison officer. We were expecting you early this morning."

"I tried, but…"

"They're working on the problem, but for the time being, this is the only way for you to get in. My advice is for you to get here as early as you can. No more late starts, agreed?"

Before Khafaji can do anything, Citrone takes him by the arm. They don't talk at all as they stroll across a vast space of broken sidewalks and streets, shot-up signs, and monumental buildings in the Baathist Babylonian style. At first, even the clusters of desiccated acacia and eucalyptus look browner than green. Half of the palms are decapitated, their feet covered in piles of things that look more like dead roaches than fallen dates. Gazebos and sheds scattered behind untended hedges, and people walking alone and in small groups, some with guns slung casually across their backs. Clouds of small birds swirling around a thick stand of shrubs, filling the air with screeches.

"Do you prefer English, Mr Muhsin, or Arabic?" Citrone raises his voice over the growing chatter of the birds. His chin never stops moving.

Khafaji decides to flatter the man. "You speak Arabic well. Do you have Arab roots?" The chirping of the birds grows into a roar, and the shadows stretch across the steps they take.

"I studied it in college. And then even more after I converted."

Never argue with a convert. Khafaji nods again and tries to look serious.

Toward the Republican Palace, the lawns begin and then the topiary and flowers. By the time they get there, the city seems miles behind. No sounds but a soft pulsing from somewhere or everywhere.

Citrone begins to confide. "I left my career to come to Iraq. Call it a personal sense of duty. You Iraqis need all the help you can get during this transition period. As a Muslim, I have a special role to play."

In the distance, a call to prayer is heard, then another and another. As if on a single cue, the birds abruptly stop.

"I assume you know about my daughter?"

"Yes, yes, Mr Muhsin."

"Can I...?"

"Of course you can. But first, you might be hungry."

"I am."

The American looks at his watch and says, "If you want Iraqi food, you can always get something at the Hajji shop. They got pizza there too. But I would suggest we go to the PX, it's not far from here and we can set you up."

At a squat, domed concrete and marble pavilion, Citrone flashes his badge to the guard, and tells Khafaji to do the same. Citrone takes a shiny .357 out of a holster and places it on the table as he steps through a metal detector, then puts it back.

No palace has ever rejected new owners, especially when they come as barbarians. Around the sides of the ballroom stand forests of upholstered furniture and cardboard outcroppings. Under carved and painted ceilings, the old chandeliers still hang, though the crystal is long gone.

Glued to the walls are oversize technicolor landscapes. A lush forest with a roaring white stream on one wall. A flowery pink meadow framed by snow-covered granite peaks on another. A pristine tropical beachfront on yet another. And colorful banners: "Flu Shots, Bldg 121", "Freedom Ain't free!", "Go Pats!"

Khafaji weaves through a crowd and makes a list: *Everyone is so young. No one walks empty-handed. Paper cups with plastic lids. Electronic devices.*

At the end of the hall, Khafaji and Citrone walk through double doors.

"In the Bubble, we call this place the DFAC. Dining facility. You'll find everything here. It's all shipped in fresh from home."

One of the walls is covered with large television screens tuned to the same sports channel. There is only one dissident screen; it shows weather. In a single minute, Khafaji learns the scores of football games and the weather in Singapore, Berlin and Washington, DC. Muted, the words scurry across the bottom of each screen then disappear.

"There's where we get the trays." Citrone has switched to English. "It's self-service. Hot food's over there. Salads and sandwiches over here. Soft drinks at the Beverage Bar."

Khafaji stands paralyzed. Roast beef, cold cuts, steamed vegetables, rice, macaroni, soups and stews and salads, breads, drinks, cakes, puddings and ice cream. He eventually decides to eat something that looks like lamb. Citrone comes up. "You don't want to eat that. Come over here and I'll show you where the halal meat is."

Khafaji shrugs and follows, then copies Citrone gesture for gesture: a mound of fried chicken, one of cabbage salad and a large cup of ice. They sit down at a square table. Citrone puts his fingers together and murmurs something into his hands before touching his food. Khafaji begins to eat with a fork. When he sees Citrone eating with his hands, he does the same.

The cafeteria fills up with people. Now and then someone waves or nods at Citrone and he mouths a few words. The workers are in constant motion, unwrapping food, wiping down counters, picking up empty plates and cups. Their hands never stop moving. Khafaji notices they are all Indian.

"Praise be to God for providing sustenance," Citrone says in English, and rubs his belly. He wipes his mouth and looks at his watch. "How about we grab dessert and coffee and go straight to the office? We'll talk there."

"As you like." Khafaji notices that Citrone's jaw is busy again.

Citrone takes him to a large table filled with cakes and picks one out. Khafaji says, "Tea, please."

There is no tea at the Beverage Bar.

Citrone frowns. "Sorry about that. They're supposed to serve everything. Nothing held back." He glances over the heads of the workers.

"Tea?"

Khafaji looks up to see a dark-skinned man with a shock of straight black hair cleaning the coffee machines. "I will bring a cup of tea right away, sir. But they have already put sugar and milk in it. I hope that is not a problem for you."

Khafaji watches him walk around the counter toward a cluster of brown men relaxing on metal chairs. Behind a collection of rags, cleaning bottles, brooms and mops, Khafaji spies an old kerosene stove with a large, battered brass teapot. The man returns with a paper cup of hot, milky tea. Khafaji sips it. Too sweet. But it is tea. With cardamom. The Indian adds, "We always have tea, sir. Come and ask any time. We are at your service."

Citrone takes Khafaji by the arm again. They walk down another hall. Before they leave the building, a man shouts,

"Still on for fifty, Citrone? You sure you want to bet against the Packers?"

Citrone roars, "Never been surer!"

It takes about five minutes to walk to their building.

"This is the Republican Palace." Khafaji can't hide the shock in his voice.

"Only the best for the Reconstruction Team. Anyway, that was about the only thing Bremer and Garner agreed on, and who's going to argue with that? Get your ID out, you'll need it here and again upstairs."

They walk through a checkpoint, and Citrone takes his gun out again. The office is on the second floor. Only it's not really an office. It's mostly an empty cavern under gold-leaf ceilings, a few computers and a long bank of file cabinets. Aside from colored ropes of wire taped to the floor, there are few signs that anything might ever happen in this room.

As Khafaji and Citrone enter, a red-headed man in his twenties gets up from one of the computers. He smooths his blue suit with both hands and introduces himself. He speaks so quickly Khafaji doesn't catch his name.

Citrone pulls up three chairs around a small table. He places the clear plastic box with the cake in front of him. The assistant steps over to set a file down on the table next to the cake. "Let's all sit down. Inspector Khafaji, let me begin by repeating what I first said to you earlier: we are eager to begin. I don't have any sermons for you. You know how badly this country needs law and order. You've already talked to our colleagues, so you know what we're up to."

He pauses and looks Khafaji in the eye. In the light, Citrone's face seems different, his eyes are darker. His jaw seems softer now that he has stopped chewing gum. His ears also seem too small for his head. Khafaji wonders if they were added later as an afterthought. Citrone's fingers work at the plastic box. It finally opens with a loud crack.

"Before we start, I want to clarify something. Some of the people we work with were reluctant to work with the US military. So let me say from the outset, we are not military. You're not being enlisted, you don't have to take an oath. This is not the US Army or NATO or anything of that sort."

"So what are you?"

"The CPA is the civilian government of Iraq. Our authority comes from the UN and only for a limited time. We pack up and leave as soon as you have your own government. So, when you work with us, you're working for Iraq. Just like before. You're an employee of the Iraqi state."

"OK. What do you want me to do?"

"Our office is charged with rebuilding the Iraq Police Service as a civilian force under civilian command. Totally separate from the military and security. The IPS is wholly autonomous, wholly civilian, and wholly Iraqi."

Khafaji begins to realize how exhausted he is. He tries to focus, but the headache doesn't help. He blinks hard, then looks around. He sees a deck of playing cards stacked together at the desk where the younger man was sitting. A fragile, leaning house.

"Inspector Khafaji, do you understand why the IPS needs to be a purely civilian institution?"

"I want to know why you need police when you've already got an army."

"I'd be happy to have that philosophical conversation later. But first let me tell you what's happening right now – since that's why we brought you here. In the coming weeks KBR is going to finish building Baghdad's new main police station. No expense is being spared. It'll have everything a twenty-first-century police force needs. They say the new central station will be ready to move into by June 1, and it will be."

"There's no police. Who do you think's going to work in that new building?"

"That's where you come in, Inspector. You're going to help us recruit and retrain the best men we can."

"The best aren't going to come work for you."

"You did, didn't you? And we have reason to think you're good at your job."

"That's not why I was hired."

"It doesn't matter how you were hired. You have the right credentials."

"So I am your recruiter?"

"Not at this stage. You're going to start by going through the files to determine who is still around and how we get them to come back. Without you, we don't know who's willing to come back."

Khafaji laughs. "And you think I do?"

"Look, Inspector. Here's what we're asking you to do. We need to find out who the decent guys are and get them back to work. We don't want any rotten apples. No Special Section, and no Military. ISP mainly. Some General Security if they're clean enough. You're going to help us decide who makes the cut. You review the rosters, name by name, we work with you and send them up the line for the second round of reviews."

Citrone picks up a bite of the cake on the table, and eats it before he goes on. "We won't have a complete force ready by June. But we are hoping to have enough cops on the street by then to show Baghdad that the police are back."

"You want me to find you a new chief, too?" Khafaji laughs again.

The assistant answers, "We've already got somebody for that. Authentic Iraqi, born in Baghdad. He hasn't arrived yet, but he's perfect for the job. Professional. He's been on the force in Chicago for twenty years. Speaks fluent. Knows how to work with business leaders. I can't say more than that until it's all final."

Hank Citrone leans back in his chair, lazily chewing cake. He looks at his assistant, takes a deep breath, and wipes his mouth. He looks at Khafaji again and the tone of his voice drops. "That's all you need to know right now, Inspector Khafaji. You've got your work cut out for you. I envy you. Few of us are ever in the right place at the right time in history to make the kind of impact you're going to make. Your job in the coming months won't be easy, but at least you'll know you're doing the right thing." Khafaji struggles to stay awake, but the conversation is like a sleeping pill. He stares at the cards again but his eyes can't focus. He finally puts a halt to the conversation. "I am sorry, but I am very tired. I asked about my daughter earlier. Can I see her now?"

Citrone nods. "Of course. Should have taken you there first thing. You go see your daughter, and tomorrow, get here early so we can really start, OK?"

He hands the assistant a piece of paper from the folder in his hands. The assistant smiles and says, "I'll call to arrange a visit right now, Mr Khafaji."

Citrone stands and brushes crumbs off his pants. He looks at his watch and turns to the assistant. "I have to get there before they close. Be right back."

Minutes go by, and the assistant also leaves. Khafaji looks over at the tiny house of cards. Now it's just a mess of clubs, hearts, spades and diamonds.

Fifteen minutes later, Citrone walks back in with a red

duffel bag. When he sets it down, it makes a heavy thud. He digs around in his pocket for keys, then opens a drawer under his desk and stows the bag there.

Remembering that someone else is in the room, Citrone looks over at Khafaji, his jaw moving furiously again. He smiles. "Khafaji, I was just thinking. We're going to get you a place inside the Bubble. It'll make your life a lot easier, and ours as well."

"Where?"

"Here. In the Green Zone."

"Yes, please. That would be helpful."

"There is some housing stock over in the new neighborhood that just got added to the Zone. It's going to take a few days for us to figure it out. And it does mean you'll be going through a more thorough vetting. In the meantime, I'd like to propose that we arrange for a morning pick-up and evening drop-off. It's a bit dangerous, considering."

"I think it's safer for me to make my own arrangements for the time being."

"If you need a driver, we can help with that too."

Khafaji nods.

Citrone shakes Khafaji's hand. "Inspector Khafaji, it's been a pleasure to meet you. We're very glad you're joining our little team. Right now, Louis will escort you to the hospital. It's after visiting hours, but they'll be expecting you."

As Khafaji walks down the hall with the assistant, they pass by an enormous room identical to the one they were just in. Khafaji glances in and imagines that he sees the Mosuli sitting with his back to the door. The Mosuli's voice is what makes him slow. But what makes him stop in his tracks is the man across the table, smoking and drinking tea as if he were sitting in his own home. The man stops in mid-sentence and looks at Khafaji standing at the door. By the time the Mosuli turns around, Khafaji is gone.

They walk for half an hour, first through the shadows of the palace grounds and then out into the empty streets of the Green Zone. More than once, Khafaji and the assistant hear people somewhere nearby splashing water, shouting and singing. A pool party. The assistant calls out to someone in the dark, and laughs to himself.

They flash their tags at the door of the hospital and walk in. In the foyer, the assistant shakes Khafaji's hand and disappears. Khafaji looks around, and finds a nurse who looks at him askance before telling him to go to the fourth floor. He presses the elevator call button, but gives up after waiting for several minutes. After climbing up the stairs, he starts walking down a long, dim corridor. The American nurse at the first desk explains, "This end is for our guys. The other end is for Iraqi civilians. I bet that's where your daughter is."

He starts walking, toward the bright lights at the other end of the long hall. He passes a row of rooms with closed doors and guards posted outside. They stare at him and he walks faster. He passes dark rooms, with doors wide open. From inside some, he hears rough breathing, the rustle of sheets, or the electronic bip and ping of monitors. From others, he hears nothing at all, but sees the rigid profiles of bedside vigils.

The hospital is still Ibn Sina, but it's not the one he knew from Suheir's visit. The windows are closed. The doors are secure and guarded. The cabinets appear to be filled with medicine. The doctors and nurses are American, their uniforms clean and pressed. Generators mean electricity that never falters.

When Khafaji arrives at the reception desk on the fourth floor, the orderly tells him that visiting hours are over. Khafaji looks over his shoulder at the rooms down the hall. He looks down at the clipboards on the desk to see if he can recognize anything.

"Can you tell me where my daughter is?"

"Pardon? Oh, hmm. I cannot divulge the private information of our patients. You need to come back during regular hours."

"But we called just now."

"I don't know anything about that. I'm sorry." After a few minutes of this, the man places a call and tells Khafaji to stay put. Khafaji reads notices on a community board on the wall. *AA Baghdad Sands of Recovery Group, Meetings, Mondays and Thursdays 7:30PM. Tuesday–Friday Salsa Class. 6PM. Annex 1.* Five minutes go by before two soldiers emerge from the hallway. They insist on escorting Khafaji all the way to the front gate.

On the way home in the taxi, Khafaji closes his eyes and goes over the scene he saw at CPA headquarters: Izzat Ibrahim al-Durri drinking tea with the exiles. *How is that possible? He was supposed to be in hiding with Saddam.* Every few minutes, Khafaji lets out a snort of disbelief. Each time, the driver stares at him again.

1960

The teacher looked down at the textbook on the desk, then spoke to the class. "The next poem in our book is Ibn al-Rumi's masterpiece on the devastation of war. In this poem, he describes how the Zanj laid waste to the great city of Basra. How the rebels destroyed its schools and mosques. Now, you will notice there is a tension between the beautiful imagery of the lines and the ugliness of the subject matter – which is death and destruction. Consider this."

The chalk shrieked across the blackboard as the teacher began to write out lines from the middle of the poem. Most of the cadets covered their ears as they exchanged looks of disbelief, as they did during every poetry lesson. Muhsin focused on the powdered words taking form on the black slate.

> *Exchanged, those palaces, for mounds and hills*
> *Of ash and piles of dirt.*
> *Fire and flood are lorded upon them*
> *And their columns collapsed into nothingness*

Muhsin was not aware his mouth was moving until the words were out, "Don't you mean *into total ruin?*"

The teacher turned around slowly and stared in disbelief.

Muhsin's mouth moved again. "Sir, don't you mean, *And their columns collapsed into total ruin?*"

The teacher put down the chalk and walked over to the desk. His fingers unconsciously touched the peak of his cap before he spoke. "And perhaps Cadet Muhsin would like to tell us why he is interrupting the lesson today?"

"Sir, if I remember correctly, the last words of the line are *into total ruin.* I didn't mean any disrespect, sir."

The teacher looked at his textbook and then looked up again, the anger on his brow more intense. "If you had been right, I would have forgiven the interruption. But if you look at the textbook, you will notice that the word is *nothingness.*"

The other cadets glanced at the page and then at Muhsin.

"I'm sorry, sir. But I think there's a mistake in the book then."

"And why do you think that?"

"That doesn't fit the meter, sir."

The class watched the teacher's fingers move on a strange abacus as he slowly read the line over out loud.

"No, it scans perfectly. Thank you, Cadet. Let's move on."

"Actually, it doesn't scan, sir. It's the light meter, correct? Listen." As Muhsin read the words back to the class, the mistake in the textbook showed itself.

"Total ruin doesn't only make more sense in the context of the meaning, it actually fits the meter in this case. Sir. And this is a central part of the tension of the poem – using the light meter to talk about such a heavy event."

Red-faced, the teacher sat down in his chair and closed the book. "You need to learn basic respect, Cadet Muhsin, even when you believe you are in the right. Please report to the Director's office."

Monday
1 December 2003

Khafaji wakes up with a headache. The bathroom light hurts his eyes, so he turns it off and shaves in the dark.

He leaves first thing, before making tea, before he hears any of the neighbors stirring. He greets the beards at the front door. The men last night were exceedingly polite when he came in. And these ones are even more so. They rise to their feet and salute as he walks by. He arrives at the end of the street, relieved.

Khafaji wanders far and wide before he looks for a taxi. He arrives at the front gate. The small crowd tells him he needs to arrive even earlier. Hungry, he eats a fat falafel sandwich with extra amba sauce at Haydar Double's.

This time, Khafaji has a book to read for the wait. When he takes his place in line and looks at the cover, he realizes he took the wrong book from the piles on the floor. This one isn't Jawahari's *Diwan*. It's not even poetry. It's a history of the Qaramatian revolt against the caliphate. Annoyed, Khafaji begins to read half-heartedly about the Africans and Persians who, according to the author, created a utopian state that lasted more than a hundred years. Even without a headache, reading prose sometimes seems like work, even if the story's good. This is no exception. The words jiggle and squirm on the page, and Khafaji's eyes can't follow. He closes the book and rubs his temples. He can't remember why he owned the book in the first place. He looks at the title page and it comes back. Spring 1985. Two years before Uday was conscripted. A dinner party. People talking about how nothing ever changed and nothing ever would change. A familiar, coded kind of conversation about how nothing on the inside could ever unseat the regime, and how no one on the outside would be foolish enough to try it. Discussions like this usually took place only in families. Or between close friends. But this was different. There was a history professor from Damascus that night. He started it all by asking whether the regime really was as coup-proof as people really claimed. Between his provocations and the alcohol, otherwise stiff tongues became loose.

Someone asked the professor about his work and he began to lecture about the Qaramatians. He kept insisting they were the first Muslims with a genuine anti-imperialist ideology. Someone recounted the infamous stories. Tales of desecrations, massacres of pilgrim caravans and fire worship. But the professor protested, "No, no, no! That's nothing but Abbasid propaganda!" He didn't hesitate to explain. "Look, Islam is the only religion that was founded as a state. What do states do?" He looked around at the others holding glasses of wine and Scotch.

"They expand and conquer, they take and they absorb. They eliminate those who dare to resist."

"Are you saying Islam was imperialist?"

"Not like the British or the Americans. It could have been, and it would have been, had it not been challenged and subverted from within. That's why the movements like the

Zanj and Qaramatians are so important. These were the first Muslims to challenge the imperial character of the Islamic state. The Qaramatians shared their property communally, and made their decisions collectively. Between trying to suppress the slave revolt in the south and trying to eliminate the Qaramatians in the Gulf, the whole northern flank of the Abbasids lay wide open and vulnerable. We remember the Mongols, but we forget they would not have been able to conquer Baghdad had the Abbasids not been so busy with their counter-insurgency campaigns down south."

"Well then – it doesn't sound like we have much to thank them for, does it?" It was Suheir who challenged the man on this point. "I mean, why should we celebrate them if they're the ones responsible for destroying our city at the height of its glory?"

Pushing his glasses back on his nose, the professor continued. "We're so used to celebrating the Abbasids that we forget the political realities that made their accomplishments possible. We forget the secret police and the coups and the repression of dissent. The Qaramatians were a downtrodden people who built a commune that lasted more than a hundred years – that's why we should study them and remember them. The Abbasids fell trying to put down a popular, democratic movement – and we're supposed to feel bad for them? If you want to celebrate all-powerful caliphs and their slave armies, feel free. I'd rather celebrate those who struggle to make a better world."

Someone proposed a toast to his rebels that night, and everyone raised their glasses and smiled. Afterwards, everyone was embarrassed. At least Khafaji was. The next week, however, Suheir had found a copy of the man's book and read it. Then she wrote "Celebrate our anti-imperialist past!"

on the title page and gave it to Khafaji. And today it made its way into Khafaji's hands, perfect reading for anyone standing at the gates of empire.

The line moves fast eventually. Khafaji has to look up from the page every few minutes to take a step forward. At some point, the same photographer from yesterday returns, strutting across the street and photographing the circus playing out across the square – the traffic jam, the vendors and their carts, the children playing on the mounds of debris, and the line of petitioners at the gate. After a few moments, someone appears on the ramparts and tells the photographer to leave. He disappears the same way he entered.

At the outer gate, Khafaji removes his jacket and goes through. At the second gate, he finds an identification card waiting for him.

"Wear it around your neck at all times," the man says.

In the morning light, the Green Zone looks more parched and neglected than the day before. Khafaji passes rocky outcroppings, and then a large abandoned cage. He pauses and lights a cigarette.

"Palace zoo. You missed the cheetahs, brother." Khafaji hears Arabic and turns to smile at the man behind him. If his overalls and plastic flip-flops don't give him away as a gardener, the shears in his hand do. Khafaji lights a cigarette for the man.

"I was here the day they got out, believe it or not. They were hungry. They howled like someone was stabbing their bellies. They hadn't been fed for weeks. Someone opened the gate and they bolted across the lawns and ran into the palace. No one saw them again for weeks. In May, the Americans caught two of them at the pool. Kept the skins as trophies."

Khafaji smiles and thanks him. He is almost at Ibn Sina when he hears someone calling out, "Inspector Khafaji!"

He turns to see Citrone wearing shorts and running shoes.

"Peace be upon you, Inspector Khafaji! I'm glad I ran into you. I'll be in the office shortly – there's something I need to fill you in on. It's urgent."

Khafaji looks at the entrance to the hospital, then again at Citrone.

"Can I meet you after I visit —"

"No, this can't wait. I'll be right there."

When Khafaji gets to the office, Citrone isn't there. Neither is the assistant. A uniformed soldier sits at an empty desk by the door. He stands when Khafaji enters, and shakes his hand so hard it smarts.

"Yes. Inspector Khafaji."

The man speaks so fast Khafaji doesn't catch his name. "Citrone wants you to start with these."

"I was told he wanted to see me."

"He'll be here any minute." The man points to a stack of files on a desk, then hands Khafaji a key and points over to a set of long filing cabinets. "When you finish the ones on your desk, start over there on the left. Let me know if you need anything else."

Khafaji spends an hour looking through personnel files of middle-ranking officers from various branches of the police and state security. The subject matter doesn't help the throbbing in his head. Most names he doesn't know at all. Some he knows by reputation. Others are people he's worked with. Khafaji finds himself dozing off and waking up again more than once. The pictures and biographical information begin to seep off the pages and spread like stains across the desk. Where are they now? The photographs are mostly years old. Most with moustaches, some with glasses, a couple with a cockeye – but always the same portrait stares at the camera. The blank look in their eyes – was it fear or defiance? But now, these are the photos of officers gone missing. Hundreds and hundreds of officers. Departed. Decamped. Detained. Disappeared.

Khafaji rubs his eyes and refocuses on the next file: Yezid al-Aamiri, lieutenant, Special Security Organization. Commendations for physical fitness. Three courses in the Party Preparatory School. Two essays, one on Iraq as the natural leader of the Arab nation, the other on Zionism. The first photo is from the 1970s. It shows a small wiry man, with thick black hair, thin moustache and obsidian eyes. He leans forward into the camera, his neck and chin stretching out toward the lens. The last photo is from 1995. It shows the same wiry man, older and no longer leaning into the camera. The last update is from January, and shows him as serving in Karmah, Anbar province. If that was true then, it isn't true now. There's nothing about Aamiri's face to say where he went. Each one of them has gone somewhere. Some to places no one can follow them to. *But for my luck*, Khafaji thinks, *someone else could be in this office today, looking at my picture and my dossier and wondering the same thing.*

Khafaji finishes the pile and takes them over to the cabinets and attempts to put them back where they belong. But it is not so simple. He begins to scan through the tabs, hoping to get a sense of how the dossiers are organized. There are IPS files mixed in with General Security Directorate and some Special Security, and a couple of Military Intelligence. It makes no sense. Not just because it's hodge-podge, but because whoever arranged these files worked hard to put them in this particular order. Khafaji makes a note, looks at his watch, and puts his head down on his desk for a moment.

Khafaji wakes up as soon as Citrone and the assistant walk in.

"Good morning, Inspector! How is the work coming along?"

Khafaji rubs his eyes, and smiles. After a minute, he answers, "Exciting reading."

"I knew it would be. Need some coffee?"

"No thanks. I'm awake."

"Find anything?"

"I won't be able to find anything until I know a little more about where these files are from."

The assistant goes over to his desk and opens his computer. Citrone pulls up a chair next to Khafaji.

"What do you mean?"

"I need to understand why they've been put in the order they're in."

"We were told that the files are ready for review. Aren't they?"

"But a file doesn't mean much on its own. You need to understand the archive as a general principle before you can read its constituent parts."

Citrone laughs. "So, here we are, having that philosophical discussion after all. I will take your question up with the people who gave us the records. But in the meantime, I need you to focus on reading them for what they are."

Khafaji understands that Citrone wants him to agree. Needs him to agree. So he nods. The assistant comes over and sits down, then runs his hand down his red tie.

"Yesterday, you asked me why you need a police force if you have an army," Citrone says.

"No, I asked why *you* needed the police…"

"Do you believe that Iraqis are fully capable of governing themselves democratically?"

"Of course," Khafaji shrugs.

"Did you know that in my country there are people who were opposed to the idea of us liberating you from tyranny? Some of them said, and continue to say, that Iraqi culture is incompatible with democracy."

"That's their problem."

"There are people in my country who want this experiment to fail, Inspector. And there are also people in your country who want this experiment to fail. Some of the people in my country say that western democracy has no place in an Islamic society, and some of the people in your country say the same thing."

"Ironic."

"We need to prove the doubters wrong. We need to show them that we were right. We need to prove that Iraqis can have democracy too – we need that to secure our win."

The assistant chimes in, "Mr Khafaji, in our country we have something called 'the free market'. Most of the time, we take it for granted and don't even think about how great it is. We're lucky because we can take it for granted. When Iraqis experience it, they will start to feel that Iraq belongs to them, probably for the first time in their lives. That's when they'll know what liberty feels like."

"I have never thought about that," Khafaji admits, then immediately regrets it. Sermons discouraged end fastest.

"And it all begins with law and order. No matter how you look at it, the key to the puzzle is rule of law. That's why it's so crucial you have decided to make a stand. Without you, this country doesn't stand a chance. We know it and the terrorists know it – that's why they focus their attacks on the police. As soon as the IPS is back on its feet, coalition troops go home. And the sooner Iraqis see this, the sooner they'll realize their country belongs to them. That's the whole point. To let Iraqis know that from now on, they're in charge. When Iraqis see Iraqi police on the streets, they'll understand that the CPA is working for them, not for the UN or for America or whatever conspiracy they imagine us to be."

Citrone leans forward. "That's the big picture you should have in mind. The whole justice system is being redesigned top to bottom. We've got experts who are making sure that the whole criminal code is all in complete accordance with Sharia law. We have advisors who know how to cut out red tape and streamline admin law. Iraq is going to be the economic powerhouse of the region. And Inspector, now you see where you fit in."

"Thanks for the explanation." Khafaji turns toward the assistant and says, "Is that what you wanted to talk to me about so badly earlier?"

Citrone clears his throat and lowers his voice. "Actually no. We need to tell you about something that has come up, Inspector. One of our interpreters has disappeared. With everything that's happening, we have no illusions about finding her, but…"

The assistant hands Khafaji a photograph of a bright face in a hijab. "Zahra Boustani was one of the first 'terps we hired." For the second time in a week, Khafaji is staring at the image of a beautiful young woman. He looks up, puzzled.

"Interpreters. Zahra is young and bright. She joined because she wanted to help her country. She got a few of her friends to sign on too. Without people like them, we'd be nowhere."

He wipes his mouth again. "It's been ten days since Zahra

last showed up for work. The other girls tell us her family haven't seen her in a week. She's probably been kidnapped. Probably nothing can be done. But we have to try. Our interpreters put their lives on the line every day. Most of them can never even tell their own family what they're doing when they leave the house. We need to find out what's happened. If a crime has been committed, we want the perpetrators brought to justice."

Citrone closes the file in front of him and fixes his eyes on Khafaji. "Look, we're not stupid. There's a war going on here. Lots of people go missing for all sorts of reasons. But we have to try. We owe it to every Iraqi who works with us. We take care of our own."

They offer Khafaji more information. Zahra only recently graduated from the university. She went to work for the Americans in late May. Since then, she recruited five girlfriends of hers to join up as well.

Khafaji studies the photograph some more. When he looks up, he notices Citrone's jaw working at its frantic pace.

"I will look into this for you. Do you have anything else I could study?"

The assistant answers before Khafaji can finish. "No, sorry. Nothing."

Citrone gently claps the conversation to a close. "Spend a couple days on this, maximum. No more. Go ask the other interpreters what they know. They know she's gone missing. It'll help them to talk about it. It'll ease their anxiety to know that you're on the case."

If any place symbolizes what was lost in Baghdad during the sanctions years, it's Ibn Sina Hospital. People continued to call it a "hospital" long after the medicine ran out. It was a hospital partly because patients kept coming, but mostly because doctors kept the place open. It was the sick who first discovered how bad things had gotten in the country. There was no avoiding it. Khafaji would not have learned so quickly if the cancer hadn't appeared. It ate at Suheir's stomach and forced them to go from hospital to hospital in the hope of finding a cure. Or, barring that, relief. Each hospital they arrived at withered and died before their eyes.

It was a decade of hospital doors closing, one after another. But so many other doors closed too. Painkillers – closed. Antiseptic – closed. Penicillin – closed. But Ibn Sina's doors never closed. That didn't mean there was much use in them staying open. The doctors who remained were saints. They stayed and they continued to do all they could. Patients treated without anesthesia. Without antibiotics. Without aspirin. But never without hope.

Khafaji walks through the lobby and climbs the stairs to the fourth floor. When he gets there, he notices that the elevators are now working. He walks down the corridor, looking in here and there at the rooms whose doors are open. Many of the beds are empty this morning – certainly more than last night. The halls are clean and polished – and as Khafaji walks, he watches the reflection of lights on the floor.

At the reception desk, the nurse is friendly and helpful even before Khafaji shows his ID.

"She's here all right," she smiles, and asks Khafaji to sign in. A moment later, she leads him down the hall, to the last door on the right. Suddenly Khafaji wishes he'd brought something with him. A book, flowers, something to eat. Anything.

But when he sees Mrouj's smile, his doubts disappear. She sits upright and still in a wide bed, looking right at the door as he enters. As if she knew he would walk in at that moment. They say nothing, but hold hands and look at one another for a long minute. At last Khafaji hugs her and breaks the silence. "How are you feeling, Mrouji?"

"Baba, I'm OK. I'm OK."

"Are they treating you…?"

"I'm fine, Baba. They're nice."

"I know. I'm sorry I…"

"Don't be sorry, Baba. I'm here and I'm OK. I still can't believe what they did to you."

Mrouj reaches over and touches Khafaji's upper lip. "I'll get used to it," she whispers as she pulls the sheets up around her.

Khafaji looks around, and only now notices there's another bed and another patient in the room. Khafaji looks back at Mrouj, who smiles. "She's nice, Baba. I'm asleep a lot, and so is she. We haven't seen each other awake very much."

Khafaji studies the machines at Mrouj's bedside. Lights blink and lines move in waves. Numbers flash and change. Mrouj smiles and says, "That's the dialysis machine, Baba. They did it the first day I was here and they're going to do it today. They say I'll feel much better. Did you bring something to read to me?"

Khafaji looks at his hands and apologizes for the book he's holding. "Tell me what you'd like me to read you and I'll bring it."

Mrouj looks at him and says, "How about Nazik?"

"Of course. I'll bring the diwan. We'll read it over and over. How long did they say before you can go home?"

"They're doing tests, Baba."

"You don't need tests, do you? We already know what the problem is."

"They said there may be complications and they want to check."

"But you can come home soon, right? After you're stabilized, we can do the treatments at home."

"Baba, the doctors want me here for more tests. And they didn't say anything about coming home."

"At least that means they're giving you good care." The look of pain on Khafaji's face makes Mrouj squeeze his hand. He bites his lip and says, "I'll come every day to see you. We'll read Nazik from beginning to end. We'll go poem by poem. Line by line."

"I'd like that, Baba."

"Aunt Maha and Uncle Nidal send their wishes. How is the food here?"

"Edible, Baba. Everything is fine."

Just then, an American doctor walks into the room and grins at Mrouj. "Shaku maku?" She forces a smile back and says in a tired voice, "Safya dafya." He turns to introduce himself to Khafaji, and seems sincerely glad to meet his patient's father. "We don't have many interpreters up here, so if you don't mind, I might use you to find out more about your daughter's condition." He then calls the nurse and asks Khafaji to tell Mrouj that they are going to run other tests on her today, as well as another round of dialysis.

"She's lucky she made it in when she did, Mr Khafaji. She's got a long way to go, but I'm optimistic. She's a fighter."

"My daughter said there were complications."

The doctor tries to remain smiling as he talks. "In the US, we'd say she has all the symptoms of stage five CKD. Hematuria, ischemia, hypocalcemia. You already knew about the dehydration, the blood in the urine, muscle cramps, the itching and dizziness. We'd expect to see this kind of uremia in any chronic case that isn't treated. She's been sick for five years, correct?"

Khafaji nods. "Maybe longer. We didn't get a diagnosis right away."

"Right now, we're using hemodialysis to stabilize her condition. We've got to do that before we can see where we are. I'd like to see some improvement before we go ahead and call it stage five. My hope is that it's going to be treatable. We're running tests – cardio, vascular – to see what complications there may be."

"So, it's complicated?"

"Yes, you might put it that way."

Khafaji translates, and Mrouj smiles again despite herself.

"Do you have any questions before we get going today?"

Khafaji and Mrouj shake their heads. The doctor leaves the room while they hold hands and say goodbye. He kisses her forehead. "I'll be back tomorrow with our Nazik. Be strong."

"Yes, Baba. Tell me a line before you go."

Khafaji thinks for a moment. "*I'm not quick to thirst, nor one whose herd is ill-pastured at night, whose calves remain unfed while their mother's udders hang free. / Nor am I a mean coward, nor one who clings to his wife and asks her what to do. / Nor am I one who is slow to do a good deed, or someone who stays in the tent all day covering himself with perfumed...*"

Mrouj pauses and asks, "The long meter?"

Khafaji nods. Mrouj closes her eyes and guesses. "Oils and kohl? *Nor am I one who is slow to do a good deed, or someone who stays in the tent all day covering himself with perfumed oils and kohl.*"

Khafaji laughs. "Yes! Good – you're not so sick at all."

Khafaji takes the elevator instead of the stairs. Exiting the lobby, he reaches for his cigarettes. His hand touches something and he takes it out to look at it. It's the picture of the interpreter Citrone had handed him. He turns and walks back into the hospital, then downstairs to the basement.

The nurse at the morgue calls her supervisor, and in an instant the coroner appears – a large, lively man with blue eyes that never stop moving. "What can I do for you?" The warmth of the man's hand surprises Khafaji and reminds him how cold the room is. He offers Khafaji a cup of tea, and they sit and talk about the previous coroner, a man Khafaji knew. Khafaji offers him a cigarette. He declines, but encourages Khafaji to smoke as much as he pleases. The coroner walks over to a desk and pulls out a drawer full of unopened packs of Rothmans and Marlboros. He invites Khafaji to help himself. "By the time these arrive in my lab, their owners don't need them any more. No one will miss them."

Khafaji takes out Zahra Boustani's picture from his jacket and hands it gently to the coroner, who cocks his head. As the man studies the girl's face, Khafaji rifles through the drawer and picks out every pack of Rothmans. He fills his jacket, shirt and pants pockets with them. When the coroner is done, he hands the photograph back to Khafaji. He looks at a clipboard, and glances at the refrigerator. They walk along the rusty steel doors. The coroner stops to pull out a drawer from the bottom row. A young woman's body. Head wounds cleaned and partially filled. Her face is not unrecognizable. Khafaji peers at her. Not Zahra Boustani. A second drawer reveals a middle-aged woman whose feet are missing. Not Zahra Boustani. A teenager with gunshot wounds to her abdomen. Not Zahra Boustani. After closer inspection, a badly burnt body that turns out to be that of a boy. Not a girl. Not Zahra Boustani.

Khafaji pauses and looks around at the rest of the drawers. He lights a cigarette and the smoke is not just sweet, but a relief. The coroner leaves the room and gives Khafaji a moment to reflect. When he comes back, they walk down the row, pausing now and then to open the drawers of women whose descriptions overlap with the girl Khafaji's looking for. They're not Zahra Boustani.

After twenty, Khafaji comments, "What's with all the rot? I don't remember bodies like this."

"Mostly it's the power cuts." The man's face widens into a frown. "The refrigerator goes off for hours. We try to do our best and make do. We don't open the doors very often, in any case. What we need, of course, is a generator. But it's hard to argue that we need it more than the people upstairs who are still alive."

He laughs. "But don't worry, I'm told we're right after them in line." Khafaji lights another cigarette and laughs too. The more he smokes, the less he has to smell the formaldehyde.

Khafaji shakes the coroner's hand again and is again surprised by its warmth. He writes down Citrone's name on a piece of paper and says, "Let us know if you come across a body matching the description."

The coroner smiles and says, "I'll be calling you every day, my friend."

When Khafaji arrives at the stairs, the power goes out. He stands in the darkness, listening to the rustle of living bodies. Footsteps, breath, conversation, even laughter. Then matches striking and the hissing of gas lanterns. Someone offers to lead a small group up the stairwell and out to the lobby. There, Khafaji joins the crowd of people streaming out, leaving the building to its doctors and patients, both those above and those below.

1965

The first time Khafaji was handed a deskful of informants' reports, he was at a complete loss.

"Here's the Baghdad 'B' Set," is all the Colonel told him. "Get to work. I've got meetings in Tashree all afternoon. I want you to brief me on them first thing tomorrow. We've got problems we need to identify."

"Yes, sir," Khafaji replied. "Would you like me to look for anything in particular?"

The man squinted at Khafaji while putting on his jacket and cap. "You're supposed to be one of the smart ones."

"Yes, sir. Is this a complete set?"

"Should be. All I want is for you to tell me what they mean." He looked at his watch and added, "You've got fourteen hours."

Khafaji sat reading for the next four hours before he reached the bottom of the pile. He got up and found another pack of cigarettes in his jacket, and sat thinking about what he had just read. The reports were from all over the city, and filled with miscellaneous accounts of treachery, fraud and betrayal. It seemed as if the whole of society needed to be put under watch. But still, there was something wrong. These reports contained only information, but no system and no intelligence. As his colleagues went home for the day, Khafaji sat circling names and words and phrases that recurred, but still it meant nothing. He called Suheir to explain and she was forgiving. "That's OK, I'll go over to Nidal's. You get your work done and I'll see you as soon as you can come home."

As Khafaji was saying goodbye, Suheir interrupted him. "*So be content with what God has divided amongst us, for verily, He who allocated the qualities amongst us also knows them better than anyone else / And when righteousness was apportioned amongst the people, He gave us more than our fair...*"

Khafaji didn't have to think about it at all. "Fair share. *And when righteousness was apportioned amongst the people, He gave us more than our fair share.* Labid. I love you, Suheir. I'll be home as soon as I can get there."

Khafaji sat down with the rest of the reports, determined to go through all of them until he found their pattern. Their rhyme. Their meter.

By the time the Colonel reappeared in the morning, Khafaji was able to show that the importance of the reports wasn't to be found in what they contained, but rather in the way they shed light on how the network was functioning. There were clusters of supposedly disconnected informants producing remarkably similar claims, and others who were connected, but producing disparate reports.

"The latest attempt hit the networks hard, and now they're full of holes."

"Explain," the Colonel merely said.

"The holes are like lines of poetry that are missing feet. And then there are entire lines that are missing too, and we need to find out where they've gone."

The Colonel looked at Khafaji, puzzled.

"What I mean, sir, is that it is not a complete set at all – and that's what's so interesting about it. And we can't know what they mean until we put them back together." Khafaji had drawn a chart of the informants, their chains of reporting, and the places in the structure where information was missing or duplicated, or where it had been corrupted.

"I can't tell you what information belongs in the empty spaces. I can only point out that they're there. It's patterns, sir. In poetry, if you know the rhyme and you know the meter, you can make intelligent guesses about pieces that go missing. Each report in this set is like a line, but they were out of order and missing all sorts of feet. First I had to put the lines back into their right order, and then I had to figure out where they were missing pieces. Then I..."

The Colonel stared as Khafaji talked.

Monday
1 December 2003

At the cafeteria, one of the Indian men waves to Khafaji from behind the counter. Khafaji walks over and the man smiles and serves him a cup of hot sweet tea. Khafaji thanks him and goes over to an empty table where he sits down by himself. He watches a discussion of an American sport on television as he eats. He follows every word, but can't understand a thing. He finishes quickly, reaches for a cigarette and lights it. He looks around him for an ashtray, but someone shouts, "No smoking! Excuse me – there's no smoking here!"

Embarrassed and angry, Khafaji gets up and walks toward the nearest door. As he walks down the hall, he hears a frantic voice behind him. "Khafaji! Khafaji!"

The assistant is at his arm as he turns. "Citrone called and needs you now. You need to put that out."

Khafaji throws the butt on the ground and stamps on it and the assistant shakes his head. Then they start quickly down another hall, and a narrow set of stairs. They are almost running, and the assistant speaks in a rushed voice. "They just turned up something at a safe house. Bodies. Citrone was on his way there. He thinks our missing interpreter may be among them. They're holding the place. Crime-scene protocol – he wants you to see what you can find. A carrier is coming to take you there right now."

They wait in an alley until a Humvee pulls up. The assistant walks forward, shows his identification and begins talking to the driver. The door opens and a hand motions for Khafaji to get in. There are two black men in the front seat, and one white boy in the back. Khafaji slides into the open seat and straps on his seat belt before they tell him to. Then they are off. From the window, Khafaji watches the Victory Arch. It seems to turn and spin as they drive around it. When they drive closer, he can see the bulging muscles. The forearms grasping giant swords. Khafaji turns to look at his feet, some-how embarrassed.

They depart from a small gate onto Damascus Street. They're speeding toward Mutanabbi, then veer right at Mansur Street. When that ends, they turn right onto 14th of Ramadan. Khafaji never looks up and his companions are pretty quiet. The soldier in the front passenger seat reads out directions and the driver answers him, but in a voice so small Khafaji can't make out a word. The soldier next to him looks out the window the whole time. Though Khafaji looks over at him a few times, he never once sees the man's face. The car is quiet. The traffic thin. They speed.

Khafaji's heart explodes when the car is hit. Not once, but lots of times. At first it sounds like bullets and he imagines the worst. But then he notices that no one else reacts in the slightest. The navigator turns on the stereo. Khafaji peers out the window for the first time and watches as a crowd of boys hurling clods and bottles recedes in their wake. He keeps his eyes on the floor after they turn left at 14th of July Street.

When they hit traffic, Khafaji speaks up. "Mosul Street is easier." The navigator looks at Khafaji in confusion. Khafaji looks at the map, and points. "Michigan Avenue, right? It'll be easier."

Two troop carriers stand at one end to the street. A third blocks off the far end. Khafaji moves to get out, but is stopped by the hand of the soldier who's been sitting next to him. The man shoulders his weapon as he gets out and walks over to the other Humvee parked in front of a long row of villas. Khafaji stares at them. *This could have been my street.*

A brown-skinned sergeant gets out of the other vehicle and the two men talk for a moment. Then the soldier walks back, and waves Khafaji over. Khafaji shakes the sergeant's hand. He is young and friendly, with piercing green eyes. He explains the situation. "Our informants have been telling us about this villa for a couple weeks. Abandoned months ago. Then suddenly men coming through at all hours of the day and night. Jihadis. We wanted to make sure we knew who we were dealing with, so the place was put under round-the-clock surveillance. Yesterday, there was a spike in chatter, and so we decided to go in. They had a loud night in the house last night. Must have been a party!"

He laughs and shakes his head in fatigue. "We waited as long as we could then went in when the first call to prayer went out. Most had already split. By the time we came in, there were only four of them. Two were killed in the gunfight. The other two were pretty badly hurt."

Khafaji nods and looks around the street again. Not a person in sight. The other man takes out a pack of cigarettes and offers Khafaji one. Khafaji lights both their cigarettes.

"Where is Citrone?" Khafaji finally asks.

"He got called away. He was one of the first to get here, you know. We've seen some shit out here, but nothing like this. These are the bad guys. Kidnapping girls for sex or ransom.

They must have killed their victims last night, but that's not our business. We had our orders to wait until you got here."

"Where did they take the ones they captured?"

"The PUCs? It looked like they were going to take them to the hospital before sending them to hell. Need anything else? No? We're out of here."

He shakes Khafaji's hand, slaps the top of his jeep and they drive off. Khafaji looks around and realizes that the other soldiers aren't Americans. It's not even clear if they are soldiers at all. The logo on their troop carrier reads Meteoric Tactical Solutions.

Khafaji turns, and notices the jeep that delivered him has also sped off. As the two jeeps drive away, neighbors begin to come out of their houses.

Khafaji flashes his ID to the armed men at the gate and walks in. He doesn't ask for a tour of the place because he already knows the two-story layout. Men's sitting room, women's sitting room, two bathrooms, a kitchen and then upstairs.

The smell in the front room nearly makes Khafaji vomit. He doesn't have to look hard to know it's coming from the downstairs bathroom. Who knows how many men were staying here when the toilet stopped working? Khafaji lights a cigarette and keeps it perched on his lips to block out the stench. He peeks into the kitchen. Trash cans overflowing with garbage. Piles of plastic bags and plastic Coke bottles on the counters. Carcasses of roast chicken. Pieces of dry bread on the floor. The refrigerator wide open. Nothing in the cupboards. A shell of a house.

If the living room looks like a filthy barracks it's because that's what it was. Blankets and clothes strewn across old threadbare couches and the floor. Khafaji walks through a dining room that is filled with dirty cots. More than a dozen in all. A single bare light bulb. A quick check on the back patio tells nothing. The smell in the bathroom makes Khafaji avoid it completely. He turns toward the stairs, but pauses at the open door. He opens it and shuts it and looks closely at the unusual configuration of thick deadbolts. *Could be locked on both sides.* Khafaji taps on the thick metal and wonders why such a heavy door was put here.

Before he even reaches the landing on the second floor, he can hear the flies. From below a voice calls out, "Hello there, Hajji! Come here! Arms up and easy."

Khafaji turns to see a blond man with a saccharine smile. His puffy face stuffed under a tight blue beret. His puffy chest stuffed into a black T-shirt.

"This is a closed military zone, Hajji. Arms up. That's right. Easy now." The man's accent is peculiar. English, but not English. "What are you doing here?"

He fingers the identity badge hanging around Khafaji's neck.

"What's this?" He removes it, and holds the picture up next to Khafaji's face. Khafaji's smile has disappeared.

"Listen. Do you speak English?"

"Do you?"

The man stops and takes a step back. "Whoa now, Hajji." He looks at Khafaji's ID again, then begins to speak deliberately slowly. As if Khafaji were a child. "You're down range, Hajji. This area is secure, as you can see. And then suddenly you show up. What the hell are you doing?"

"I was sent here to investigate."

"You need to explain, Hajji – I don't know about this."

"I was explaining. If you can't understand my English, talk to Citrone." For the next fifteen minutes, Khafaji gets to know his new cigarettes.

"…well, you can understand why we needed to ask. We don't even know yet if the place is secure. We knew you were sending someone, but we weren't expecting natives."

"…"

He looks Khafaji over from head to toe, then turns away. "Well then, don't send them out in civvies."

"…"

"I'll let him get on with it."

The man tries to make peace with Khafaji by offering one of his cigarettes, but Khafaji ignores him. He takes out one of his Rothmans and lights it as he walks back upstairs. The cloud of flies is buzzing even more furiously. The door to the master bedroom is cracked open. Khafaji pulls out a dirty paper napkin and opens it the rest of the way. The first thing he sees are three splatters in the middle of the wall. Then the three women, face-down in a row. Long, loose peasant robes flare up and outwards to reveal bare legs and thighs and torn underwear. The spectacle is indecent. Khafaji pulls the cloth down past their knees, and notices that their wrists are deeply lacerated. They were bound at some point, then released. He looks around and finds some plastic cuffs on the ground, covered in blood. As he picks one up, his leather soles start to slide in a sticky, slippery half-congealed pool. He throws the cuffs in an empty pillowcase.

Each was shot in the back of the neck with something small. It could have been a lot messier. The killers must have forced them to stand facing the wall before he shot them. Their wrists were still bound when they were shot. The killer was tall – tall enough to hold and shoot a steady pistol at their neck so the bullet would travel down into their torsos. *An inefficient way to do things*, Khafaji thinks. *Plenty of mess. But it would silence the noise.*

Walking into another bedroom, Khafaji stumbles across a fourth body sprawled across a bed. This one has multiple cuts to the neck and torso, and sits in a pool of filth. The stench of emptied bowels fills the room. She must have seen her attackers. Death did not come quickly. The sheets and mattress are saturated with blood and shit and piss. A banquet for the flies. This one is facing up, staring at the ceiling. She's young. Her brown eyes are small but pretty, darkened with heavy kohl and blue eyeshadow. Her painted purple lips are strangely serene. Khafaji looks at her fragile, pale wrists. This one was never bound. He picks up her right hand and lets it drop. The rigor mortis has just started to set in. He looks at her fingers and glimpses blood and skin under her nails, though the filth of the scene makes it hard to tell for sure.

Khafaji pulls on her necklace, and jostles a plastic identification card. Almost identical to the one around Khafaji's neck. There's her picture. There's her name. In English: Sally Riyadi. US Army issue. Khafaji takes it, then goes to the bathroom to rinse it off. He cleans his hands on a pink bathrobe, then he puts the card in the pillowcase.

Now he goes back to the other bodies. One by one, he rolls them over. They're all just beginning to stiffen up. He imagines that one is almost warm, then checks again. The first one wears an identification card, and Khafaji removes it. The picture matches the face. Another name, Candy Firdawsi. He can't find an ID on the next girl, but as Khafaji looks at her, he's struck by how pretty she is. How pretty they all are. And made up like they were going out dancing.

As soon as Khafaji rolls the third body over, he regrets it.

He regrets coming to this house. He regrets his deal with the Americans. He regrets having to see any of this.

Khafaji doesn't need to read the girl's card to know who she is. For the second time in three days, he sees Suheir's face staring at him. She looks at Khafaji with the same eyes, the same faint smile. The same beauty mark. The same beauty. Only now it's cold and stiff.

Khafaji collapses on the ground. He beats on the concrete floor until his knuckles start to bleed. At first he's crying over Suheir, then over his niece Sawsan whose body he never intended to find. Then he weeps for the other girls.

Khafaji slumps against the wall and takes in the scene for a second time. Only then does he see how neat the room is. Except for the bodies and blood splatters, it could have been any rich girl's room. The purple overstuffed sofa, the purple pillows, the purple drapes. The poster of Kadhim al-Sahir. He wipes his eyes and puts Sawsan's card into the bag with all the others. Then he starts to explore the other bedrooms on the second floor. Each is decorated with the kind of bordello luxury you expect to see in the home of any high-ranking member of the Party. Lush feminine pinks, fuchsias and lavenders. Lace and satin and velvet textures. He opens one closet door. It leads to a separate staircase on the outside of the building.

Each floor of the house tells a separate story. Downstairs, it's all guerrilla safe house. Upstairs, all Baathist brothel, complete with murder. Khafaji walks downstairs and stops at the wall just behind the bathroom. He taps at the concrete, but doesn't need to. He can picture Uday and Mrouj as children. Playing and hiding in the same crawl space.

Before leaving, Khafaji tries to tell the soldier about the crawl space. The man looks at him confused, and Khafaji walks him over to the access panel in the bathroom. Khafaji holds his breath until he is outside again. Then he lights another Rothman and breathes the fresh air. Outside, over the wall, he sees the neighbors attempting to talk with the men in the troop carriers.

Later, as they drive Khafaji to a checkpoint in Karrada, the South African shakes his head and says, "My God, man. That was a huge stockpile. We thought we'd cleaned that house top to bottom."

"If you want to find the explosives, you need to bring the sniffing dogs."

The man insists on shaking hands when Khafaji gets out and walks into the night.

1975

The Director of the Information and Operations Branch of the Political Department writes to confirm the following:

While investigating the disturbances that followed the cancelation of the sectarian pilgrimage to Kerbala, our office stumbled upon the information that led to the uncovering of the Dawa Party leadership in the capital. That our officers were able to do this relying solely on secondary police reports filed in Najaf is an indication of our superior professionalism and unflagging attention to detail. The Iranian agents captured during the initial rounds of arrest had, prior to our investigation, operated with unusual confidence and total impunity. Interrogations in Branch headquarters (Muthana) rendered further actionable information across the enemy network, and we believe that this poison has now been completely driven out of the body of the Arab Iraqi people.

Special commendation needs to be given to Insp. Muhsin

Khadr al-Khafaji for tireless research and for following up on leads ignored during the primary investigation of Najaf office. Without Khafaji's skills in combing through mountains of previously analyzed information, this subversive foreign network would still be targeting the safety and security of the Arab Iraqi people. We recommend he be awarded *sharat al-hizb*, with full party honors and official compensation for his efforts and accomplishments. He is a credit to the DGS, and we expect his promotion in due course.

May you live to continue the struggle,

MUHAMMAD AL-DULAIMI

Tuesday
2 December 2003

When Khafaji wakes up, his headache is back, even worse. When they mess with your body, they mess with your head. That's the whole point – even he knew that and he was only a desk man.

Khafaji holds his head under the cold water until the pain goes away. Then he shaves in the dark. He spends half an hour looking for the book for Mrouj before giving up. He grabs a poetry anthology and walks out the door and fixes it shut. Two new young men are sitting at the front door, sipping tea, AK-47s resting next to them.

"God's grace! Peace upon you!"

They invite Khafaji to share their tea, and he forgets to scowl at them. They're as polite and friendly as the other details.

As his foot hits the curb, Khafaji feels a tap on his shoulder. One of the men smiles apologetically and hands him a note. "Sorry, Brother. I was supposed to give this when you came down."

As Khafaji walks to Abu Nuwas, he reads: *In the name of God, the Compassionate, the Merciful. Brother Muhsin, Greetings. Please stop by the apartment today. I'd like to have a word with you about what we discussed the other day. May God keep you safe. Yours, Ali.*

Khafaji puts the note into his pocket and walks to the corner. In the cab he ignores the young driver who tries to engage him in conversation. When the kid realizes Khafaji's not going to talk, he turns up the music on the stereo. His fingers tap along as an Egyptian pop singer belts out a love song. Khafaji's head is about to explode.

"Who're we listening to?" Khafaji frowns.

The driver mumbles a name Khafaji has never heard before. Then he turns up the volume.

Khafaji spends an hour at the gate shuffling through the book in his hands. He can't read because of his head.

Everyone in line is quiet today. They keep to themselves. And so Khafaji begins to see how nervous they are. They look over the concertina wire, as if they were waiting for someone to come over it. They stare at approaching cars, as if they were waiting for one to drive into them. By the time Khafaji takes off his jacket and his belt, he is relieved to be leaving the line behind. As he walks through the first gate, guards shout at someone to move away from the wall outside.

One of the guards recognizes Khafaji's face, looks at his badge and tries to pronounce his name. She gives up and asks, "Can I just call you Moe?"

Khafaji can only laugh. "Moe? OK. What should I call you?"

"You're talking to the Florida National Guard," she grins.

"OK, Florida!" He laughs back.

Citrone is in the office when Khafaji walks in and hands him a plastic bag.

"Peace be upon you, Inspector! Before I congratulate you, I want you to put these on."

Khafaji looks inside and sees a camouflage uniform. He takes it out and holds it over his body. It's a size too large. Or two.

"That's the closest they had. Go change in the bathroom, Inspector. We didn't know your shoe size, otherwise we would have got you the whole thing. I can take you down later to pick the boots that go along with it."

Khafaji returns to the room, looking like a scarecrow in uniform.

Citrone laughs. "Mashallah! You won't have to wear it for very long. The new IPS uniforms should be delivered in a couple weeks. Did I show you what they look like? We're pretty happy with how they turned out."

Citrone shows Khafaji a picture of a white man wearing an American baseball cap, black pants, and a neat blue shirt, with the words "Iraq Police" inscribed in both Arabic and English. In a second picture there is a woman modeling a feminine version of the uniform, complete with hijab.

Citrone smiles proudly and asks, "What do you think? We worked with the designers to make sure they were culturally sensitive."

Khafaji nods. "They are… um, very sensitive."

"You're supposed to wear those from now on when you're on duty." He fixes the collar on Khafaji's shirt before adding, "I've got a meeting upstairs. I'll see you in a bit."

Alone, Khafaji looks over at the filing cabinets. He starts to open drawers, looking for any pattern in the tabs and labels. Anything that will tell him about how the thing is supposed to work as a set. For two hours, he makes lists of names, divisions and sections. By now, Khafaji has wandered halfway across the room opening the drawers.

"Not those files. Citrone wants you to start with those back there." Khafaji turns around to see the same clerk from yesterday, pointing at the cabinets Khafaji looked at the day before. He must have come in at some point.

"Thank you." Khafaji notices the game of solitaire on the man's computer screen.

Khafaji takes out a stack of dossiers and begins reading them. Every so often, the pain in Khafaji's mind makes him close his eyes. When he does, all he can see is Sawsan's cold smile. Khafaji opens his eyes and looks over at the man playing cards. All by himself, so far from home.

At some point, the assistant walks into the office, leading a group of other young men behind him. All of them are wearing ties, sports jackets, and combat boots. Playfully, the assistant grabs Khafaji's arm and shouts, "Hey, everybody! Tell Bremer I'm the one who found Tariq Aziz, and he was working right here! I want my million dollars now! Where do I pick it up?" He slaps Khafaji on the back.

Everyone laughs. Khafaji closes his eyes, and finds Sawsan's frozen eyes staring back at him.

"No, seriously, this guy's the new star of our team. He's going to help us make quota. But it almost wasn't so."

One by one, Khafaji shakes their hands while the assistant recounts how Khafaji was arrested as one of the most wanted. "That's an amazing story. I love telling it," he adds.

"Listen, we've got a thing over at Prosperity. I'll be back in the office after lunch."

"OK, see you then."

Right before he walks out the door, he stops. "Listen, Citrone told me about what happened yesterday. Amazing work. Did you talk to the guys they captured?"

"Umm?" Khafaji squints and tries to forget the pain in his head.

"They're over in Ibn Sina. Citrone got them admitted there so we could talk to them."

"Should I go talk to them?"

"Yeah. You and Citrone. That's what he said."

"All right, I'll wait till I see him then." Khafaji goes back to the files on his desk. Out of habit, he reaches into his pocket for his cigarettes, but realizes they're in his jacket. He pulls out a pack of Rothmans and also the picture of Zahra Boustani. The soldier at the computer doesn't say anything. Khafaji finds a coffee cup on the assistant's desk and uses it as an ashtray. He smokes and closes his eyes and finds that Sawsan is still there, looking straight at him. He blinks and starts staring at the picture of Zahra Boustani instead. He stares until his cigarette is done. His headache is almost gone.

"Is there an office for the interpreters?" Khafaji wonders out loud.

Without looking up from the screen, the soldier calls back, "I'll check for you." He picks up the phone and a moment later calls out, "The linguist pool has an office trailer over in the West Villas. If you go there and ask, shouldn't be hard to find."

Khafaji looks at his watch. He stuffs the Rothmans in his shirt pocket and announces that he'll be back in an hour or so. As he walks down the stairs, he looks at his cracked leather shoes and imagines how odd they look with his uniform.

Lighting a cigarette, he wanders around the side of the palace until he arrives at the back, then he starts walking. When he gets there, he finds a dozen white trailers sitting behind a cluster of eucalyptus and jojobe. It takes some work and a cigarette before Khafaji finds the right one.

Maybe because the only image he had of interpreters was the black hood, when he opens the door Khafaji is surprised to find humans at desks and in cubicles. No one wears a mask. Khafaji shows his ID to the American at the front desk, and asks if there are any interpreters he can talk to.

The man points to a small group sitting in a cubicle, sipping tea in the back.

Khafaji greets them, and they shake his hand. There are five of them – three men and two women – and they are all in their early twenties.

"I'm Muhsin Khafaji. I'm here to ask about one of your co-workers. Zahra Boustani."

"Yes?"

Khafaji decides to start from the beginning. "One of the people you work with is apparently missing. Did you know that?"

Two of them shake their heads. One answers, "No one is missing from our group."

"Not that we've heard, at least."

Khafaji shows them Zahra's picture, and at first no one says anything.

"I recognize her," one of the women says. "She used to work with us, I think. But that was before my time. I'm pretty sure she works for the Army now."

The others nod and Khafaji asks, "Who do you work for?"

"This is the CPA group."

Khafaji frowns, and one of the men explains, "The Army has its own pool of interpreters. And so do the Marines. And the other countries. And security companies."

"Where are their offices?"

"On the bases, mostly. Some are probably over at Prosperity."

Khafaji asks, "Where's that?"

"Al-Salam Palace. Army HQ. But they keep us separate."

The other girl looks directly at Khafaji and adds, "Sometimes we end up working with interpreters from the other pools, and so we meet them. But they keep us all separate."

The others nod.

"Why?"

"They're pretty strict about security," the man adds.

"Of course it's impossible to keep us totally apart. Once in a while, we run into them eating at the cafeteria or en route. When that happens, we talk."

"But not too much."

"Yes. Anyway, I might recognize translators from other groups, but that doesn't mean I could tell you what name they use, let alone what their real name might be."

When he sees the look on Khafaji's face, one of the young men explains, "Look, you don't use your actual name, do you? So why should we?"

A woman says, "Look, our work is dangerous, isn't it? Who is the first target they go after? Us, that's who."

Another one continues, "There are two ways to eliminate interpreters. The first is at the checkpoints."

One of the women gets up and walks back with a bullet-proof vest and a black mask. "That's why interpreters get to wear the latest fashions even before the Americans do."

"What's the second way?"

"Infiltrate. Stick one or two in with the rest of us and wait for someone to talk."

"Like you're talking to me right now?"

"No. This doesn't mean anything. You don't know anything about me. Nothing dangerous about this."

"So, you assume they're already here and whatever you say goes straight to them."

"Everything. Or at least the things they want to know: who you are, where you live, who your family is."

"Of course, it's hard to not talk," a young man with long hair and glasses adds. "You work with someone for months, you're going to want to talk about your real life."

Khafaji takes out a cigarette and taps it on his knee while he looks at his notes. "So let me get this right," he finally says. He turns to the first woman. "*You* recognize this girl. She's an interpreter, you think, maybe for the Army? And you're sure she doesn't work for the CPA?"

"Yes."

"Good. And now for the hard part. If I told you her name was Zahra Boustani it might not mean anything even if you knew her?"

"Right," two others answer at the same time. Another adds, "None of us use our real names. Ever."

Khafaji looks at his notes, and then writes down some questions: *What is Zahra Boustani's real name? Who knows their actual names? Does somebody actually know these things? Does Citrone? If Zahra Boustani doesn't work for the CPA, what am I doing asking about her?*

When Khafaji looks up, he sees five young faces anxiously studying him.

Suddenly, they all laugh at once, even Khafaji. Nervous laughter, the kind that happens spontaneously when you're talking to someone about your problems and you realize their life is even more screwed up than yours. They're laughing together, but the way they look at Khafaji makes him squirm.

The throbbing in Khafaji's head is back. He decides to end the conversation as quickly as he can. "Would you mind me reading a list of names? Could you tell me if you recognize any?"

He flips the pages of his notepad and reads: "Sally Riyadi." Silence. "Candy Firdawsi." Nothing. "Sawsan Faraj." Nothing again.

Desperate, Khafaji digs into his pocket and takes out

Sawsan's picture. He passes it around the group. One girl draws her breath and sighs, "This one I do know. Her name's Suzy."

The other girl nods her head. "Yes. She works for the Army."

"The Army prefers girl 'terps," one of the men jokes, but no one laughs.

Khafaji asks again, "Are you sure you know this girl?"

They both nod. "Pretty sure," one of them murmurs.

"How do you know?"

"Like I said, once in a while you end up meeting each other by accident. I met her a few times at an Army base. She always talked to us, always. I am pretty sure she worked there with the Army group."

Khafaji digs around his pockets before he remembers he'd left the other girls' IDs back in his apartment. He makes a note to return to this office with those pictures.

1988

Topzawa was a vast camp that looked more like a busy petrol depot than what it really was. The early-spring air froze in their lungs when they went out to meet the new arrivals. Balagjar village, in the Qara Dagh region. The backs of the cattle trucks opened and steam rose up from the huddled crowd inside. Soldiers jostled the first line of villagers, and an old woman fell to the mud. Two younger men hitched up their baggy pants and climbed down to help the others.

The men were separated to one side. Sixty in all. The women and children were led away somewhere else. Then the process began. They had them remove everything. Watches and rings. Then hats, scarves, belts, and shoes. Piled onto a canvas tarp that was bundled up and sent off.

When, finally, the men were cuffed to each other in pairs, the officers set down their teacups and began to go about their business. The intelligence officer from Tikrit went first, stripping the men of their wallets and identification cards as the man at the table matched each with the names on the lists.

"Omar Askari. Father, Ozer. Mother, Khadija."

"You know what you've done, don't you?"

"Sir, no. I have done nothing."

"You have been found in prohibited areas."

"That is my village. That is my home."

The officer slaps the boy to the ground. "You are subversives."

"No sir, we are farmers."

The officer turned to the man at the desk and said, "*Peshmerga*. Next!"

An old man fainted and the officer ordered him back on his feet. The teenager cuffed to the old man tried to plead. "He is still suffering from breathing the —"

The boy did not have a chance to finish. The intelligence officer began beating and kicking the two men savagely until both fell motionless to the ground.

At some point, the man from General Security tapped the intelligence officer on the shoulder. "Let me have these two."

Something about the way he said it made the Tikriti walk away. He knelt down in the mud, and asked for someone to bring them water. When the men could stand again, he walked them over to the office where they drank hot tea and talked in hushed voices. He had hot meals brought in, then cigarettes. Every now and then, the Tikriti came over and he waved him away again. He went over the names on the lists twice before letting the prisoners go to sleep. When he saw the boy could read, he sent the old man off. He shared the documents in the folder and together they read them out loud.

The next day, he continued his conversations with the boy. He didn't interrogate. He didn't threaten. He just continued reading with the boy by his side. By nightfall, he had the names of all KDP operatives in the village, including two who also worked for intelligence. After that, resistance in Qara Dagh crumbled. After that, the men from Tikrit gave him more respect.

Tuesday Afternoon
2 December 2003

Back in the office, Khafaji tries to stare at a dossier. His head still throbs, and he leans back in his chair, looking for a distraction of any kind. Fumbling through his wallet, he comes across the number of the man who drove the taxi. On a whim, he dials it, with the idea of offering the man a job. The man picks up before Khafaji knows what he's going to say.

"Good afternoon, Karl. It's Muhsin. You gave me a ride a couple days ago. Rusafi."

"Glad to hear from you. Still alive? How are your American friends?"

Khafaji laughs. Remembering Citrone hasn't authorized him to hire his own driver, Khafaji is vague. "I've got an idea I want to run by you. It involves a regular salary. And you'd get to keep driving."

Karl chuckles. "Personal driver, huh? You paying in dollars?"

"Could be. Can we talk about it in person? When's a good time?"

"Tomorrow, 8 p.m. Dijla Café. Outside the gates. Backgammon?"

"*Mahbousa.* Loser pays. See you there."

*

Khafaji walks over to the DFAC and eats a late lunch. The food is heavy and warm and he realizes it won't help him stay awake on the job, but it helps his head. As he eats, he watches the large television screens on the wall. Someone changed the channel. No more sports. There's a report on the falling dollar. Commentators offer terse pronouncements that scroll across the bottom of the screen: "Nervous investors", "Concerns over impact on oil markets". Transfixed, Khafaji decides to keep watching even after he's finished his lunch. He pours a cup of American coffee and gets a piece of cake. By the time he returns, the news programs are running a story about a street battle that took place yesterday in Samarra. More than fifty people killed in a gunfight. Gang attempts hijacking of US Army trucks carrying load of freshly printed Iraqi dinars.

Khafaji takes a sip of the watery coffee and spits it back into the cup. He walks back to the counter and asks for a cup of tea. The man brings him a paper cup of the milky sweet confection. Khafaji smiles and offers him a cigarette. The man touches his chest with his open hand and goes back to his work.

Walking over to Ibn Sina, Khafaji remembers the poetry anthology he brought to read to Mrouj. Sitting right on his desk in the palace. A panic sets in and it takes Khafaji a few cigarettes to understand why he's so upset. It's only when he asks himself what he'll talk about with Mrouj that it begins to become clear.

Sometime in the last day he'd made a vow with himself not to tell his daughter anything. Not to talk about his arrangement with the Americans. Not to talk about being forced out of their apartment. Not to talk about the interpreters, neither those who came to work nor those who disappeared.

Not to talk about the girls whose cold bodies he touched. Mrouj didn't need to hear any of it. Only now does it occur to Khafaji that at some point he'll have to tell Mrouj about her cousin.

He walks down the long hall on the fourth floor, from the American side to the Iraqi civilian side, and the guarded rooms in the middle to keep them apart.

Mrouj's room is dark when Khafaji enters. He coughs, but no one answers. It takes a few moments for his eyes to adjust. She lies propped up in bed, her eyes closed, and her arms stretched out by her sides. Khafaji walks toward the chair beside her bed and sits down. The quiet in the room is only interrupted by the blips and ticks of the medical equipment. Khafaji looks at the wires and tubes in Mrouj's arms and closes his eyes. Immediately, he falls asleep.

An hour later, he awakens to the sounds of moaning and a sudden rush of movement. He blinks and watches as two nurses attend to the other patient in the room. When he turns back, Mrouj is looking into his face. They both smile and Khafaji unconsciously reaches for her hand. They sit silently as the nurses speak in hushed tones and give the other woman something that calms her. When they leave, Mrouj speaks up and breaks the spell. "Hi, Baba. I wasn't sure you'd come. I still almost don't recognize you."

Without thinking, Khafaji runs his fingers over his upper lip. "Of course I'm here. I'll come every day." His headache is still there, but not as bad as it was.

"Did you bring me some poetry?" Mrouj closes her eyes and Khafaji's panic returns.

When she opens her eyes again, she notices the pained look on his face. "What's wrong, Baba?"

"Nothing, Mrouji. Nothing. A little headache is all. I left the book I'd brought for you back in my office."

"We can just talk then. It's not a big deal."

"Yes, we can just talk."

A heavy silence falls over them as they listen to the labored breathing of the other patient.

"We're in Ibn Sina, I know that. Is your office nearby?"

Khafaji looks at her, but can't speak.

"Baba, what's wrong?"

"I'm sorry, Mrouj. It's just that I can't talk about it. I'm feeling overwhelmed."

"Of course. We don't have to talk about anything."

They sit there, hand in hand for minutes until Khafaji finally relents. "It's just hard, that's all."

Mrouj doesn't answer. Khafaji continues speaking. "They're asking the impossible of me. But I didn't have a choice."

Mrouj squeezes his hand and says, "We don't have to talk about it, Baba."

The pain in his head returns, and despite his intentions Khafaji starts talking. In his state, he imagines that if he can limit himself to talking about the easy stuff, he might just get through without saying anything about the hard stuff. He begins by telling her about the office work and the files.

"All they want me to do is read dossiers. Thousands of them."

"Sounds like your idea of heaven, Baba!" She manages half a smile.

"Lucky me. My own dream job, with the greatest employers you can imagine. They're not so bad, they're only deluded. Who the hell do they think is going to come work for their police force?"

After a pause, Mrouj says, "Someone with a sick daughter, I guess."

Khafaji looks at her, but she smiles before he can say anything. "You can laugh, Baba. It won't hurt you."

"It's all going to work out fine, Mrouj. Other than showing up for work, they're not asking me to do anything that would compromise me."

Now Mrouj laughs. "I'm glad, Baba. I'm just worried now that you're a real collaborator."

"Worry about yourself," he laughs back. "I spend my days in a room protected by an army."

"My room is protected by an army, too."

Khafaji falls quiet again, and Mrouj asks, "Really? All they're asking you to do is look at files?"

"For now, yes. Later on, I guess we'll approach the ones they want to take back. Who's going to say yes?"

Mrouj is sitting up alert now. "Why would someone join the Americans, Baba?"

"That's exactly the problem. People who are compromised, who can be blackmailed. People with scores to settle. People with ambitions. You might even find a couple who actually believe in the new cause. And then, some will join because they want to sabotage the whole thing."

"So the problem won't be about finding people."

"I guess so. The problem will be identifying their motivation." Khafaji pauses. "Motivation, and identity. How will we even know if they are who they say they are any more?"

They sit holding each other's hands for a few minutes before Khafaji murmurs, "*Time will reveal to you those things of which you were ignorant. / And the man who delivers such news may well be he toward whom you were once...*"

"You don't always have to give me such easy ones, Baba. 'Stingy'. Tarafa's ode. *And the man who delivers such news may well be he toward whom you were once stingy.* You should have given me the next line, it's better: *Time is only ever but borrowed, so take as much of its goodness as you can.*"

Khafaji kisses her and promises to return the next day.

When he walks back, a guard outside the middle corridor rooms greets him. Khafaji decides to try his luck and flashes his ID. "Citrone sent me over to talk to the men we picked up yesterday. This is where they are, right?"

The man looks at Khafaji's ID, and then again at Khafaji.

"I work for Citrone. You can go ahead and check if you like."

The man rifles through a clipboard, then inspects Khafaji's ID again.

Finally, he writes down a number and steps aside. "OK. They're yours. By the way, the doctors were trying to get a hold of you this morning to find out how long they're being held. These beds are in demand."

"I should know when I'm through with them."

Khafaji walks in and sees one old and one young. The man on the left is at least sixty years old. Maybe older. His arm is set in a heavy cast, but other than that, he seems to be in one piece. His other arm is handcuffed to the metal rail of the bed. The man's eyes are tired, though Khafaji doesn't miss the look of scorn in his eyes. Suddenly self-conscious, Khafaji's hands try to smooth out his baggy uniform.

The other man is much younger. Maybe twenty-five. It's nearly impossible to tell. The part of his face that isn't hidden by the oxygen mask is bruised and swollen. His breathing makes a muffled hissing sound. The only other sound in the room is the hum of the machines connected to him. His eyelids flutter slightly as Khafaji approaches. Then they close again. Each of his wrists is cuffed to the bed.

These men aren't jihadis. That much is clear. Their

moustaches and haircuts give them away. Tattered and dirty. Probably Fedayeen Saddam. The kind of gunslinging assholes everyone had to watch out for, especially cops.

Minutes go by as Khafaji sits down and stares at them. He hesitates. This was something he was never very good at. Give him a desk, give him files, and he could make the whole world talk. Give him a script, maybe he could improvise. But getting information talking face to face? That was for someone else to do.

"Comrades, I need to ask you a few questions about yesterday."

Silence.

"It's fine by me if you don't want to talk." Khafaji remembers hearing that timing is everything. He holds his tongue and goes back to silent mode. Things get heavy and weird. Khafaji lights a cigarette, and notices the glint in the young man's black eyes. *A smoker.*

Khafaji turns toward the older man, and says, "Father, how about one?" The man stares at Khafaji, but says nothing. "I only have Rothmans on me. Hope that's OK." Khafaji lights a cigarette and puts it on his lips. The old man never takes his eyes off Khafaji as he tries to lift his broken arm. He winces from the pain and his hand falls back on his lap. His eyes are glued to Khafaji's, then finally break. With all his might, he spits the cigarette out of his mouth. It almost clears the bed to land on the floor. Almost. Instead, it falls and rolls back onto his lap. The cigarette begins to smolder on the sheet.

Khafaji now has a script, even if it's rough. He leaves the cigarette burning and turns to the younger man. "You want one too? Let me get this out of the way so you can have one."

Khafaji removes the oxygen mask and puts it on the man's lap.

"Comfortable?" Khafaji makes a show of smoothing over the pillows and sheets on the man's bed. Then slowly he takes out another cigarette, lights it, then rests it on the young man's lips. The panic in his eyes makes Khafaji turn. He reaches over and switches off the oxygen machine. This whole time, Khafaji looks at the old man.

When the first smell of burning cloth hits his nostrils, Khafaji doesn't bother turning around. "How are you doing over there, Father?"

The young man tries to peer around Khafaji, but Khafaji grabs his face. "Is that better? You relaxing now? How about a glass of water?"

Khafaji lets go and they sit for a few more minutes. Finally Khafaji turns around to see small flames flickering on the old man's crotch. Khafaji grabs a plastic clipboard and begins beating at the man's legs and stomach. With the sheet fabric burnt and torn away, Khafaji notices that the flames have burned through the bandages on the man's legs and licked at his bloodied skin. Khafaji looks at the man and he stares back. He never once flinches. By now, Khafaji realizes how out of his depth he is.

Khafaji turns to the younger man and says, "Look, I really don't care who you are. I don't care what you may have done to the Americans. I just want to know about the crime you committed. Why the hell did you kill those girls?"

Again, a long, awkward pause. Khafaji decides to change his tack. "You know these guys are going to throw you in Abu Ghraib as soon as I'm done. If you think by not talking, I'll tell them to keep you longer, you've got it all backwards. You clam up, I'll say, 'Fuck you. Go to Hell.' And you know what? You will. They say you're criminals, so that makes you criminals.

"If on the other hand, you decide to answer my questions, I'll have them go easy on you. I'll have them put some televisions in here or something."

Finally, the old man breaks the silence. "Fuck you, you puppet. What crime is it to defend our home? What shame is there in standing up like a man? You should be the one answering questions."

Khafaji wishes he were back at his desk. Somehow paper could never get to you that way. Before he knows it, Khafaji feels his fist driving into the man's face. Blood gushes out of the man's nose and across his chest and lap.

Khafaji wipes his hand on the sheets before taking out another cigarette. He smokes without saying a word, then opens the window and flicks the butt into the sky. "I'm not talking about that – I'm talking about what you did to those girls. Who kidnapped them? Whichever of you talks first, I help."

Silence. "Who killed them?"

Silence. "Who raped them?"

The younger man tries to talk, but winces in pain. It takes him a minute before he can whisper, "What are you talking about? What girls are you talking about?"

Khafaji stares out the window. "The girls upstairs. There were four of them. It'd be pretty hard to forget them."

The younger one looks nervously at the old man, and then back at Khafaji. The older man closes his eyes, and the younger man talks. "We don't know anything about any girls. We arrived at the house. We were told to stay downstairs. They told us not to go upstairs."

"Go on."

"When they delivered us, they told us, 'Stay on the ground floor.' Who knows why we weren't supposed to go upstairs?

All I know is that there are reasons why people tell you to follow instructions. I followed them."

"You never saw people on the second floor? Never heard anything? Four women were shot while you were there and you didn't even hear it?"

"We knew people were upstairs. It was a separate apartment. They were having a party. We heard music. But no gunshots. And we didn't go up there. Most of us were so tired we just ate dinner and went to sleep. We weren't going to be there for more than one night anyway."

"But you went upstairs when the raid started?"

"There was no time."

"I mean, when the fighting broke out, some of you went upstairs to escape or…? There were four of you. One of you might have gone upstairs during the chaos."

The younger man doubles forward in distress. "Not possible," he manages to blurt out before he loses his voice in a bout of wheezing. Khafaji reaches over and turns on the oxygen machine again, then places the mask over the man's face.

The older man speaks now. "All of us were out when the door burst in. I was supposed to be sentry, but I'd dozed off. There was no warning. None of us heard a thing. They were sound asleep and their guns were in the next room. There was no gunfight."

Khafaji leans forward. "So what was all the shooting about?"

"There was shooting, but no gunfight."

Khafaji turns the conversation back to the subject. "Then what the hell happened?"

"What happened happened."

The man seems to be telling the truth, but it doesn't help at all.

"Look. I need to know. Four girls were shot upstairs in the house you were staying at. Someone tied them up and shot them. Then someone untied them again. All this happened while you were staying in the house. There's no way they could have been killed in that house without you knowing about it, or at least hearing it."

Utter silence. They look back at Khafaji as if he were speaking about a far-off country. Without thinking, Khafaji adds, "And one of them was my niece."

To his surprise, the words improve the tone of the conversation. Khafaji stays with them for another hour, going over and over the same details. Despite his doubts, he realizes they're telling him everything they know. Which is nothing. Each time he asks a question, they give more or less the same answer. Their story is consistent, even if it doesn't mesh with the facts he saw. And even though they don't like Khafaji, they no longer show any hesitation in talking about the details of this event. For them, it has no importance.

Entirely unsatisfied, Khafaji leaves. On his way out, he stops to speak with the doctor. "Their bandages need changing. Also, television. They need television in the room. These prisoners are VIP. So important to us."

The man nods and assures Khafaji that he'll make it happen. For the first time in hours, Khafaji's head feels clear.

Khafaji walks back to the office. Citrone is not there, but he has left a note asking Khafaji to meet in the morning to talk about the issue of housing. The soldier is still sitting at his computer. Still playing solitaire. Khafaji takes out his civilian clothes and goes to the bathroom to change. On his way out of the palace, Khafaji's hunger drives him toward the cafeteria. The place has closed, and the Indian workers are cleaning up the various counters. One of them spots Khafaji and signals him to come over. He offers to make a sandwich, and Khafaji accepts. The man hands it to Khafaji in a paper bag, along with a plastic bottle of Coke. Khafaji offers him a cigarette. He takes it and puts it behind his ear as he goes back to work. As Khafaji walks through the shadows of the palace gardens, he unwraps the sandwich and eats it while walking back to the gate.

Khafaji walks out of the American Zone, then down many blocks before he looks for a ride. By the time he gets to the gate at the end of his street, it's late. Too late to visit Ali, not that he wanted to. The guards smile and invite Khafaji to drink tea with them as he goes upstairs.

1988

"Thank God, you're home again."

Khafaji looked at Suheir, then buried his face in her neck and breathed her in. She held onto him, happy but confused. "You didn't call. We weren't expecting you."

Mrouj interrupted her, running down the stairs and throwing herself onto her father.

"My girl, my girl! I missed you both so much."

"We're so glad to have you back."

Mrouj did not let go of her father, not even when he knelt down to unlace his boots. As he pulled them off, thick pieces of dried mud scattered across the floor of the front room. Khafaji pulled off socks that were stiff with old sweat, then felt the cool tiles beneath his toes.

Mrouj just pointed. "Stinky, stinky! Get them out of here!"

Suheir picked up his boots and socks and put them outside. She shut the door and turned and smiled. "How long is your leave this time, Mhaysin?"

Khafaji only shook his head. Suheir walked into the kitchen, calling out behind her, "Mrouj, come get something for your father. He's tired and thirsty. Ask him what he wants to drink."

Mrouj ran off toward her mother, then spun around. "Baba, what do you want? I'll get it! Look how fast I am!"

Khafaji tried to smile, but failed. "Anything. Water's fine."

When Mrouj came back and saw the state her father was in, she ran back into the kitchen. She came back, dragging her mother by the hand.

"Mrouj, go outside and play. Be back for dinner, OK?"

"Yes, Mama."

Suheir held him for minutes before he finally looked at her.

"Have you heard from Uday?"

"What's wrong, Muhsin?"

"When was the last time you heard from him, Suheir?"

"What's this got to do with him? We talked on the phone in February, I think. He can't call because he's at the front. But he's managed to send letters every week all spring. I've been getting one every Thursday. I haven't gotten one in two weeks." She looked at the ceiling, and added, "Three weeks, tomorrow."

"Show me one, I need to see one."

"Why? What's this about?"

"Just get me a letter. Get me the last letter. Or any letter."

Suheir came back into the room with a stack of envelopes. Khafaji looked at them one after the other.

"Aren't you even going to open them? I saved everything."

"They fired me, Suheir. They didn't say why, but they put me on a bus and told me to wait at home until I received my next orders."

"You mean they transferred you?"

"Fired. Demoted. Transferred. I'm not sure. But whatever it is, it's not a good thing. And it's got to be punishment for something. It's coming from somewhere up high. I had a long bus ride to think about what it could be, and the more I thought, the more I began to worry about Uday."

Only then did Suheir notice the empty spots on his chest and shoulders where badges and medals used to be. She reached out and held his arm.

"What does this have to do with Uday?"

"Look at these postmarks, Suheir. He's not at the front. That means he's not with his unit."

"God help him," Suheir muttered. He looked out the window and added, "And us."

Khafaji turned suddenly to Suheir and asked, "Is this everything? We need to get rid of it all right now."

Suheir nodded as they set to work.

Wednesday Morning
3 December 2003

Khafaji wakes up late. As he makes a pot of tea, he remembers the dream that woke him once, just before dawn. A nightmare in the guise of an Egyptian musical. The band strikes up a song, and a dancing girl suddenly appears in the middle of the dance floor. Close-up on the smile that flashes across white teeth furiously chewing on gum. Other dancing girls swirl around her as she moves forward toward small round tables where the audience sits drinking wine and smoking cigarettes. The girl whirls around, and the other girls disappear into the wings. Suddenly, the violins fade out and the music becomes a purely percussive beat. Dum-tik, tik-dum-tik. Dum-tik, tik-dum-tik. Close-up of the girl's midriff as it shakes with increasing frenzy. She whirls around and around violently. Spinning and spinning as the music's tempo rises to a crescendo. Montage of mad musicians. This one blowing furiously on a reed flute, that one hitting the strings of an oud, another banging on a tambour. Finally, the girl collapses in a heap in the middle of the dance floor. Close-up on the girl's face, her lips contorted in ecstasy and pain. The audience explodes in loud applause, and the girl is carried off the floor.

After a pause, the scene begins on the same stage with another girl, another dance, and another collapse. It repeats five times in all – each girl with her own individual features and flourishes. One is athletic and kicks her legs improbably high into the air. One flips her wrists and fingers like a Hindu goddess. Another curls her lips like an Andalusian gypsy. The last shakes a round belly while rolling her hips in small jerks.

Only later in the morning does Khafaji realize that the faces of the first four are those of the dead girls. And then came the grand finale that ripped him from sleep. At first the body of the last dancer seems to belong to Sawsan. Or Suheir. She circles around Khafaji's table, but he can't get a glimpse of her face. She pulls on his tie and swings past him, but he still can't see who it is. Then, as she begins to shake and bend, she suddenly turns over him, so close Khafaji can feel her breath on his face. Zubeida Rashid.

Khafaji went back to sleep. When he woke up again, he was exhausted, but his headache was gone.

While making tea, he decides to break the news to Nidal. He washes his face, shaves slowly, and gets dressed. As he's walking out, he remembers the ID cards from the villa, and goes to find the pillowcase. He stuffs them in his pocket and walks out, fixing the door shut behind him.

For the first time in days, there is no one sitting in the building's entrance. Khafaji salutes the guards at the gate down the street, then walks a slow zigzag through the neighborhood, in the opposite direction from the day before. He looks behind him more than once before heading to Kamal Jumblatt Square, where he catches a taxi. Khafaji mentions the address in Saadun, and the young driver says "As you wish" in a polite voice. The young man pauses, then asks, "Would you mind if I played some music?"

Khafaji replies, "By all means."

The driver chuckles and slips an old cassette tape into the stereo. Khafaji is glad to hear what he hears. Fayruz's *Immortal Songs*. Khafaji closes his eyes and listens to the songs. Music is the only element that has the power to reverse time. The more he listens, the more present the past seems. And it fills him with a warm feeling. A checkpoint diverts traffic, and the detour adds twenty minutes to their drive. Each time they pass a gas station, the flow of cars comes to a halt, then opens up again on the other side.

The building Khafaji gets out at overflows with the bustle of life. Children are everywhere, playing in the street out front. In the garage below. Their laughing voices fill the stairwell.

As soon as Nidal's wife Maha sees Khafaji at the door, she guesses the news he's come to deliver. She collapses on the floor. The other women of the house lift her onto the couch and she faints again. They urge her to retreat into the bedroom, and she disappears with one of them. Nidal returns home fifteen minutes later carrying a plastic bag of fresh bread. He hears his wife and sees Khafaji and immediately understands that his daughter is dead. He sits down on the couch next to his brother-in-law. Khafaji's hand rests lightly on the man's heaving shoulders. Khafaji looks up and sees a crowd of children thronging around them.

"Go downstairs and play," Khafaji murmurs. The older siblings grab the younger ones and disappear.

Minutes pass before Nidal recovers his composure. He wipes his eyes with the back of his hand, and says, "We're done. We're leaving."

Khafaji looks away but keeps his hand resting on Nidal's shoulder. He notices the row of over-packed suitcases along the wall.

After a long pause, Nidal pulls gently on Khafaji's hand until they're looking at one another.

"Why?"

"I'm sorry, Nidal. I don't have any answers."

"Tell me what happened, then. You found her?"

"Day before yesterday."

Nidal squints and looks away. Embarrassed, Khafaji continues talking. "There were three others. Murdered."

Khafaji lets it sink in for a minute before continuing. "I think they were kidnapped. Maybe for ransom. Maybe just because they were working for the Americans. They were killed right when the Americans showed up."

Khafaji attempts to catch the man's eye, but now it's Nidal who's looking away. "Her body was taken to Yarmouk Hospital, they said. I can go with you when you're ready."

A new torrent of wailing spills from the bedroom.

Finally, Khafaji asks, "Did you know that Sawsan was working for the Americans?"

"I knew she was getting paid in dollars. She never talked about what she was doing. So we thought that was a possibility. What did her professor say?"

"She told me nothing. It was someone else who told me. For what it's worth, Sawsan was only doing what a lot of other kids are doing. Working as translators."

After a pause, he adds, "There's a lot worse that kids might do, you know."

Nidal shakes his head. "Like what?"

"Don't get me wrong, but there aren't many decent ways to make a decent living. So what if she worked for the Americans?"

Nidal shakes his head and laughs bitterly. "Is this a joke? Why did you come here?"

"I'm not joking…"

Nidal glares at Khafaji. Finally, he speaks. "So, what was Sawsan translating, then?"

"What do you mean?"

"I mean, how was she translating for the Americans when she didn't know more than a few words of English?"

Now it's Khafaji's turn to glare.

"Everyone knew that about Susu. She was no good with languages. Her brothers used to tease her in English because they knew she wouldn't understand them. And she never did."

He laughs and blows his nose. He shakes his head again and again.

"Only a fool would have hired Susu as a translator. You found the wrong girl."

Khafaji doesn't know what to think. He makes a show of looking at his watch and decides to leave. He stands up and tells Nidal, "I swear to you, Nidal, the body I saw was your daughter's. It makes no sense, I know. Maybe I was wrong. I promise I'll find out."

As Khafaji walks downstairs and into the street, he begins to consider the possibility there was a mistake. *But you saw her with your own eyes.* He rubs his bleary eyes and lets the exhaustion pour across his body. When the headache returns, it comes on fast.

The children swarm around Khafaji as he walks down the street. Their laughter suddenly annoys him. A ball hits a pothole and bounces over to Khafaji. He tries to kick it back, but misses. They scream and take off running after it while he curses under his breath.

1988

To: Iraq Intelligence Service, D4
RE: Uday Muhsin Khadr al-Khafaji

This formal clarification is prompted by interviews with officers from D4 (Date: July 30) and the Directorate of Military Intelligence (Date: July 22) concerning the desertion of my nephew, Uday Muhsin Khadr al-Khafaji. Let it be known that I have only met my nephew a handful of times and that my relations with his family were distant long before he committed his crime. It is true that my nephew had, for many months, attempted to contact me via post. It needs to be emphasized that this gesture on his part was uninvited and ceased more than three years ago. I believe he was motivated more by a desire to practice his English than by any particular sense of familial connection to me.

It will not be difficult for you to prove that, as instructed, I have maintained nothing more than cordial relations with my relatives in Iraq since my appointment at Exeter. I believe that a fair consideration of my actions will absolve me of all responsibility and connection to this case, and have refrained from contacting my brother since I was notified of my nephew's execution.

At the risk of overstepping, I would be remiss if I did not enter a plea on behalf of my brother, Muhsin Khadr al-Khafaji. I understood from my interviews that he has been relieved of the post he has held for more than a decade, and this would appear to me to be a mistake. I admit that I am not so estranged as to have lost all fraternal sentiment, yet my reasoning remains objective and my motive professional. My brother's reputation in the service is exemplary. He is known to be a diligent investigator and a talented handler of networks and information systems. If you find that his commitment to our Glorious Party remains unwavering, and that his loyalty to the Great Leader (May God protect Him) remains steadfast in the wake of this incident, I would recommend that he be rehabilitated. One might even consider him for a post in the Office of Information and Records. As they say, an archive is only as good as its minder.

May you live to continue the struggle,

HASSAN KHADR AL-KHAFAJI

Wednesday Afternoon
3 December 2003

By the time Khafaji goes to the American Zone, the sun is sitting high in the sky. And so is the pain in his head. The air is unseasonably warm, even hot. The wait at the gate looks daunting, so Khafaji retreats to the Dijla Café. He drinks a cup of coffee and looks across the road, glad that he is not standing there.

At first he thinks of sitting outside in the air. But his head forces him to move into the shadows. At this hour, the square is cluttered with people and traffic. Hundreds of automobiles and trucks. Most driving west, out of town. A few pulling over to wait in line to enter. Pedestrians cross the melee in all directions. It looks like a parking lot. From a distance, the people standing in line look no different than the fluttering plastic bags caught in the spools of razor wire. Khafaji picks up some discarded newspapers and begins to read. The front pages are filled with conjecture about the seven Spaniards killed outside al-Hilla. Spanish military intelligence? CIA? Mossad? Inside, Khafaji reads about the killing of two police sergeants in Mosul. He folds the papers and throws them back on the table. His head hurts too much to keep reading. He stands and decides to try his luck at the gate.

Khafaji is most of the way across the intersection before the chaos erupts. The first sign there's something wrong are the gunshots. Then all at once everyone ducks onto the ground. Pedestrians dash behind large vehicles. At first, car passengers try to lean under dashboards and seats. Then they open car doors and flee. The shots stop, but now there is commotion at the gate. Sirens explode and soldiers appear on the ramparts. A loudspeaker barks commands, too garbled to make out. But it doesn't take long for the simple message to travel: leave the area now.

Khafaji jogs back to the café, and orders a tea. Within a minute, the tables around him fill with people anxiously watching the street. Pedestrians stream away from the gate. Cars and trucks and buses back up and then speed off. Twenty minutes later, the street is empty except for a dozen abandoned cars. Periodically, the garbled announcement issues from a distant loudspeaker. Khafaji hears words, but their meaning dissolves in the wind. He notices that the line at the gate has vanished, and decides to seize the opportunity.

As Khafaji approaches, he sees a large water truck parked directly in front of the gate. The doors to the cab are wide open. A man in a thick armored suit slowly walks around, periodically inspecting pieces of the vehicle. To Khafaji's right, a voice begins to shout, "Imshi minna! Imshi minna!"

Khafaji turns and sees one of the regular guards at the gate. Khafaji smiles and holds his hands over his head. "Hi there, Florida! It's me – Moe!" He walks over slowly. "I am sorry, Florida. I could not understand what they say. Is everything OK?"

The woman studies Khafaji's face for a moment and then notices the ID hanging around his neck. Finally she nods in recognition.

"What is going on?"

"We've got a situation. Probable bomb in that truck. It's huge. Come over here." She speaks into a radio and then waves Khafaji to come over. From this angle, they are separated from the truck by one hundred meters and a shoulder-high concrete slab. The minutes tick by slowly as they watch the bomb squad inspect the truck. The man in the suit runs his fingers along the shiny metal of the tank, feeling, listening, walking a few steps, then feeling and listening again. It takes a quarter of an hour of watching this before Khafaji notices the crumpled human form on the ground near the cab. One of its legs quivers and kicks. Khafaji turns and catches the eye of the soldier. She explains. "This guy cuts in at the front of the line, believe it or not, and the cars start honking. That gets everyone's attention. Then, when somebody goes out to see what's going on, the driver bolts. He leaves the keys in the ignition, and takes off running. Didn't get very far."

Khafaji watches as the man in the suit takes off the thick metal helmet. He waves with both arms a few times and walks away. A few minutes later, the soldier's radio crackles. All clear. Not a bomb. A couple of medics exit the gate, and rush toward the man on the ground. But by then his body has stopped moving. Khafaji follows twenty meters or so behind the soldier, curious, but not sure what he's supposed to do. One of the other soldiers nods when Khafaji waves. Khafaji sees two interpreters among them, now wearing fatigues and thick body armor. Curious, Khafaji walks over to where they're standing. Within a few minutes, there's a crowd of men and women in fatigues around the tanker. Among them is the soldier who first confronted the driver. "FODA! He was suicide!" The man is trembling with fear and excitement.

His comrades attempt to calm him down, but he just paces back and forth yelling, "Fuckin' A!"

When they open the seals on the tank, the escaping air makes a hiss. A soldier puts his face into the hole and peers into the darkness. The heat makes him come out and wait for a moment before putting his face in again. He frowns and rubs his nose and asks for a flashlight. Someone tosses one up to him. He aims it down into the tank and looks again. He looks for a long time, then shouts something into the hole. Finally, he shouts, "Sergeant, you better come up here and look at this. There are men down in there. It's an oven. You better get the medics."

One of the interpreters climbs onto the tank and begins to call out into the darkness. He calls and calls, his voice frantic, then weak. The soldier waves him off and sits down on the top of the tank. The interpreter slides back down the side, murmuring, "There are twenty of them in there. Like they're sleeping. Twenty sleeping men."

Khafaji decides to get away as fast as possible. He turns and walks up to the outer gate. No one is there, and he walks through without stopping. When he gets to the inside gate, they stop him and ask him to wait by the side until they receive orders to reopen the gate. Khafaji sits down next to a metal box with a hole in the side. A strong smell of cordite wafts out from inside. Khafaji lights a cigarette and reads the weapons clearing procedures on the side of the box.

Fifteen minutes later, they let him and some others through the second gate. He doesn't break pace until he walks through the metal detector at the DFAC.

Khafaji picks up a paper cup of tea from the cafeteria and offers the man a cigarette in exchange. Speaking in halting Arabic, the man introduces himself as Noman. Khafaji follows him through the kitchen to a door that opens onto a loading deck. Noman mentions that he learned some Arabic in Riyadh.

"Ten years. I did Omra twice and Hajj once."

"What was it like?" Khafaji asks.

"What?"

"Riyadh? What was it like?"

"Highways and mosques. Highways and malls," he laughs. "I don't know. We worked a lot and we weren't allowed in." He pauses and then adds, "Ten years driving a Cadillac equals one apartment in Delhi. That's what it was like."

They smoke in silence, then Noman whispers, "It was not so bad until the war came. My boss went to Europe for six months and fired everyone except me. Fired the gardeners, the cooks, the maids. God knows why they kept me on and left me behind to take care of everything until they got back. Gardening, maintenance, cleaning, car repair. Everything! I did the jobs of ten people. And when he got back and saw what I did, my boss decided he could save money. He cut back permanently. Only me after that. I never had a moment of rest after the war! No offence, but I wish Saddam knew how to aim better. Maybe the boss would never have come back!"

"Maybe you would have gotten to keep the villa!"

Noman laughs and insists on shaking Khafaji's hand. Khafaji gives him two more cigarettes. At first Noman tries to put them both behind his ear. Then he slips them into his shirt pocket.

Wednesday Evening
3 December 2003

Khafaji feels a headache coming back on when he finally walks into the office. The first thing that catches his eye is the book of poetry sitting on the desk. Right where he left it. The second thing he sees is the pair of thick-necked men in their shiny suits. Khafaji notices their barrel chests and pauses. By the time he notices their arms, he's being pushed into a chair. One of them disappears into the hallway. For five minutes, Khafaji sits in Citrone's chair with a stranger's hand on his chest. He nods and asks, "Looking for Citrone?" No answer.

Khafaji adds, "Well, he's not here. Let me go get him for you."

The man pushes hard then leans forward into Khafaji's face. His whisper is almost imperceptible: "Shut up."

Khafaji and his guest sit face to face, their knees kissing. Khafaji tries to look away from the man's eyes without being too obvious. Khafaji looks left and right, then his eyes settle on the window. Shutters closed like every day. He studies the filing cabinets instead, then closes his eyes and goes looking for Sawsan.

At some point, the other man returns from his errand. He pivots as he walks though the door. By now Khafaji has considered the scene and guessed his options. He is not surprised when the Mosuli strolls through the door, looking as serious as a popular referendum. The other man flashes a shoulder holster as he straightens his jacket. If he were quick, Khafaji could almost grab the man's gun. The Mosuli sits down. He straightens his suit with smooth, soft hands. Khafaji looks at his shoes. Still new, still shiny. Like he still hasn't set foot on Iraqi soil.

He doesn't say a word, he just snorts like a horse. Khafaji starts to fidget and looks at the ceiling then out the door. In the hallway, everything continues as normal. Young Americans in suits walk by with paper cups and cellphones. No one looks in. No one looks around. The man by the door carefully shuts it. Suddenly, the Mosuli leans over and throws a Manila envelope on Khafaji's lap. I know this script: *File and Dossier.* Khafaji smiles.

"Open it."

Khafaji's fingers uncoil the red thread and pull out a small sheaf of paper. Two photographs slide out onto the floor. When Khafaji leans over to pick them up, he realizes that he does not remember this script at all. When his fingers touch the photos, he begins to wish he was sitting somewhere else in some other room. One is an image of a group of men in uniform, sitting in an office, dated 1988. It takes Khafaji a second to remember. The regional HQ in Sulaimaniya. You can tell they're laughing even though they are all wearing the old Soviet gas masks. Some are holding up small glasses of tea. Like they were raising a toast.

Khafaji spent 1987 in Kirkuk, dealing with the chaos of resettling thousands of southerners into the city as fast as possible. The next year, he was transferred to the mountains and the front. This was the only year of his life he wished he had never lived. He wrote reams about it, draft memos and reports. But he spoke about it only once – to Suheir. Then never to anyone again. He went to the north, and he managed to survive. And for his service, they stripped him of everything and sent him home.

Those days were long gone. Forgotten, erased. Sixteen years later, Khafaji stares at a picture, and it stares back, dragging behind it a mule-train of memories. Khafaji's father always said that a secret in the hands of a stranger is a weapon. And he was rarely wrong.

The Mosuli leans forward and waves at Khafaji. "Keep reading. Don't worry about them getting dirty. The originals are in California."

The other photograph is from winter. The gates of a place he allowed himself to believe was never anything but a bad dream. He suddenly feels the bitter air and shivers. Houses and horses, mules and boots, tires and pants – everything splattered with mud.

"Recognize that? It's a place called Topzawa. The Directorate was highly efficient. Some units kept meticulous records of everything. You made sure that yours did."

Topzawa. The name slashes across the years. It was a name Khafaji used for a year until its sound became so sharp it could cut. A year of ferocious activity, of flying over valleys and diving through reports, of driving headlong through the fog of war.

For years, all he ever remembered were the wildflowers. He arrived with spring. The mountains were carpets, with cicatrix stitches and fantastical designs. He never saw anything so beautiful. Whites and reds and purples. And greens rolling off into forever. And the red narcissi, bleeding veins in the hills. The air was wild herbs. His driver taught him the Kurdish names for each flower and plant. But now, at this moment, Khafaji can only remember a scent – a green sweet smell. Death. The fragrance of green apples, spring onions and young garlic that would hang for days in the valleys. Mustard gas. Khafaji goes limp in his chair. The papers slide off his lap onto the ground.

Khafaji is not fully conscious of what transpires next, nor even of how long it lasts. He is aware that the Mosuli is talking to him, but it's as if the room has gone dark. His eyes are wide open and the lights are on, but he sees nothing. Periodically, he hears noises out in the corridor, but they pass by and fade away. Footsteps and conversations that come and go.

At some point, the door flies open, and the assistant walks in with two other young men. They're laughing at a joke of some kind and holding paper coffee cups.

"Inspector!" he cries out. He then turns to the Mosuli and, suddenly serious, adds, "Very pleased to meet you, sir." The other young men step forward in turn, eager to shake the exile's hand. "It's an honor to meet you, sir."

In reply, the Mosuli has risen to his feet and is busy smoothing over his jacket. He smiles broadly. All too easy.

Khafaji feels the anxiousness of the thick necks at the door, and it wakes him up from his nightmare. He has only a few seconds to take advantage of the situation, so he does. Khafaji stands up and says to the assistant, "Good to see you. We are talking about how to coordinate efforts better." He shakes the hands of the assistant's friends, then rests his hand casually on the Mosuli's shoulder as if they were friends. "Everyone sit down. We might as well start now."

The assistant sits and asks, "If it's not an imposition?"

Khafaji replies, "Not at all."

The assistant introduces the other two young men in suits. "These guys may as well join us too. They're from Prosperity, but they're connected to everything we're doing down here. They may even have some fresh ideas about the coordination process."

One of them laughs, "Don't know about that!" They all smile and look at Khafaji.

The Mosuli begins to say something, but Khafaji interrupts. "The process is delicate, but that shouldn't stop us, should it? Why don't I get coffee?" The assistant and the others hold up their paper cups and decline. The Mosuli leans back and smiles grimly. Khafaji tries to be gracious as he grabs his jacket from the coat rack. He fails.

"I'll be back then," Khafaji announces to the room in a glad voice. He even pats the arm of the man at the door as he walks by.

On the steps of the hospital, he lights a cigarette and tries to think. But all the nicotine in the world would not solve this problem. He flicks the butt away and walks in.

As Khafaji signs in on the fourth floor of the hospital, he remembers the book sitting on his desk. By the time he walks into Mrouj's room, it's all he can talk about. "I'm sorry, Mrouji. I haven't brought you anything. I forgot the damned book again."

Mrouj looks up with tired eyes and tries to smile. Khafaji looks for a chair, then comes back to sit down next to her. She takes his hand and pats it gently. Mrouj's hand is warm to the touch. Minutes go by before Mrouj breaks the silence. "What's making you so upset, Baba?"

Khafaji strokes her hair and murmurs, "I don't want to talk about it."

Her eyes closed, Mrouj whispers, "Talk if you need to. Otherwise, just go."

Khafaji says nothing. Minutes go by before Mrouj repeats, "Talk."

Khafaji's silence drags on, interrupted only by the coughing of the other patient in the room and the gentle pings of medical equipment. Khafaji feels suddenly cold. He begins to shake.

"Baba, are you sick?"

Mrouj's voice is no comfort. When he opens his mouth to speak, his anger and frustration pour out. He tells Mrouj about her cousin. He tells her about the bodies on the floor and the blood and the flies. He tells her about the traffic and the checkpoints and the morgue. He tells her about the men down the hall. He tells her, though none of it makes any sense. He tells her about the new neighbors in the apartment building. He tells her about the boys with guns in the foyer. He tells her about the roundabout ways he comes and goes home. He tells her they're being evicted. He stares out the window as he talks, and never once looks at her. Mrouj listens and reaches for his hand. Eventually, Khafaji starts talking about Sulaimaniya. About Topzawa. And he is surprised to find he hasn't forgotten a thing. He talks for what seems like hours. He tells her everything.

When he finally looks at her, he sees that she's asleep. He takes his hand out of hers and strokes her cheeks. He pulls the blankets up around her chin. Glancing around at the room, he notices the other patient wide awake and staring at him as if he was a ghost. With a start, he gets up, and Mrouj calls out softly, "I'm here, Baba. Tell me a line."

"OK, Mrouj." He pauses before answering, "*Man is half tongue, and half mind, and between them is nothing but a sketch of flesh and blood. / While fools that are old have no wisdom to look forward to, young fools may sometimes..."*

Khafaji listens for Mrouj's voice, but hears nothing.

"May sometimes become wise. Zuheir. Goodnight, Mrouj," Khafaji whispers, "I'll be back tomorrow."

As he walks away, he looks over at the other patient, and she withers beneath her blankets.

When Khafaji arrives home, he finds the guards are back at their posts. He rushes past them at the gate, and again in the foyer. As usual, they try to stop him with an offer of tea. Khafaji notices the hall is filled with suitcases and cartons. At the stairs, he hears a commotion above.

On the landing on the second floor a group of men throngs around someone wearing black robes and a turban. A cleric. It takes Khafaji a minute to work halfway through the thick crowd. Now they are speaking Persian. Along with Arabic. Ali stands beside the man, trying to calm the crowd. Khafaji sneaks past the last men when Ali catches his eye.

Khafaji goes to unlock his apartment and notices the door is already wide open. Walking through the rooms, Khafaji finds the shutters to the balcony open as well. When he goes to shut them, he looks down at the street. Stopped at the gate is a black Mercedes. The guards signal for him to turn around. The driver leans forward over the dashboard, looking up at the building, scanning each floor. The men at the gate finally force the driver to disappear.

Khafaji goes to the sideboard and finds a bottle of Johnnie Walker. He gulps one shot, then sips a second. He goes back to the balcony and stares past the roofs at the night sky. At some point, he feels someone staring at him and looks around. He looks at the gate, and sees that there's nobody there. Then he notices the man in the shadows on the street below, looking up at him. Khafaji takes two steps back from the railing. He waits, then looks again to see the same man disappearing into the entrance below. Seconds later, Khafaji sees the man jogging back to his car, followed by one of the guards. As he runs off, Khafaji imagines he knows him. The bodyguard from the university. Down in the street, the guard trots after him.

Khafaji sees that the water is on, so he rushes to take a shower. Quickly, the water turns into a trickle, then dies. By the time Khafaji reaches for his towel, the lights also go out. Khafaji dries off in the darkness. Shivering, he looks for a gas lantern. When he can't find any matches in the kitchen, he fumbles through his jacket for a lighter. For the first time since the morning, his hand finds the ID cards. In the flickering light, he studies them one by one. Candy Firdawsi. Sally Riyadi. Sawsan.

Khafaji studies the girl's face, but soon he is looking at Suheir. Aunt and niece. Past and present. Then he remembers what Nidal said. *You wanted to find Sawsan so much, you imagined it. You still imagine it.* He reaches for the photograph of Sawsan that Nidal gave him. He looks at the two images side by side, and begins to see the differences.

He pours himself another shot to forget these girls. Another to forget memories spilling down from the mountains. Another to forget the Mosuli. The minutes pass. Then hours. It goes quiet outside. The bottle is half empty, but Khafaji's mind is fuller than ever.

Khafaji picks up the IDs again and studies them one last time. Candy Firdawsi. Sally Riyadi. He picks up the photo of Sawsan and imagines that her smile is meant for a lover. Suddenly, Khafaji is not thinking of Sawsan or Suheir, but

Zubeida. Sawsan's face belongs to Suheir, but the make-up belongs to her professor. Only then, in the daze of the Scotch and the whisper of the gas flame, does he notice that the name on the ID is not Sawsan Faraj, but Suzy Jinna. He wasn't wrong. He wasn't imagining anything.

Thursday
4 December 2003

Khafaji's head is almost clear when he wakes up. He shaves and leaves the house quickly. Coming downstairs, he bumps into Jaafar, who is walking up, carrying a tray of empty tea glasses. The boy smiles and shouts, "Good morning, Mr Muhsin!"

On the landing below, Khafaji almost stumbles over the new guard. He stands alert and salutes Khafaji, with a pious "Peace upon you, and God's mercy and blessings". The guards at the door rise to their feet and ask Khafaji to join them for a cup of tea.

As Khafaji turns out the door, he sees two other men posted at the end of the street. They stand, weapons on shoulders, looking the other way. Khafaji is nearly past them before they notice. A voice calls out from the building, and the guards wave and smile to their comrades in the street. Half-smiling, one grunts, "God's grace."

Khafaji is the first through the gates today, and the first to arrive at the office.

He looks over at the bag with his uniform, but decides not to wear it. He leans back and lights a cigarette, and then he starts reading.

Some files are like compact, short stories. Others are like fat novels. This one wanted to be a teacher. Failed out of high school, limited success at the police academy. Twice failed in Party courses. Reassigned to Mosul vice during the Faith Campaign of 1990s. Another man studied engineering in college. He alludes to the fact in each of his unsolicited lengthy memoranda, which are composed of extensive statistical analyses of crime. He produces charts for each year of the sanctions. Rates for begging, prostitution, smuggling, drug sales, addiction, and black-market trading. Very interesting if accurate. Another man probably killed someone in a family feud when he was young. His file does not come out and say this, but there is a note which explains that he should not be assigned to Irbil. One dossier, belonging to a colonel in the DGS, contains multiple studies on the importance of women's rights and family planning. It makes no sense until Khafaji reads a note in the margins: "Has nine children." Today, the dossiers seem like fiction. Some might even qualify as good literature.

Later, he goes to the DFAC for a quick meal of stale bread and plastic cheese.

In the afternoon, Khafaji begins reading the dossier on Basra's last police chief. Even before he picks it up, Khafaji understands that the man was someone to stay away from. Most files from the sanctions years are like that, either pitiful or filthy. This man's hands were so dirty you could see the shit on his elbows. Nothing extraordinary until '91, then promotion after promotion until last year. This guy learns to fly right when the sky falls. Khafaji throws the file down on the table. The file says he's civilian police, but the story makes him out to be intelligence. He lights a cigarette. *Why should it bother you?* Maybe because files lie. Maybe it's like reading files that could be yours. *But you weren't like this at all. Your generation had hopes and dreams. And ideology.*

In the Directorate, they had wanted him to read files quickly. But he showed them that he also knew how to read closely. Creatively. He could make an autopsy look like a birth certificate. If he had enough reports, he could make dead informants talk for years.

Read them like a poem, he used to say. Study them. Learn to see their rhythms. Look for the deeper structures. If you weren't reading for the patterns underneath, you weren't reading at all.

When he first arrived in the police, they wanted him to write reports, not read them. They knew what he did before, but they wanted to put him through the hoops just the same. They sent him out to arrest men selling black-market DVDs, then made him compose an arrest report. They sent him out to bust an unwanted brothel, then made him transcribe the initial interrogation.

But he showed them that it was no use writing dossiers if no one was going to read them. Read them properly. After two months on the streets, they decided he was more useful inside the station. He was not only good behind a desk, he was happiest there. Looking for missing feet and broken rhymes. Looking for poetry.

Khafaji looks up as he stamps out his cigarette. The coffee cup is full of butts, so he walks over to empty them in the waste bin. *What did ideology do for you?* He stares at the ashes as they fall. *They won. You lost. Today, the patriot is the one who holds the fork while the stranger carves up his country. Today, the terrorist is the one who dares to complain while strangers devour his limbs.*

Khafaji reaches into his drawer and opens another pack of Rothmans before going back to the dossier on his desk. *Why so defensive? You're not the one on trial here. Not today at least...* He smokes two more before he can admit that the scene with the Mosuli threw him.

Khafaji thumbs through the dossier and stands up. He opens up drawers and looks through papers on desks, searching for the file – the dossier on him – the Mosuli had handed him. When he can't find it, he lights another cigarette, then looks at his watch. By the time he stamps out this cigarette, he has decided he needs to read his own dossier.

It takes an hour to find it. Or, rather, to find the place where it should have been. The hanging folder is there. His name is on it. But the dossier is missing. Khafaji closes the door, then sits down on a desk. Citrone's desk. Curious, he tries the drawers, but none open.

He lights another cigarette and thinks. He flicks the ashes then tosses the butt on the floor before stepping on it and losing his balance. His hand comes down on a computer keyboard and the screen blinks to life. Khafaji looks at it, then plays with the keys. When nothing happens, he gives up. He looks over at the computer on the assistant's desk and walks over. His hand brushes the mouse, and the screen turns on. Again, this one is locked. Khafaji goes over to each of the other computers in the room. Each turns on. To Khafaji's relief, one monitor is accessible. He sits down and begins to play with the cursor. He scrolls up and down, clicking on folders. He comes across lists of documents. He recognizes nothing.

When he hears voices outside in the corridor, he imagines the Mosuli again. Slowly, Khafaji locks the door and turns off the light. A moment later, someone is knocking at the door and jiggling the handle. Then silence. Khafaji waits at the door, making no sound. Someone knocks again, and then there's a shuffling sound next to the door. Khafaji hears footsteps in the corridor, and imagines the same voice again. He leans over, and sees the silhouette of someone trying to peer through the crack beneath the door. A few minutes later, there are knocks once more. Khafaji's heart pounds so loud he is sure they can hear it outside. Eventually, the person walks away.

In the darkness, Khafaji goes back to the computer, and opens a document that contains another list. He begins to recognize the names of people with dossiers in the cabinets. Khafaji opens another list, then sees the same names on another list. He opens one and sees it contains an electronic copy of a file he read two days ago. He opens another and sees the same. The minutes go by and he slowly begins to glimpse a system. He works backwards through lists, now paying attention to the titles. As in the cabinets, there is no sharp line between agencies. Military. Civilian. Foreign Intelligence. Domestic Intelligence. General Security. Special Security. Party Intelligence. They bleed into one another without rhyme, without order. Khafaji experiments opening and closing windows and documents in the hopes of uncovering other designs in the catalog. He clicks further up the chain and finds the two largest files, "Former Structure" and "Reorganization".

He opens Reorganization and begins working through files quickly. In one, he finds a document labeled "Payments". It lists pages of what might be addresses and also phone numbers. One appears to be account sheets. On another page, he reads through a long list of Iraqi names. He skims over hundreds, but recognizes none. He looks through it twice before noticing that no men's names are included in it. Another file, entitled "Clearance", contains dozens of completed applications. Scrolling over it twice, Khafaji finally recognizes the name of one applicant, Candy Firdawsi.

Khafaji walks over and turns on the lights. He blinks for a moment, grabs his notebook and returns to the computer. He scrolls to the top of the file, going back over the addresses on the list. Most are located nearby. In the American Zone, in fact. Others are located in other parts of the city. One address stands out. Khafaji lights a cigarette and struggles to understand. Minutes later, it dawns on him: *it's the same street as the murder scene.* Khafaji looks at it again closely, then flips through his notebook. *Same house, actually.* Khafaji begins to underline as many of the other addresses as he can: 126 Salhia. 44 Sheikh Maarouf. 19 Shawaka. 77 Fatih. *Why are they grouped together here?*

Khafaji turns to the sheets of numbers. He stares, trying to figure out what they refer to. Each seems to be a dated triple entry, but the numbers in the columns do not add up in any pattern. Like fragments of lines. On a separate sheet, Khafaji finds a single entry list with large numbers and dates. He jots down a few, then looks again. He reads these files closely, as if they were lines of poetry. He looks for meter and rhyme, then for missing feet and broken sounds.

Khafaji sits on the edge of the desk. On one page, he draws a chart of the database as best he can. He lights another cigarette and decides to go back to the files again. Without knowing their system, the individual points of information mean nothing.

As he touches the keyboard, the screen changes. Suddenly, a half-played game of solitaire appears and fills the screen.

Khafaji throws the butt on the ground, and then tries pressing various keys. But he cannot make the game disappear. And he cannot return to the previous screen. He begins to punch the keys, then ends up throwing the whole keyboard on the ground. Khafaji hears the faint rattle of the door after the crashing sounds subside. He freezes, then hears the voice of the assistant calling out, "Hey, Khafaji! Are you in there?" Khafaji looks at the smashed keyboard on the ground and the monitors around the room, their screens brightly lit. The assistant knocks and calls out again, "Khafaji! Are you in there?"

At last, Khafaji yells, "Yes!" Unsure what to do, he scrambles under the desks and unplugs each computer. One by one, the screens go dead. He gathers up the keyboard as best he can, and throws it into the back of a filing-cabinet drawer.

Khafaji takes a deep breath and opens the door, rubbing his eyes and mumbling, "Sorry. I must have drifted off." Khafaji slumps back into his usual chair and picks up the file on the desk. He looks at the Basran Police Chief again. After a few minutes of silence, Khafaji asks, "When is Citrone coming in?" His eyes never lift from the page.

The assistant doesn't look up when he answers. "Huh? He's in meetings all day. He'll be in tomorrow morning. By the by, Citrone wants to know where things stand with the list."

"What list?"

"Our list of cops we're going to approach."

Khafaji says nothing. The assistant finally looks up. "The IPS recruits."

"I am working on it. I'll have it by Friday."

"Is that what you agreed on?"

"Yes." Khafaji shrugs. As the words come out, he becomes conscious of what he knew in his gut all along: they know nothing except what he tells them.

"And I talked to him about your idea of setting up a coordination meeting with the HR task force. He's on board."

Khafaji finally looks over at the assistant.

"Good," he lies, then says, "I need to know about my housing situation. It's dangerous for me to be out there, you know."

The assistant is now on his computer. He curses, then looks up. "What? Oh, right. Hank's been on that, I'm pretty sure."

As Khafaji exits, the assistant asks, "Do you know what happened to my computer?"

Khafaji shrugs again. "Sorry."

Khafaji is halfway down the hall when he remembers the book for Mrouj. When he walks back into the room, he sees the assistant on his hands and knees looking at keyboard letters in the palm of his hand. He calls out from beneath the desk. "Hey, Khafaji! Did the cleaning people come in this morning?"

Thursday Afternoon
4 December 2003

For the first time Khafaji is happy to sign in at the reception desk. For the first time he also comes bearing gifts. In one of the corridors of the palace, he found fresh roses in a vase. He looked around quickly before grabbing the stems. Then he went back for the vase and took that too.

Mrouj sits up in bed when she sees Khafaji walk into the room. Even her eyes smile. "Good afternoon, Baba. Are all those for me?"

"Just don't ask where I got them," Khafaji laughs. He looks around the room for an empty place, then sets the flowers on the windowsill. Mrouj grins the whole time.

"And what's that, Baba?"

"This is the book I've been forgetting all week. I finally remembered to bring it today."

"Will you read?"

"That's why I'm here, Mrouji. Where shall I start?" He pauses, then adds, "But before I do, I have bad news. I can't find Nazik anywhere."

Mrouj begins to speak, then hesitates.

"But I will find it, and when I do, I'll bring it here and read as much as you like."

"So what did you bring?"

Khafaji opens to the title page. "Poetry Primer. Volume 2. The Moderns."

"You brought a textbook, Baba?!"

Khafaji attempts to make her laugh. "Don't interrupt, me, Mrouj. Let me read the rest of what it says here: 'Ninth Edition. Approved by the Ministry of Education, 1978.'"

"That's not mine. Let me see that, Baba." And Khafaji hands it to Mrouj. She opens it and looks at something. The book falls out of her hands. She closes her eyes.

When Khafaji looks at the page, he sees the handwriting in the margins. He looks more closely, and sees it's not Mrouj's. It's not his either, or Suheir's. He flips the pages until he sees Uday's signature. Tamim Middle School, 1982. This was not Mrouj's copy. He reaches out for her hand and holds it. He closes his eyes and listens to her as she sobs. Finally, she takes a deep breath and then another and wipes her eyes. Then she whispers, "It's OK, Baba. Read."

"What would you like?" Khafaji begins reading the names from the table of contents. "Mahmoud Sami al-Baroudi. Ma'ruf al-Rusafi. Hafez Ibrahim. Ahmad Shawqi."

Mrouj moans, "No mummies please!"

"Khalil Mutran. Abu Shadi. Abu Shabaka."

Mrouj groans, "If I wanted poems about trees, I'd read French."

"You don't even know French…"

"That's what I mean!"

He keeps reading names, and Mrouj keeps dismissing them. When he calls out, "Abul-Qasim al-Shabbi," she finally relents.

"Just the first stanza or two. The rest is just tree poetry."

Khafaji closes the book. As he starts, Mrouj recites the lines with him:

"If, one day, a people wills to live, then fate will answer the call.
And their night will then begin to fade, and their chains break
   and fall.
For he who is not embraced by a passion for life will dissipate
   into thin air,
At least that is what all creation has told me, and what its
   hidden spirits declare..."

After the first stanza Mrouj scowls at Khafaji, but doesn't stop him from reading. In the last stanza, she finally objects. "I told you I only wanted the first stanza. But now that you recited it, I want you to start over and read it. And read with more passion please."

Khafaji begins again, this time dutifully only reading from the page. After a few stanzas, Mrouj interrupts him again. "You skipped something, Baba."

He looks down at the page and rereads the same stanza. She nods. He rereads the stanza just before it, and then she shakes her head. "No. That's wrong."

He holds up the page. "Look for yourself." She glances at the poem for a moment, then puts her finger on one line and says, "OK, found it. Listen to me and tell me what's wrong." She begins to read from the book while Khafaji listens with his eyes closed. He stops her and says, "You missed a line: 'Then comes winter, season of mists, season of rains, season of frost. The enchantment of life is extinguished, and with it sapling branches, blossoms and fruit are all lost.'"

Mrouj hands the book back to him. "Keep reading, Baba."

"Should I really stick to reading?"

"Yes. But when something's missing on the page, it's your job to correct it."

"Think what would happen if everyone ignored what was on pages!"

As he reads, he watches her lips soften and her breathing slow. He continues reading for an hour. Rereading poems they both know by heart. He doesn't stop until long after she's fallen asleep. He closes the book and stares out the window at an empty building nearby.

"I've been thinking, Baba." Mrouj's voice wakes Khafaji. Outside, night has fallen. He stretches his arms and stands up, then sits back down.

"About what?"

"I've been thinking about the story you told me. There's something that doesn't make sense."

"What do you mean 'something'? Nothing about the story makes sense."

"No, what I mean is that first you go out looking for Sawsan. Then you go out looking for this other girl. What's her name?"

Khafaji thinks for a second, then answers, "Zahra Boustani. I think. Supposedly."

"Then when you're looking for Zahra you stumble across Sawsan. And then the only way you can identify Sawsan is by the name on her ID, which isn't hers at all. I mean, practically the only thing that makes you think it was Sawsan is that she's got a made-up name."

Khafaji says nothing.

"From our perspective these look like coincidences, right? But from another perspective maybe they aren't."

"I'm sure you're right!" Khafaji laughs. "Tell me about the other perspective."

"I don't know, Baba. I am just thinking about it. Both girls went to college. Did this other girl also work for that professor?"

Khafaji says nothing. He thumbs through his notebook to keep his eyes busy.

"You didn't ask, did you? So, Citrone asks you to find the missing interpreter, right?"

"Right."

"Even though she's supposedly not in the CPA. So how does he know her?"

"What do you mean?"

"How does he know this girl? Zahra?"

Khafaji tries to remember their conversation, then admits, "I don't know." He thinks again, then says, "Maybe he knows her in some other way. He took a special interest in the case, but that's because he wanted me to talk to the other interpreters about it."

"He's the one who gave you her picture?"

"Yes. Him or his assistant. I don't remember which."

"So he knows what she looks like, at least. And you can assume he didn't give you the only copy of the photograph he had. So does the assistant know this girl then?"

"I don't know."

"Well, you might ask, Baba," Mrouj says in a raised voice. "If I were you, I would begin by asking." She closes her eyes.

"You're right, of course. What's wrong?"

"I'm not upset, I'm just frustrated. I sit around here all day with nothing to do. Every day."

Khafaji laughs. "OK, I'll bring you things to read. You'll see how exciting things can get!"

"It's not that. Some days I feel better. Not much, but a little better. But most days I feel the same. I'm not sure if this is doing any good."

Khafaji puts down his notebook and strokes her cheek.

Mrouj sits up and asks, "So, Citrone knows what this girl looks like, right?"

"I guess."

"And Citrone was one of the first to arrive at that house, right?"

"Yes," Khafaji picks up his pen.

"He could have easily identified Zahra Boustani by himself."

After a pause, Khafaji says, "You're right, Citrone didn't need to send me on that errand at all."

Thursday Night
4 December 2003

In the cafeteria, Khafaji fills a tray with some kind of stewed meat and rice. He searches for plain yogurt, but can only find small cartons of sweetened, fruit-flavored concoctions. A man waves at Khafaji from across the dining room. Khafaji looks closely. An Iraqi in a pressed suit. Another exile. The man looks vaguely familiar, and Khafaji smiles back. By now he has stood up and is motioning for Khafaji to join him.

As Khafaji comes up, the man's voice booms with excitement, "You're Hassan's brother, right? What are the chances? Salman Jabbouri al-Ghanim. You don't remember me, but I'm an old friend of your brother's." His English is British.

Khafaji nods. Jabbouri stretches out a hand and Khafaji shakes it. "Salman Jabbouri, pleased to meet you. You're Ihsan, right?"

"Muhsin."

"Right. I was just thinking about Hassan the other day. It's been years since we've seen him. We get a card from them every Christmas, but it's been years since we've seen each other. How is he?"

Khafaji shrugs. "Same as always, I'm sure."

Khafaji eats while Jabbouri talks. "I think you and I met once years ago. I was back on holiday."

"You and Hassan were the first Iraqi students at Cambridge, right?"

"And the first ones to marry English!"

Khafaji tries to focus on what Jabbouri says, but he is distracted, trying to identify what kind of meat he is eating. Not lamb. Not beef. He pushes the tray away.

Khafaji concentrates on wiping his mouth before he realizes the other man has stopped speaking. He smiles and asks, "So you are moving back to Iraq for good?"

"Just for the time being. I'm with McCannell and Sutton. Do you know us?"

Khafaji's face is blank.

"Why would you? I'm part of a team that integrates developing economies into the global market. When the contract came through, I was sent here to head up operations. My wife doesn't like the idea at all. She thinks it's dangerous. But she's listened to me talk about Iraq for thirty years, so she couldn't very well tell me I can't come back to help rebuild things."

Khafaji nods.

"We've mostly been tasked to transition Iraqi state industries into viable market frameworks."

Khafaji looks at his plate, considering whether to take another bite, but then decides against it. When he realizes Jabbouri is waiting for him to say something, he asks, "So tell me what that means."

"Well, Iraq is a rich country, right? Oil wealth, but no industry. You go anywhere else in the Gulf and you see construction everywhere. Massive cranes. Bulldozers. Cities going up overnight. But here, no building. Nothing. Economists like me look at a place like this and see nothing but manmade disasters. You have aluminium factories here, right? They produce tiny amounts of the stuff. But why does it cost more to make one pound of aluminium foil here than it does to make a ton in Sweden? Or take the petroleum refineries. Their technologies are so antiquated that they add dollars to the price of any drop of oil they pump out. But again, that's only part of the problem. You have this needlessly expensive refining process, then you go and sell the product for almost nothing on the market. Here's how I put it: *industry* is Iraqi for 'lifetime job'. And in the meantime, look around you. Do you see any factory producing anything at all these days?"

Khafaji murmurs, "The electricity stopped working when —"

"Exactly!" Jabbouri exclaims. "The electrical grid is a total disaster. But it was totally predictable. Given the mismanagement, corruption and neglect, it's amazing there is still a grid at all. We're going to have to build a new one from scratch."

"It used to work before —" Khafaji offers, but Jabbouri begins talking about Thailand, Bolivia, Sri Lanka, and Ireland. Somehow all are directly relevant to Iraq. "We've already learned these lessons, Muhsin."

Khafaji finally interrupts him. "Would you like some tea? Indian tea?"

Jabbouri raises his eyebrows and the two men walk over to the Beverage Bar. The man at the counter hands them two cups of tea. Khafaji invites Jabbouri outside to share a cigarette.

They walk out a side door. Beyond the fluorescent light over the doorway, it is now pitch black. Next to an Evacuation Assembly Area sign, Khafaji and Jabbouri huddle in the wind as they try to light their cigarettes. The door opens, and the assistant emerges, pulling a pack of cigarettes from his jacket pocket. He smiles, though it takes him a moment to recognize Khafaji. Khafaji says hello, then introduces the two men to one another. As they speak, Khafaji hears the young man's name as if for the first time – Louis Ford. The three men smoke their cigarettes. Khafaji offers them Rothmans, and they both accept. When the tea is gone, Jabbouri wishes out loud for Scotch. Ford begins to tell them about the Rashid Hotel bar. Somehow, Khafaji finds himself dragged along.

On the walk over, Khafaji listens to Jabbouri ask Ford about his life.

"I wrote my senior thesis on the financial connectivities of emerging threats, then I got a great internship in security studies. One day, I'm talking to my boss about converting threats into opportunities. The next day, he's asking me to join the Iraq Future Group. No interview. And here I am," Ford laughs and lights another round of cigarettes. As Jabbouri and Louis talk, they quickly establish that they share the same networks.

At the hotel, many people come up to greet Ford. He makes a point of introducing Jabbouri to some. Out of politeness, a couple smile and shake Khafaji's hand as well. Suddenly, Khafaji's exhaustion catches up with him and so does his headache. "I am sorry, friends. I'm tired."

"You can't leave. If you're really tired, just have one," Jabbouri pleads.

The doorman at the bar stops Khafaji. Louis clasps the man's hand and says, "He's all right, Tommy, he's with me." They click their fingers together in a ritual Khafaji has only seen in American movies.

The room could be anywhere. A dusty mirrored ball sparkles under the long, low acoustic ceiling. It is dark and smoky and very crowded. Louis explains, "It's one of the few places where you can get a drink."

At first glance, the clientele seems to be identical to that of the cafeteria. But gradually Khafaji recognizes slight variations.

Mostly Americans, but Europeans too. Jabbouri invites them to the first round and sends Khafaji and Ford to find a table. Ford points out the different groups – the British and Australians together, the Italians and Spaniards, the Poles and Ukrainians. "They're all here. Every Thursday night. I'll be right back." Ford strolls over to some friends.

Ten minutes later, Jabbouri returns with three tumblers. Khafaji takes the ice cubes out of his glass and throws them on the floor. The two men sip their Scotch and scan the room. It's too loud to have a conversation. Twice, Jabbouri excuses himself as he walks over to shake someone's hand. It doesn't take long before Khafaji has finished his glass. As soon as he stands up to leave, Jabbouri returns in an excited mood. "Great place, huh?"

Jabbouri looks at Khafaji's empty glass and then at the other one, still untouched. He hands it to Khafaji and yells over the din, "Here's your next round." Soon, Khafaji finishes his second watered Scotch. The edges of the night begin to soften. Jabbouri points out various people in the room. Journalists. Contractors. Businessmen. "Really amazing collection of people in this room, you know? Amazing. Baghdad hasn't seen this much talent in a thousand years!"

Ford returns at some point with more drinks. Khafaji doesn't bother to remove the ice. Soon he has finished his fourth tumbler. Jabbouri and Ford go on talking. In the noise, Khafaji finds it difficult to follow. Khafaji is no longer tired. His head begins to swim. Jabbouri slaps him on the back and asks, "So, tell me about what you're up to. What sort of projects are you working on?"

Khafaji stammers out something, then stops when Ford returns to the table. Jabbouri and Ford go back to their conversation.

Annoyed, Khafaji looks around the room with bloodshot eyes. He becomes conscious of the fact that there are almost no women here. He notices one woman surrounded by men. They are all flirting with her, trying to buy her drinks.

Khafaji asks a question, but his words come out garbled. He asks it again, only now very slow and deliberate. "Where are the women?" He should not have stayed this long.

Jabbouri laughs. "Yes, Muhsin has a point. Where are you keeping all the women, Louis?" He winks at Khafaji and continues, "My old knees may be weak, but I still know how to dance."

Ford takes a moment to think. "That's a more serious question than you know. Imagine what would have happened if there were a lot of women here."

He pauses, but Jabbouri and Khafaji say nothing.

Ford continues. "We did that in Saudi, and it nearly caused a revolution. They limited the number of women in this operation. They say they did it out of respect for Islamic culture. We can't come into their places and flaunt our women. It would be insensitive. I'm not defending it per se. And it certainly does make it difficult to get laid around here." He grins.

"Laid?" Khafaji blurts out.

There's an uncomfortable pause before Ford turns back to Jabbouri and adds, "I get by just fine."

The three men laugh. Jabbouri asks, "Really? I've worked in a lot of places. Some, a lot worse than this. But whenever I have, it's always been quite obvious how men get by. No secret about that. But what about here in Iraq? You've got thousands of men stationed here for months. You can't tell me that they take it lying down?" He winks at Khafaji.

Ford laughs. "A lot of porn. Movies. Magazines. You name it, the military supplies it."

"And the bases?"

Louis laughs again. "You always hear stuff about the Army. Planes flown in from Bangkok. Rumors and gossip about a whorehouse here in the Green Zone."

He stands up. "Let me get the next round."

By the time he comes back, the conversation has gone in other directions. Jabbouri and Ford talk for a while about the untapped riches of Iraq. Khafaji yawns and wonders why he's still there, empties his glass, then gets up to leave.

Jabbouri clasps Khafaji's hand and talks about getting together again soon. Ford looks across the room for his friends.

The air outside has turned cold and dark. Khafaji thinks he sees the outlines of the Victory Arch in the distance. Drunk, he starts to walk toward it. He lights a cigarette and imagines what it would be like to touch the giant sculptures. Three cigarettes later, Khafaji is wandering down a road whose asphalt has been chewed up by heavy machinery and tank treads. Khafaji hesitates when he can no longer see anything in the gloom. No lights. No sounds. Nothing but the empty, quiet night. He walks on, hearing nothing but his own footsteps kicking up dirt and gravel. The concrete monument begins to materialize in the darkness. Khafaji stops and stares, the sky spins for a moment before it catches itself. It takes a few moments for Khafaji to realize it is something else. A mosque. Or a tomb. Khafaji walks along the round exterior walls. The textured concrete feels like giant cuneiform writing. Khafaji drags his hands across it for balance, and eventually comes to an entrance. He walks into the shadows. The smell of shit and garbage almost makes him turn back. He lights a match and looks around. The floor is covered with dirt and debris and something else. He walks over to what looks like a gravestone. When the match goes out, he lights another, and gazes up at the crystal chandelier and the Quranic verses. The brilliant gold calligraphy glitters faintly like a distant constellation. Khafaji knows whose tomb it is. The great Baathist intellectual no one would ever read unless the Party made them. The philosopher who insisted that politics be composed as poetry, and who ruined both in the process. Khafaji remembers hearing about the man's burial. Like everyone else, he wasn't surprised to learn that Michel Aflaq was dead. The only surprise in hearing the news was finding out that Michel Aflaq had been alive all that time.

A whimper in the corner makes Khafaji jump. The match goes out. It takes a few tries to light the next one, and then a moment to see the eyes glowing in the blackness. The match has gone out again by the time he registers what he saw. A feral bitch nursing a litter in the garbage pile. Khafaji steps back to the door.

The night air is even colder now. Khafaji shivers and pulls the jacket collar up around his ears. And now he begins the long walk back. The bracing wind revives him. He lights a cigarette and then another, determined to cover the smell of alcohol by the time he sets foot in a taxi.

He asks the taxi driver to drop him off on Abu Nuwas. Half stumbling, Khafaji traces another long zigzag across his neighborhood before arriving at his street. The guards at the street gate receive Khafaji warily. One of them escorts Khafaji to the front door of the building and leaves only when the guards there can vouch for him. The young man apologizes, and wishes Khafaji a good evening. Khafaji stumbles upstairs and falls into bed without even turning on the lights.

Friday
5 December 2003

Khafaji sleeps so soundly, he doesn't even dream. He wakes up early, surprised to find his headache gone and his mind clear. The water is back on, so he fills a kettle, then goes to shave and shower. The aluminium pot squeaks and pops on the gas stove. When it boils, the kettle spits hot water and steam. The tea steeps while Khafaji washes days of dirty teacups sitting in the sink. He listens to the clinking sound each cup makes as he sets them on the drying rack. He sweeps the floor and wipes off the counters. By the time he is done, the kitchen is as clean as it ever was.

Tea in hand, Khafaji returns to the living room. At first he reaches for a book of poetry, *Diwan Jarir*. But the stacks of books sitting on the ground shame him into work. For Khafaji, reshelving books is like meditation. Or like moving into a new home. He starts to put some in their places, but then gets sidetracked when he comes across a title from his teenage years, *Awatif*, by Muhammad Salih Bahr al-Oloom. He browses another book for an hour before putting it on the shelf. *Kitab Alf Layla wa-Layla Min Usulih al-Ula*.

He gets another glass of tea and tries to reshelve others. Eventually, he finds himself sitting on his favorite chair, reading a book he didn't know he owned. And so it goes for a few hours. Shelving. Book. Tea. And then all over again. By eleven, Khafaji has finished. All the books are back on the shelves, but not the same shelves as before. This time, Khafaji decides to separate Arabic titles from English ones. That solved the issue of alphabetization that had plagued the books before. Granted, it meant mixing genres. But Khafaji gives up and leaves it as is. Imperfect. As he sorts through his collection, he notices just how many of his books are missing. By the time he's done, there's nearly an entire shelf gone. All of it poetry. The bare shelf is incontrovertible proof of theft. And now he understands why he couldn't find Nazik's diwan.

Khafaji goes to the kitchen to pour another glass of tea. The pot is empty, so he decides that he might as well go to work. Walking out the door, Khafaji finds Ali on the landing.

"Peace upon you, Brother. Are you coming to pray with us?"

"God keep you, Ali. Bless you. I would like to, but…"

Ali quietly adds, "Sunday. The day after tomorrow. I'm sorry it's got to be like this. But we did give you more time. I trust you've found a solution?"

"Yes, I have, thank you."

He nods and shakes Ali's hand. Ali's expression is as warm and sincere as ever, only his eyes are dark. Khafaji grins, almost laughs. *It really is not personal. He may even like you.* The guards at the door signal to the guards on the corner. Everyone smiles at Khafaji as he walks to the river.

There's only a handful of people waiting at the gate, and Khafaji walks through quickly. Jacket off. Arms up. Shirt up. He looks at the faces of the guards as he goes through, but doesn't recognize any of them. He attempts to smile to one, but it goes nowhere. A new group.

Ford is working at his computer and waves to Khafaji when

he comes in. He doesn't get up or turn around. "Hey!" he calls out. "How do you feel this morning?"

Khafaji flips through his notepad instead of answering him. He reaches for a fresh pack of Rothmans in the drawer, tears off the plastic wrapper and tries to toss it in the trash can but misses. He takes out a cigarette and lights it. Then he asks, "Where is Citrone? I need to talk to him."

Ford smells the tobacco smoke and turns around. "It's Friday. I know he's got something later, so he'll probably come in before. You can't smoke here, you know."

"It is a free country now, no?"

"And my cup is not an ashtray. Disgusting."

Khafaji looks at his watch. It's nearly 2 p.m. He hangs up his jacket and scarf on the hook and sees the clear plastic garment bag under his desk. The uniform. Khafaji wonders if he should ask about the boots, but decides not to bother.

Khafaji turns to the filing cabinets. By now he's gone through hundreds of dossiers. He takes a drag and decides to wait until after his next cigarette before he starts.

As if reading his mind, Ford calls out, "Citrone's expecting your list today."

Khafaji mumbles, "Yes. Sure. OK." There is no list.

A few minutes later, Ford shuts off his computer and walks out the door. "I'll be back later. We've got a new clerk coming in this afternoon. Let him know I'll be back. See you later, Khafaji."

Khafaji looks at his watch. 3.00 p.m. Citrone still hasn't shown up. Khafaji calls out, "Hold on! When is Citrone getting here?"

Ford shrugs.

"You are sure he is coming in?"

"He sometimes does on Friday mornings."

"He said I'd be able to move into a house by now."

"Sorry."

"Is there another way I could talk to Citrone?"

"Citrone said he'd be in, but technically it's his day off." Ford runs his fingers over his hair.

"But you said he wanted the list today."

Ford shrugs. "You can give the list to me now. Or tomorrow, when he comes in. I know for a fact he'll be here early, we've got a 9 a.m. You'll be there, too."

"What?"

"Our meeting. I told you last night."

"…?"

"Coordination with the HR team. You asked me to set it up."

"Oh… Right," Khafaji says, stubbing out the butt. Ford frowns and walks out into the corridor.

Khafaji continues working at his desk for a few more minutes, before walking over to the door. A 9 a.m. with the Mosuli. Wonder what the hell they were going to talk about?

Khafaji looks at the wall next to the door and sees something he hadn't paid attention to before.

Warning Siren. High Wailing Tone. 1. Secure all classified documents. 2. Close all windows, lock all doors. 3. Immediately leave building.

Low Wailing Tone. 1. Get away from all windows. 2. Duck and cover. 3. Wait for clear siren, then meet at Evacuation Assembly Area.

Khafaji tries to lock the door, but the key is gone.

He attempts to turn on the computers, but gives up. He goes to Citrone's desk looking for keys. When he doesn't find any, he tries the drawers. This time, one is unlocked. Khafaji slides it open. The only things he finds are a few duffel bags. Empty. He takes them out and turns each one upside down. Nothing. He leans back and feels for his cigarettes in his pocket.

Outside, someone tries the door handle, but it does not open. Then a hand raps softly on the door. Khafaji gently closes the drawer and goes back to his desk. "It's open," he calls out.

Zubeida Rashid is halfway across the room before she recognizes Khafaji. When she sees him, she stops. At first he breathes a sigh of relief when he sees she's alone.

"Professor. Come in. Please." He does his best to sound forceful.

"You?" Her voice is colder than he remembered. "I'm looking for Mr Citrone. Where is he?"

Khafaji smiles and shakes his head. "No, Professor. Sorry to disappoint." A moment later, he adds, "But we expect him back any minute. Would you like to wait?"

Khafaji gestures to an empty chair. She looks at her watch. Her foot has not stopped tapping since she walked in. She is not trying to hide it. She looks up and says nothing. When she does answer, it comes out like she's doing him a favor or making a threat. "If that's what I have to do."

Khafaji walks over and pulls out the chair for her. "Please, sit down. Can I bring you a cup of tea while you wait?"

"What are you doing here?" she snaps.

Khafaji tries to explain, but his words make no sense. She pretends not to listen. At some point, she simply interrupts. "Yes. Tea, please." She stops looking at him.

Five minutes later, Khafaji returns from the cafeteria with two paper cups of sweet, milky tea. As he enters, the phone is ringing. Khafaji puts the hot cups down on the desk. By the time he picks up the receiver, the caller has hung up.

"May I join you?"

"Of course." She turns to the window, even though the shutters are closed. Khafaji opens the windows and then unclasps the shutters and throws them wide open. Fuzzy lines of orange and pink streak through late-afternoon haze. For the first time, the room learns what a slight breeze feels like. Khafaji closes the window quickly, but the room is already cold. Khafaji puts on his jacket and sits down, warming his hands with the hot cup. He drinks slowly, gazing out at the dusk as it gathers itself up.

Without sound or motion, tears begin to stream down her cheeks.

"I've done something very stupid, Muhsin. I'm in over my head." She sniffles. Her words come across as an invitation. Khafaji begins to reach out to touch her hands, then pulls back. She stares down at her feet. Khafaji's eyes follow hers, and suddenly he's staring at thighs, knees, calves, ankles, and finally feet. She is wearing open sandals. Khafaji looks at her painted toenails.

By the time Khafaji remembers his tea, it has gone cold. He hesitates, and finally breaks the silence. "Zubeida, it's OK. Whatever it is, it'll be OK."

"It is not OK, Muhsin."

"Maybe I can help?"

"I don't think so, Muhsin."

"You don't know that."

"No, Muhsin. It's you who don't know."

A minute goes by, then Khafaji ventures, "Tell me about what happened to Sawsan then."

She doesn't look at Khafaji. He continues, "It's about Sawsan, isn't it? And Zahra and the others, too."

Now she looks at Khafaji. "What do you know?"

"I know they were working for you. I know they got killed because they worked for you." Khafaji pauses, then lies, "And I know that you work for Citrone. I know how much you are paid."

She pauses, and dries her eyes. She looks out the window and begins to talk. "The other day, I heard an American reporter talking about how the lives of Iraqi women have improved since the invasion. Imagine – our lives, improved!"

Khafaji notices he's still staring at her feet. Embarrassed, he looks up at the ceiling. The phone rings, but he ignores it.

"They want to rescue us women. They want to free us. They invent stories about American women captured by Bedouins. It almost worked, until it turned out the stories weren't true. You'd think after that, they would shut up about saving women."

Khafaji's smile dies. She goes on. "They do not have the slightest idea about what they're doing here. They got on a horse, but they don't know how to ride. And now they're just beginning to understand it's more dangerous to get off than to keep riding."

Khafaji takes out a cigarette and lights it. He leaves the pack on the table in front of her, and goes over to get Ford's coffee cup.

"So the Americans will sign on anybody they think might be an ally. But do any of them care about women's rights? Do the Mullahs think I should be allowed to go out at night? Will Kurdish grandfathers stick up for sisters in the south?"

She turns to look at the door, then picks up her cup. She takes a sip, frowns and sets it back down. Now she is looking directly at Khafaji. "Maybe this strategy was stupid."

"It was stupid," Khafaji agrees, then remembers it's best to let others talk themselves out. He nods for her to continue.

"It was better than some of the alternatives. What would you have them do? There's no other work."

"Yes, but it's dangerous."

"We had promises. My girls had assurances. Only now, something has broken down. Can you help us?"

"With what?" Khafaji regrets saying it as soon as it comes out.

"I need to talk to Citrone. He needs to do more like he said he would."

"What should I tell him when I see him?" Khafaji asks.

"Tell him that I know I can count on him. And tell him to make things right, or it's over."

There's no warning siren when she leans forward and kisses Khafaji's cheek. No high wailing tone, no low wailing tone. Just the scent of her perfume burying itself deep in his mind. He tries to look away, but her fingers catch him gently by the chin. She takes a tissue from her purse and wipes lipstick off his skin. Then she walks out without saying another word.

Khafaji leans back in his chair, more seriously confused than ever. Outside, the sky is dark, the sun has set. As he sits there, the phone begins to ring again. He ignores it and slowly smokes his cigarette. The ringing stops, then starts again. Khafaji drops the butt on the floor and stamps it out before he picks up the receiver. On the other end, Ford's voice is hysterical. "Khafaji, I need you to come quick. There's been another incident. Can you meet me right now?"

Khafaji hangs up, buttons his jacket and turns out the lights as he races out.

Friday Evening
5 December 2003

As they drive, Khafaji looks over at Ford. His face is white.

"Where are we going?" Khafaji asks. Ford says nothing, as if he doesn't hear the question. The Humvee drives in fits and starts, sometimes speeding, sometimes crawling over a street torn up by construction. Khafaji bounces around in his seat and looks out the window. Dozens of bulldozers, tractors and cranes. And at the side of the road, an endless row of prefabricated concrete sections. After a couple of minutes they jerk to a stop, then begin creeping over a series of deep ruts. Khafaji sees more stacks of concrete sections and a deep trench running the entire length of the street.

They pass troop carriers and Humvees parked along the side of the trench. Khafaji looks around, and tries to guess where they are. It seems like Kindi, but he doesn't remember them leaving the American Zone. The place is entirely cordoned off, and a small traffic jam has formed. Strobe lights flash on the roofs of two military-police trucks. Khafaji watches MPs waving lighted batons in the dark air, directing cars onto side streets. As they approach, the driver rolls down his window and greets one of the policemen who waves them through. An officer approaches their car and Ford goes off to talk with him. A minute later, the two men come back. Ford pulls Khafaji by the shoulder. "Come on with us, but be careful. They're still conducting a search operation. Some of them may still be here. Let me take you to the house."

Dozens of masked special-operations soldiers appear in the light flashing from the police cars. Then the street goes black again. Flash, and lines of men swim like shadows. Flash, and the street is empty again. Flash, men and guns in motion. Flash, night again and no one is there. Khafaji walks right behind the other two men down another street also torn at the edge by a trench. In a few places, the concrete sections have been inserted into the trench and fitted together. This is the fortress wall, although here it is mostly gaps.

They arrive at a house lit by floodlights mounted on two Bradleys. To the side and behind, Khafaji hears shouting and doors crashing open. Khafaji asks the other officer, "What street is this?"

"Whiskey at Charlie."

Khafaji asks, "What's the real name?"

"Hold on. Let me get a 'terp."

A minute later, a round figure in full-body armor and a balaclava appears. He nods at Ford and Khafaji.

"Where we are? Do you know what street this is?"

"I think it's Fath Street." Khafaji holds his notebook up to the light. It takes him a moment to find it, but he does: "Fatih." When he first saw the word, he thought it was a street across town. Hack transliteration. Like Whiskey at Charlie was a hack translation.

The house was typical concrete with touches of black marble in the Italianate style. Now it is something else, because when marble and concrete explode, they do very different things. Fine white dust saturates the air, and Khafaji and the others cough and hold handkerchiefs over their faces. The steel-fortified front door was blasted out with explosives. Even through the cloth, Khafaji recognizes the elements of the stench – a cocktail of burning paint, plastic and hair. A pool of blood and the tangled limbs of three young men. An American soldier wearing latex gloves busies himself retrieving AK-47s from beneath them.

The other officer tells Khafaji to expect the MPs soon. "They're gonna fill you in on what happened here. I gotta get back to my men." Ford and Khafaji stand side by side surveying the battlefield. After a minute, Khafaji begins to walk clockwise around the ground floor. The bare bulbs cast too much light on the empty rooms. Bare concrete spaces, but heavily used. In the dining room, a dozen cots with cheap wool blankets and dirty pillows. More garbage bags and plastic bottles in the kitchen. Chicken bones and old cans of tuna. Many tea kettles, one burning empty on the stove. Khafaji turns off the gas. The door to the bathroom is wide open. At least the toilet was still working here. Khafaji walks over to the walls, tapping them at intervals. Nothing – concrete doesn't work that way anyway. He walks around to another room in the back and finds more carnage. When they blew in the wall from outside, the men inside were shredded. Body parts and clothes and shoes all around. Khafaji moves back when he realizes he's stepping on a forearm. The fingers curl around the toe of his shoe. Behind the smell of cordite, wood, and plastic Khafaji recognizes something else. He puts the handkerchief over his face, but only after the stink of burnt hair has filled his nostrils. He rushes back to the dining room and lights a cigarette. In one pantry, he finds a cache of explosive hardware – artillery shells, metal casing, spools of wire. He walks around the ground floor again. The villa has two stories, but there is no staircase to the second floor. He's feeling again at the walls in the dining room when he hears the crunch of boots behind him. Khafaji turns around to find Ford standing there, accompanied by a tall brown man in a white helmet.

The man steps forward to introduce himself. "Inspector Khafaji, Corporal Belascoaran of the 172nd MP. We had orders to contact your office if something happened here."

Khafaji looks at him, then murmurs, "Is there anything here? This looks like a war zone, not a crime scene."

"You're right – there is nothing for you down here. You need to go upstairs."

He leads Khafaji out the back patio, and then to a metal door with a heavy lock. Broken heavy lock. It leads on to a steep exterior staircase. As they approach the top of the stairs, an acid reek hits their sinuses. Tear gas. Khafaji puts a handkerchief over his mouth again and closes his eyes. Ford winces and runs down the stairs.

The MP calls out, "It's stronger down there than it is up here. Come on up."

The first thing Khafaji senses is the cool air blowing through open windows. The second thing is the same contrast between upstairs and downstairs he saw before. Oriental carpets. No chairs, only low sofas and pillows. Heavy brocade curtains on the walls. But it is the tinted light bulbs that slap Khafaji in the face. The light is so subdued, and so red and purple and blue. Even someone who never worked vice would have recognized the place.

Beyond the carpets and the broken glass and the tear-gas canisters, beyond the chandeliers, Khafaji squints to see the far side of the room. He sees the heap of color on the couch, but can't make out what it is. Khafaji walks over.

The crunching of broken glass beneath his shoes startles him. At first he recognizes bits of clothing. A scattering of bright prints, lace, scarves, beads and bangles. And then, caught in the fabric, limbs and faces. The three young girls wearing wedding-night lingerie. A macabre orgy, stopped in mid-action. Khafaji turns away and goes to find a sheet to cover them.

He walks around the room. On the ground, pairs of high-heeled shoes, strewn about as if they were kicked off. Mixed among them, a black pair of men's shoes. Khafaji looks inside, sees "Size 11" inscribed in English.

On the low glass table in the corner by the window, a small collection of wine bottles and ashtrays. On another table, small piles of white powder. Tucked beneath the table, a red duffel bag. Always a red duffel bag. Khafaji picks it up and looks at it. Like the others, empty.

Khafaji walks around the room, looking for pieces of the story. The stereo is still on, so Khafaji hits play. Loud pop music blares out and the sound of it shocks Khafaji so much that it takes him a moment to turn it off again. He opens the CD player and looks at the disk. Nancy Ajram. The name means nothing. Khafaji walks over to the window and gazes down at the scene now unfolding in front of the villa. Beyond the floodlights, Khafaji can barely make out a long row of strips of white cloth. After staring for a minute, he sees they are blindfolds on men lying face-down on the pavement. Groups of masked soldiers stand over and around them, their guns held low and ready in their hands. The last one in line is barely visible. Made to stand while he talks to an interpreter and soldier, his dark clothes and face and hair disappear in the darkness. The white blindfold seems to hang in mid-air.

Khafaji turns to face the MP. "What am I looking at?"

"Sir, at 1800 a patrol heard shots coming from the ground floor. They assumed wire breach and engaged. Then called for backup. They tried to maintain surveillance as best they could. We know a group of Hajjis fled the villa. Probably took refuge in one of the neighboring homes."

"Then what?"

"Our guys waited till they had sufficient firepower, then re-engaged. They started with tear gas. Both floors. No response. Then all hell broke out on the bottom floor. That was when we got here. These guys were armed and ready. But they had no chance. Just sitting in Allah's waiting room. Two pops and we were in. By that time, they were done. FODA. We got lucky. This could have been a nightmare."

Khafaji pauses. "So why did they call you?"

"Pardon, sir?"

"Do they call you anytime there's an engagement?"

"No."

"So why did they call you?"

"MPs have jurisdiction in the Green Zone, sir."

"We're in the Green Zone?"

"We're technically inside, even if the wall isn't fully up yet. This belongs to us, and so do the people who live here."

"Who lives here then? In this house?"

"We don't know yet. As far as we knew, everyone on this street was a friendly. They've all been cleared, in any case. We've got about five thousand locals who are cleared. But it's not one hundred per cent secure. Vehicles can't come in or go out without passing through the gates. People can walk through. But even so, we're here round the clock, and nothing happens here without our knowing it."

"So, this is a big deal?"

"If we got terrorists setting up camp here, it's a big fuck-ing deal. Heads are going to roll. What are you and Citrone looking for?"

Khafaji looks at Ford, who's standing at the door. Frozen like a statue. His face white marble. Khafaji suddenly realizes that Ford knows the girls on the couch. Ford knows this place.

Khafaji turns back to the MP. "We are here because some interpreters have gone missing." He points to the couch. "We need to examine these bodies – that might be them. You should know these houses usually have an extra crawl space or storage room in them."

The MP frowns, trying to understand. Khafaji adds, "Under the stairs, maybe." The man nods and Khafaji continues, "If you've got dogs, you should bring them in and go over the place."

The MP nods grimly. "Got it. We'll look for crawl spaces, safe rooms or whatever right away."

"Right. Could we borrow some bags from you? And gloves, too? Thank you." The man nods again and goes downstairs. Khafaji calls Ford to come over. Ford flinches.

"Do you know this place, Louis?"

When Ford says nothing, Khafaji asks, "We need to take pictures, Louis. Can you get a camera for us?" Ford disappears down the staircase.

For the next two hours, Khafaji goes through the main room on the second floor, and then the bedrooms leading off from it. He touches the powder on the glass table, then licks his fingers. When the tip of his tongue goes numb, he shakes his head and makes a note. There's a stocked liquor cabinet. With bottles never seen before. When the MP returns, Khafaji asks, "If we are inside the Green Zone, how…?"

Belascoaran snorts. "Believe me, I know what you're

thinking. The story is they were supposed to finish the new wall in two stages. The contractor doing the second stage of the job finished fast, while the contractor doing the first stage stopped. He's supposed to work round the clock until it's done, but he doesn't have enough guys to work the shifts."

Khafaji shakes his head. The other man laughs. "Believe me. We've been telling them there's a problem."

Khafaji goes through each bedroom carefully. They're mostly empty except for a few things, small nightstands, mirrors, and beds. In each, Khafaji finds personal articles. Lipstick. Lingerie. Blouses. Shoes. They don't mean anything, but he puts them into bags. He finds more ID cards, the same kind as before. In three rooms, Khafaji finds new kinds of IDs. A university identification card. A driver's license. When he matches them up, he is not surprised. Each face has multiple names.

Khafaji taps at the drywall, and notices a hollow sound in the room behind the staircase. At first he assumes it's only a crawl space, but then sees the outlines of the small panel. If the light were brighter, he would have seen it long ago – there's nothing hidden about it at all. He opens the panel and finds himself staring into a small black hole. Khafaji sees a floor lamp on the other side of the room and brings it over. He clicks on the light and points it into the hole. Something on the floor catches his eye. He reaches down and picks up a heavy piece of metal. It sits snugly into the palm of his hand like it was meant to fit there. He takes off his latex gloves and feels the heft on his bare skin. A nickel-plated Smith and Wesson Magnum, .357, short-nosed. Vanity piece. He smells it. Nothing but cold, oiled metal. Enough to confirm it wasn't fired tonight. Khafaji slips the gun into his jacket pocket.

Khafaji shoves the light bulb into the space, then crouches over and enters. In the naked light, he sees a tiny crowded closet. And in there, another body. Not just another body. The body of the last person who should be there.

They gagged and tied Citrone with steel wire before setting him in the chair. His wrists are fastened with plastic zip-ties.

The girls in the room were shot. Downward through the neck. Like before.

But Citrone is different. No blood, no wounds. His face is bright purple. Or blue. Or both. Then Khafaji notices the scarf around his throat. Silk paisley. Tied tight. He looks down at Citrone's socks. No boots tonight.

Khafaji reaches over to touch the body, but something about it looks wrong. He pulls the lamp closer, but his own body blocks the light. He looks around slowly, sees the car battery. He follows the wires with his eyes, then notices the spot where they coil into Citrone's clothes. Where they appear to enter his torso.

Khafaji jerks back. He looks again, and follows the wires again. Trip wires. Citrone isn't just dead. He's also a weapon. Aimed directly at Khafaji.

Khafaji crawls out of the closet and is halfway down the stairs when he thinks again. Slowly, he walks back to the panel and goes through again. The pockets of Citrone's jacket seem clear. Khafaji reaches in, and his fingers pull out papers. He holds them up to the light. Napkins and used tissues. Khafaji tosses them on the floor. He leans over, this time reaching across Citrone into the pocket on the other side. His fingers fumble around, but he can't feel anything. He leans into Citrone's belly and tries again. He touches a cluster of metal pieces. Khafaji's finger pulls it free and he hears the jangle of keys.

Khafaji crawls backwards then starts moving toward the stairs. He looks at the small pile of evidence bags on the floor but decides to forget about them. When he gets to the bottom of the stairs, he runs into a soldier about to enter the building, and shouts, "Do not go in! There is a bomb!"

Khafaji runs around the house and into the street. The MP sees him and comes over. Khafaji is out of breath and manages only to whisper, "There is a bomb there! Bomb!"

The MP begins barking orders at a man next to him before disappearing behind the villa gates. Khafaji looks around for Ford, but he's nowhere to be seen.

In minutes, the villa is evacuated. Two MPs come running out, latex gloves on their hands, masks over their faces. Soldiers in balaclavas mill around under the floodlights, their weapons on their hips. Khafaji lights a cigarette and starts walking down the street. He walks out of the light, back to where they parked their car. It's gone. The other jeeps are also gone, and so are the flashing lights. The men in blindfolds are gone. In the darkness, he notices the doors to the houses. One after another, all wide open. He gets to the end of the street and starts to walk back. He is fifty yards away when the first explosion hits. In an instant, glass windows turn into bursting rainclouds. And then the big explosion erupts, sending bricks and dust and fire in all directions. Khafaji is thrown to the ground. When he stands up again, he can see the bodies of men who only a minute ago had been standing at the entrance to the villa. Too close. He watches one soldier writhing on the street. He sees the man calling out, and looking around for help. Khafaji strains to hear what he is saying, then realizes there are no sounds, only ringing.

Khafaji dusts himself off and looks at the silent scene around him. He begins to run; he runs until gradually he begins to hear the world around him. First, his breath and heartbeat. Then the sounds of his shoes on the gravel and concrete. He has run half a mile before he sees flashing blue and red lights, and then he begins to hear sirens, first one, then many. When the first fire trucks appear, he leaps across the trench. He's now out of the American Zone and into the shadows. Khafaji runs and runs until he can't breathe. Hundreds of meters behind him, beyond the half-built wall, and beyond the trenches in the street, a convoy of Bradleys fly past in the dark. Khafaji leans against a wall and he reaches for his Rothmans. His fingers find Citrone's keys instead.

Friday Night– Saturday Morning 5–6 December 2003

The taxi crosses the river twice on the way home, and each time they wait at the checkpoint. Near the new headquarters of the Dawa Party, he gets out. He walks along Abu Nuwas Street, past the new headquarters of the Communist Party and past a shadow of Scheherazade entertaining a shadow of Shahryar. When he comes to the statue of Abu Nuwas, he turns off the street and down to the embankment, flooded in blue light. He sits on a low wall and lights a cigarette. He remembers sitting in the same spot thirty years ago with Suheir and her friends from school. Drinking arak on the grass. How did they keep the ice from melting? He can't remember. He flicks the half-smoked cigarette high into the air and watches it disappear over the embankment below.

He lights another cigarette and stares at the bleak orange lights of the city. The moon is almost full tonight. Its glow is useless against the haze of the city, but beneath it the black water glistens here and there. In the silent shadows, the Tigris becomes an empty flood filling the horizon. Khafaji stares at the river until it becomes a moat. Another line of defense protecting this side of the city from the American encampment in Karkh.

Khafaji leans back on the concrete wall and lets the coldness seep into his bones. He thinks about everything from the last days. And then about nothing at all. Nothing, except for the image of Citrone's body. He tries to forget it by thinking about other images. Or words. He tries, again, to remember something from Nazik. A line. A word. Anything. Eventually he has to admit it's not about poems. It's about his ability to remember. Or his ability to forget.

He closes his eyes. He tries to think of Suheir. He wishes she were with him. He imagines her smiling at him, telling him it will be all right. But the face that appears belongs to Zubeida instead. Khafaji breathes, and suddenly Nazik's words come back to him. *Days pass, extinguished. We do not meet. Not even the folds of a mirage can bring us together. Alone, I nourish my hunger with the footfalls of shadows…*

Khafaji smiles to himself. *Something has returned.* The poem's first words. *We do not meet.* He closes his eyes and his body seems to float. By the time he opens his eyes, he's forgotten the lines again. He closes them, but now there is no face smiling back at him.

Exhausted, Khafaji stumbles home. He stops to peel a plastic bag off his shoe. Near the corner of his street, he stubs his toe on a broken sidewalk and almost falls. He pauses to rest his ankle, whispering curses at the dark. It's then that he sees red brake lights snap on and then off. The black Mercedes, parked at the end of his street. The flood of red light sweeps across the black night, falls back across the street. Khafaji freezes and tries to think. When his feet begin moving, it's not because he knows what he's doing. He walks up to the window. He peers inside before the driver knows he's there. The thick-necked man from the university. Zubeida's bodyguard. And before he can do anything, Khafaji smacks his gun on the window so hard it nearly breaks the glass.

The man doesn't put up a fight when Khafaji demands to go to Zubeida. The man doesn't resist when Khafaji reaches into his jacket and takes his pistol. Khafaji takes the clip out and sticks it in his pocket. He pops the bullet out of the chamber and throws it out the window.

The man doesn't complain when Khafaji holds the .357 revolver on him and tells him to drive him to the professor's house. The man doesn't complain when Khafaji dozes off and drops the gun on the seat.

They drive south, then east. Khafaji wakes up in time to see the last slums of al-Dora. By they time they reach Highway Seven, he's asleep. When he wakes up again, they are speeding down a long dirt road. Khafaji rubs his eyes and tries to get his bearings. On the right, the Tigris flows by so slowly it looks like a lake. The car stops in front of a large gate. The driver rolls down his window, and in the darkness a man steps forward to wave them through. They drive for another minute until a villa appears. At some point, Khafaji remembers his gun and picks it up. He waves the driver out of the car and they begin walking along a gravel path toward the front door, the driver in front, Khafaji behind. In the country, the moon is bright, more blue than white. Here, there are too many stars to count. Here, the cane fields sway dark blue, gray and white. And the wind rustles like a whisper. The same lulling sound that the river makes as it pushes toward the sea. It's all enough to make Khafaji want to go to sleep then and there. The only thing keeping him awake is the crunching sound of pebbles beneath his leather shoes.

When they get to the porch, the bodyguard turns aside. Khafaji tells him to go back to the car, and the man does.

Khafaji is almost at the front door when it opens. A warm yellow light spills like a thick carpet unfurling itself across the ground. Without saying a word, Khafaji walks inside. And there is Zubeida wearing nothing but a house robe and an anxious smile.

She walks toward Khafaji, but he pushes her away. He looks at the gun in his hand, and then again at her. The traces of tears in her eyes make him regret his decision to see her.

"What the hell is going on, Zubeida?"

She stares at Khafaji, but says nothing. He raises his voice. "Citrone's dead – and you need to explain."

She starts to cry, but this time there are no tears.

Khafaji begins to shout. "Zubeida, Citrone's gone. You've got more dead girls. Now it's time to talk."

She continues to stare at Khafaji. She stares at the gun in his hand, then she stares again into his eyes. He can't tell if her silence is a challenge. Or a threat. Or just a sign that he wasted his time. It doesn't occur to him that it's an invitation.

When it happens, it's so slow he doesn't even notice it. Until her lips are on his and he's smelling her skin and her hair and holding onto her for dear life.

When Khafaji pulls back, Zubeida has got the gun in her hands, pointed into his belly. He opens his mouth but her hand stops him from saying anything. They stand there for a minute before she puts the gun into his jacket pocket and takes his hand. She leads them down a long marble hallway, turning the lights off behind them as she goes. They walk into a bedroom, then into a bathroom where she begins to draw a bath. She sits Khafaji down. She begins to wash the dirt from his face with a washcloth. He closes his eyes as she washes his forehead, his brow, his eyelids, his chin, his mouth. He feels her fingers tracing the skin on his upper lip. Half dreaming, he watches as she takes off his jacket. The gun in the pocket makes a loud clank when she hangs it on the door. She walks out and closes the door behind her. He sinks his body into the hot water. He leans back and soaks his skin, his muscles, his bones. When he closes his eyes, time stops.

When he opens his eyes, the water's gone cold. He gets out and dries himself with a thick white towel. He walks into the bedroom to find Zubeida sitting at a writing desk. She hears him approach and closes a drawer.

Hours later, Khafaji awakes to the sound of the call to prayer. Under the warm sheets he listens to the invitation in the dark. *Come pray, come pray! Prayer is better than sleep!* When the muezzin finishes, Khafaji imagines the wind in the cane fields outside, then realizes it's Zubeida's breathing. He turns over, but she is not there. When Khafaji sits up, he sees her profile at the foot of the bed. She turns toward him, though he can't see her face in the shadows.

"Muhsin, I wanted to tell you everything. But I couldn't. Now I have to. We need you."

"You don't need me." His voice is cold.

She takes a deep breath. "These are dangerous times in Iraq. Dangerous for women, that is."

"You've already said that."

"Particularly for those of us who are not protected."

"Tell me something new."

Her eyes flash in the darkness. She clasps her hands around Khafaji's.

"When men with guns are in charge, women become fair game. Especially women who don't have men. Who don't have husbands or fathers or brothers or sons. In wartime, women who have to earn a living are especially vulnerable.

Look around you. Would you want your daughter going out to work?" She shakes her head and closes her eyes. "I can't believe you need me to explain this to you, Muhsin."

"You don't have to explain these sorts of things, Zubeida. I just need you to explain what's going on."

"I provide work and protection to girls who need it. Together, we turn our vulnerability into strength."

"Prostitution is strength?"

"Where do you think my girls come from? Some are university students whose families have run out of money. Or wives whose husbands are dead. Or girls whose fathers are dead. Every one of them has her own circumstances. They are stronger as a group than they'd be as individuals. And when you're earning money, you can buy protection. That's how this world works."

"Unless it doesn't work that way. Unless something goes wrong."

"Things went wrong the day some of them started working as interpreters for real." She pauses. "Some of the girls thought they could get out of the business. The Americans were desperate. They would hire anybody who was willing to show up for work two days in a row.

"It was Zahra who first met Citrone and put me in contact with him. They were trying to fly in girls from the Philippines. The CPA didn't want to have to send contractors out to Thailand. And they knew that if the media found out, there'd be an uproar. The business plan we came up with solved all their problems. And for us, it was going to be a boom."

"That's debatable."

"Have you ever heard of a war without sex? No army of men has ever gone anywhere without an army of women right behind them. We have a captive market. A monopoly."

Khafaji closes his eyes. Zubeida is so close he can feel the breath of her words. "Our problems have always been logistical. Not moral. Not financial. The Americans wanted the girls brought in to them."

"So where did the line about interpreting fit in?"

"That was Zahra's idea. She planted it in Citrone's mind. She got him to put everyone on payroll and clearance. He got them IDs even. They could come and go without raising any red flags."

"Like the house on Fatih Street?"

"That was especially safe. The new Green Zone expansion was going to solve the problem for good. I can't believe it." She pauses. "Citrone was good about protecting us. We never had anyone take a second look at any of our houses."

"Until last week."

"Yes, until last week, no one came near us. Not coalition forces. Not neighbors. Not militias. We were as good as invisible."

"So why did Citrone ask me to investigate Zahra's disappearance? What good could come from that?"

Zubeida doesn't hesitate. "Citrone wanted to keep this under wraps. But he had his own reasons for wanting to find her."

"Like?"

Zubeida doesn't answer.

"Was the pay good?"

"God, yes. Citrone wasn't stingy. He wanted supply. And he paid enough to ensure we met the demand. A few months of this, and my girls were going to retire. It would have worked…"

"How did fedayeen set up shop there?"

She strokes Khafaji's forehead. "I don't know. It's all confusing. Maybe they were trying to blackmail the girls? Or hold them hostage?"

Khafaji adds, "They're not the ones who killed the girls."

Zubeida whispers, "I know. It makes no sense."

"So, what happened tonight?"

"No idea. All I can say is that Citrone showed up for his Friday afternoon date. As usual."

"His date with who?"

"What sort of investigator are you?"

Khafaji ignores her. "Zahra was there?"

"She was a favorite."

"Where's Zahra now?" Khafaji tries to look at Zubeida, but her face is in shadow.

"I don't control Zahra."

Khafaji sits, lost in his thoughts. Finally, he gives up. "What happens now?"

She puts a finger to his lips and silences him.

In the shadows, the words begin to flow like the river nearby. *The lover river is a god today. Didn't our city just wash its feet in his waters? Up he rises and pours treasures into her hands. His arms spread wide in the glitter of the morning. His drunken hands embrace us and drown all our terror. Have we ever had any lover but this god?*

Is that Zubeida whispering Nazik's ode to the flood in your ears? Khafaji cannot tell.

Saturday Morning
6 December 2003

The sun is rising as Khafaji leaves the villa. The air is damp and cold. Khafaji stretches and sees Venus hanging low and bright in the east. The red and orange light on the clouds looks like a scar. He thinks of Nidal and Maha – he knows they need to talk, but he doesn't know what to say.

Khafaji finds the bodyguard asleep in the back seat of the Mercedes. The man rubs his eyes, then yawns and takes a drink of water from an old plastic bottle wedged into the parking brake. He gets out of the car, stretches his legs, then gets into the driver's seat and turns the key in the ignition.

Khafaji offers the man a cigarette, and he doesn't say no. Khafaji smokes and watches the road float by like a silent film. Eventually, he gets his bearings. Somewhere near Madain. They drive a few miles through thick cane fields. When a checkpoint comes into view, they slow. The car rolls to a stop in front of concrete blast walls. Two men in body armor and black balaclavas walk forward and peer into the car. They take the bodyguard's ID, then Khafaji's, then disappear. A minute later, they return and give them back. They repeat this at two other checkpoints before they get to the first southern slums.

Khafaji offers the man another cigarette and puts out his hand. "Muhsin." The other man murmurs, "Omar."

After their third cigarette, Khafaji asks to use a cellphone. Omar hands the phone to Khafaji without taking his eyes off the empty road. Then he turns and smiles. Khafaji struggles with the phone before Omar offers to dial the number for him. Nidal sounds far away when he answers. Khafaji looks at his watch. "Sorry for waking you up."

"We're leaving tomorrow," Nidal says.

"Look, Nidal. I don't know how to —"

"You don't need to say anything, Muhsin. I know you did your best."

"That's what I need to tell you. I wasn't —"

"You don't need to tell me anything. Sawsan's gone. She might be dead, she might be alive. I can't tell you how…"

For the next minute, Khafaji listens to the sound of a father sobbing. Nidal finally speaks. "We'll never know."

"You'll never know."

"In the meantime, we can't wait. So, like I said. We're leaving tomorrow. We'll be here all day, seeing friends. Come by," he adds.

"Wouldn't miss it," Khafaji promises, though part of him does not want to go at all.

Omar drops Khafaji off at the front gate and they shake hands. By the time Khafaji closes the door, the car is speeding off.

Khafaji walks up to the outer gate, wondering what to do with the gun in his jacket. He takes it off and puts it to the side. He pulls up his shirt and walks through and turns so the man can frisk him. No alarms go off. No sirens ring. He puts his jacket back on. He repeats this at the inner gate.

Khafaji walks over to the cafeteria. He can't help smiling when he sees Noman in the kitchen. Noman invites Khafaji to share a cigarette on the loading dock. Fumbling through his pockets for a lighter, Khafaji's hand touches a cluster of jagged metal objects. Until he pulls them out and looks at them, he can't remember what they are. The whole time he is with Noman, he is thinking about what to do with Citrone's keys.

By the time they throw their butts on the ground, he knows what to do. He shouts goodbye, because he's already walking as fast as he can toward the office.

Most of the keys don't open anything. But one of them does open two large drawers. Inside Khafaji finds another red duffel bag. Only this time it's not empty. He unzips it and can't believe what he sees. Dozens of packets. Hundreds of hundred-dollar bills bundled together. Stacked neatly in rows.

Khafaji zips the bag closed and slides it out of the drawer. He is reminded of how heavy paper can be. Khafaji remembers a teacher once telling them that paper was made to retain moisture. Most of its weight was from water. When cheap paper aged, it began to lose its ability to hold water. Without moisture, it dried and cracked and died. Paper lived its strange heavy life with water. Khafaji remembered this every time his moved his books.

But money is heavier than books. Maybe because of the special ink.

He closes the bag again, and lugs it onto the floor. It feels like a bucket of water. He reaches into the second drawer, and finds another duffel bag. Khafaji feels around the bag on the outside and finds something hard and compact. When he opens the bag, he finds a cellular phone. Beneath the bag, he finds a set of dossiers. He pulls them out and skims over the names on the tabs. Women's names. Girls' names. He opens one and finds the picture of a girl with lipstick staring back at him. Suzie Habib.

Khafaji does not need a cigarette to know what to do. He rummages around the room until he finds a cardboard packing box. He throws the bag into the bottom and the dossiers on top of that. Then he places his garment bag on top along with some loose papers and office supplies, pencils, half-used notepads, even a couple of staplers. He sets the carton beside the door and plans his next step. The getaway.

Khafaji pulls out his wallet, and finds Karl's telephone number. Then he takes the cellphone and tries to dial. After a few attempts, he succeeds. A young man picks up. "My father's asleep," he says. "Could you call back later?"

"I'll hold on. Tell him," Khafaji says, trying to hide his excitement. "Tell him that Muhsin wants to talk about poetry with him."

As Khafaji waits, he lights a cigarette and plays out the possibilities in his mind. In the background, he hears footsteps, voices calling out, and shuffling. Minutes go by, then finally he hears the son's voice again. "I'm sorry, Mr Muhsin. My father likes to sleep late. Is there a number he can call you at?"

"No, that won't work," Khafaji answers. After a pause, he adds, "Tell him I'll be waiting at Dijla Café. He knows the place. I'll be there in an hour and I'll wait for him."

Khafaji hangs up. He has no plan. He throws the butt on the ground and wonders how to get Mrouj. Khafaji stands up and takes one last look around the office.

Suddenly, the door opens, and three men in uniform walk in. Khafaji reaches into his pocket and feels the pistol. He walks over and speaks in a voice loud enough to cover all fear. "Good morning, please come in. Gentlemen, please." Khafaji extends his hand to the ranking officer and introduces himself.

"Inspector Khafaji, I'm Captain John Parodi of the 267th MP."

"It is about Citrone, isn't it?" Khafaji tries to sound concerned.

"I understand you were there last night. You're the one who discovered the body, right?"

"I was. It was horrible."

"Where did you go? By the time we showed up, they couldn't find you anywhere."

"I went to the hospital."

Parodi looks at another man and says, "Make a note of that."

"Look, Khafaji, that was not the right thing for you to do. We've got a mess on our hands. Citrone might have been in the wrong place at the wrong time, but I doubt it. We have to assume they knew who Citrone was. And now we have to work backwards to understand how."

"Who was he then?"

Parodi doesn't say anything. He looks over at the computers and the other men walk over and begin to power up each machine. The man sits down at one and unrolls a pouch of small tools. He types until the screen lights up, then he works on the machine with a screwdriver and another tool Khafaji has never seen before.

Parodi's gaze returns to Khafaji. "We have reason to believe Citrone's death is linked to the targeting of interpreters."

Khafaji nods and Parodi keeps talking. "We have two tasks here, and they are at odds with one another. We need to secure protection for our 'terps. And we need to investigate them to find who's working for the other side. My men need to go through this office, starting right now. We're hoping you might be able to help us. I'm sorry we have to put you under scrutiny, but that's how it is."

"Of course, sir. I'm at your service. Let me tell you what I know. It's not much. I've been brought in to help rebuild the police force. I'm just going through old files and identifying potential recruits from among the ranks of police officers with experience."

Khafaji pauses. As he narrates, he realizes two things: that once again, the only things they'll know are what he's about to tell them, and that once again, none of this is very convincing. "We knew that the difficult work was ahead of us. I've only been here a few days."

Parodi looks at Khafaji intensely. Khafaji holds his gaze, and adds, "Now that Citrone is gone, I'm not sure what is going to happen."

At least these last words are true. When I am done with this conversation, Khafaji thinks, I am leaving for good.

"I understand, Inspector Khafaji. But I will do my best to make sure your efforts have the support they deserve. Obviously, it's not my jurisdiction. I don't have the authority to do more than convey that to the right people."

For the next hour, Parodi asks Khafaji to explain what he has been doing. He asks questions about money. He asks questions about Ford. He mentions other names, and asks about people Khafaji has not met. He asks questions about a girl named Zahra Boustani, and then about interpreters. Khafaji doesn't say anything untrue, but he also doesn't say anything about Zahra or the interpreters.

When Khafaji tells Parodi that the question of his own salary hadn't even been settled, the interview starts over.

Parodi makes notes and begins asking the same questions again. Throughout, Parodi implies that Khafaji and Citrone worked together day-to-day, and Khafaji never bothers to correct him. From the corner of his eye, Khafaji watches the two other men turn the office upside down. Gently and methodically, but upside down. One of them sits at the computers, plugging in devices and trawling through files. He unplugs one computer and sets it aside. He does the same to the others. The other man wears latex gloves, moving through filing cabinets, desks, and wastebaskets. At Citrone's desk, he uses other keys to open all the drawers. He buries his head inside, and with a small flashlight peers under the desk. Finally, the man at the computers asks the other for help. Together, they begin carrying small loads of electronic equipment out the door.

Parodi's questions come around again to the issue of money, and not to Khafaji's salary. Khafaji meditates on his one single thought: *Today is your last day.*

Ford walks in a different person. A man, almost. Ten years older than he was yesterday. Yesterday, he might have passed for a teenager with shaving problems. This morning his sideburns are white. His face is ash gray. His eyes blood red. Abruptly, he wraps Khafaji in a bony hug.

It is only then that Khafaji understands that Parodi had been waiting this whole time to see Ford. He, Khafaji, was only an extra as far as they were concerned. And now his part was over. This was not unwelcome news.

Another man steps in and introduces himself. "Inspector Khafaji? I'm Bernie Olds, CPA security. I'll be taking over the police project until we get a replacement for Citrone. You'll be working with me. Grab your stuff and come on down the hall. I'll tell you what's going on when we get there."

Khafaji goes over to his desk and fills his pockets with packs of cigarettes. He picks up his box and follows Olds down the corridor. He tries to appear casual, but has to set the heavy box down long before they arrive at the office. Olds helps Khafaji pick it up and together they carry it the rest of the way.

The meeting with Olds is rushed. In his mind, Khafaji has already left. Each minute seems like hours. Khafaji is so busy thinking about his next steps that he does not exactly hear what Olds is telling him. "For the moment, the work in Baghdad is being put on hold. You're being temporarily reassigned to a working group in Kirkuk until this is all cleared up. We're leaving tonight at 1900."

"I need to pack my bags," Khafaji mumbles.

"Go and pack, then. Be here by 1800 at the latest."

Before he knows it, Khafaji shakes Olds' hand and walks out the door with his heavy box. He manages to walk out of the palace before he has to set it down. Walking toward Ibn Sina Hospital, he has to set it down again every hundred yards or so. Finally, a soldier offers to help, and carries it all the way, even into the lobby. Khafaji gives the young man a Rothmans and they go outside to smoke together.

Saturday Afternoon
6 December 2003

Long before Khafaji sets the box down at the reception desk on the fourth floor he sees the commotion. When he tries to pass the desk, he is stopped by the nurse, who reminds him to sign in. Box clutched to chest, Khafaji walks into the melee. There are so many people crowding into Mrouj's room that at first he cannot step inside.

The room is filled with balloons and roses and flooded with bright lights. The air is hot and stuffy. Men stand around holding video cameras, microphones and electronic equipment. Khafaji tries to look over their shoulders, but he cannot see his daughter. The curtains around her bed are shut tight. Beside the bed on the other side of the room, an American reporter sits awkwardly, smiling and holding the hand of the other patient, an older Iraqi woman with two black eyes and an oxygen mask. The woman is awake, but not lucid. She looks at the men with the cameras and flashes a thumbs up sign, and the reporter asks the cameraman, "Did you get that?" He nods. "OK, let's get the doctor back in here."

Someone shuts off the spotlights, and the temperature of the room begins to drop immediately. Only then does the reporter's smile fall into a scowl.

A man walks out of the room. Politely, he points to the box in Khafaji's hands and tells him to step back into the corridor. Two others press by Khafaji, pushing him out of the room. One man holds a clipboard and shouts down the corridor, "Where's the doctor? We need him now."

Khafaji slips back into the room. Stepping over toolboxes and backpacks filled with equipment, he nearly trips. One man catches Khafaji, another catches the box then hands it back to Khafaji. Khafaji notices the reporter pointing at him. Khafaji opens the curtain and closes it quickly behind him.

Khafaji sets down the box, and then looks at Mrouj's sleeping face. She looks weaker than yesterday. Worse in fact. There's no mistaking the yellow of her skin. Khafaji looks for a chair to sit on, but sees none. He puts his hand in Mrouj's. Outside, the noise in the room grows louder. Khafaji finally loses his patience.

When he steps out from the curtain, Khafaji finds the reporter standing next to him. "Hello. I'm Caridad Macmillan. They tell me you're here visiting your daughter."

Khafaji stares at the woman but says nothing.

"We're doing a story on Iraqi patients. The human angle. Some good news for a change. Could I talk to you about your daughter's experience?"

Khafaji looks around the room and simply murmurs, "No speak English." He reaches around her for a chair. The reporter tries to engage him again, but gives up as soon as the doctor walks into the room. With a harried smile, the doctor first nods at Khafaji, then looks at the reporter. "OK. We can do it now. Let's go."

The reporter tells her assistant to bring the others back to the room, but the doctor interrupts her. "If you want to interview me, you need to start right now. You've got five minutes." He looks at his watch, then goes over to the old Iraqi woman in the other bed. She looks up at him with a pale shade of confusion in her eyes. The doctor strokes her arm, checks her pulse and then says, "It'll be all right," as the cameras begin to roll. The old woman does not understand the words, but she understands what they mean.

When the reporter gives a signal, the man with the clipboard repositions the doctor on the other side of the patient, opposite the reporter. She turns her smile on again, just as the lights flash on. In an instant, the temperature in the room begins to rise.

"In the battle for Iraqi hearts and minds, there is no weapon more powerful than medicine. And on this frontline, the frontline of healing, American doctors are paving the way for the transition to peace in the new Iraq. We're here with Dr Lewis Stone, one of the many American doctors treating patients in Baghdad."

The doctor nods and smiles grimly.

"Could you tell us about your typical day, Dr Stone?"

"Besides the mass trauma, it's not that much different from a day at home. Seeing patients, figuring out how to bring them the care they need." His lips are pencil thin.

"So tell me what is different about working in Iraq, Doctor?"

"Well, one thing that is different is that many of my patients here suffer complications from chronic diseases that are perfectly treatable."

The reporter's smile never dampens. "What sorts of diseases?"

He now looks directly at the camera for the first time. "Well, at home, I rarely see patients who have something like a kidney or liver condition that is allowed to go untreated for years. But it's one of the most common things you see here. You've got to ask yourself why that is."

"Why is that, Doctor?" She grins.

"Because for thirteen years we prevented these people from receiving the simple care they needed. For every Iraqi patient I'm seeing today, hundreds of others died in the last decade – simply because they could not get the basic medicines they needed. These problems were all caused by the sanctions system. And who put those in place, Caridad? We did. The American people did."

"But they must appreciate the care you're giving them now."

The doctor is no longer smiling at all, and no longer talking to her. "I am not sure if 'appreciate' is the right word." He looks at the old woman, who struggles to smile as she gazes up at the reporter. "Caridad – imagine being poisoned. Imagine I poison you every day for ten years. I keep on poisoning you to the point that now you're on your deathbed. Then imagine I magically come one day and tell you I've got the antidote. Would 'appreciation' describe your feelings toward me?"

The reporter's smile never fades, though confusion shows in her eyes. But before it can spread, the doctor looks at his watch and announces, "And now I have to get back to work. Thank you very much for your interest. My patients need their rest, so please leave now."

He catches Khafaji's eye, then walks over. The two men wait as the crowd exits the room. And then they are alone.

"I am very glad you came, Mr Khafaji. Mrouj's condition is not so simple."

"What's wrong, Doctor?"

The doctor draws back the curtain and feels Mrouj's wrist. He looks at her face for a minute then answers, "What's wrong is that we were hoping to reverse the deterioration quickly, but we haven't been able to. She responded favorably to some of the ACE inhibitors and ARBs and it looked like her condition was stabilizing."

Khafaji looks puzzled and the doctor explains. "Those are two classes of medication used to treat kidney disease at these levels."

"So what is happening?"

"Mrouj started to have an adverse reaction to the ARBs – that sort of thing is always a possibility. Did you know she has a heart condition as well, Mr Khafaji?" He pauses. "We are hoping that the dialysis by itself will improve her state, but there's no guarantee. And as you can see, she's weak. Lucky for her, she was able to sleep through the circus today."

Khafaji shakes the man's hand as he leaves, then sits down at Mrouj's side. He picks up the book of poetry and begins to read, but can't concentrate on the lines in front of him. Two hours go by as Khafaji strokes Mrouj's brow and reads aloud. Every so often, he stops himself. He tells Mrouj about Citrone. About the money. About Zubeida. About Nidal and Maha. About everything. He wonders aloud. He argues with himself in whispers while Mrouj sleeps. By the time Khafaji gets up on his feet again, he is forced to admit that his plan is now no longer an option.

The old woman smiles at him, and Khafaji realizes that she has been listening to him the entire time. Listening to him read poems. Listening to him talking to Mrouj. Listening to everything. Khafaji struggles with the box, then sets it down. He searches around for something to write with. He looks through files until he finds a blank piece of paper. He sets the files down on the windowsill and walks back to the reception desk and borrows a pen. He composes a short note to Mrouj, telling her that he will be away for a few days. When he finishes, he slips the note into the pages of the book, then picks the box up off the floor again. He hesitates before going and looks at Mrouj one last time. When he waves goodbye to the old woman, she holds up her fingers in a victory sign. As he walks out, he asks the receptionist to write down the phone number for him.

"Here's the main number, and the extension of the room. And I have written down the number for the desk here too, just in case."

In the back corner of the Dijla Café, Khafaji sits drinking tea. One man passes by, tapping a shoe brush against folded cardboard. Khafaji looks the other way. Another walks up and does the same, and Khafaji looks at his watch. His hands grip the box on the table. Each time he finishes one cup of tea, a man comes to take it away. And Khafaji orders another.

He places the box on the ground and rummages through the clothes and papers on top. He digs until he finds the duffel bag, then glances around the room to make sure no one is paying attention. His hands search through the bag until they find a loose bundle of bills. He slides one into a jacket pocket, then does it again. After closing the bag, he rearranges the clothes. His jacket pockets are now full, with lumps of metal, with packs of cigarettes and paper money. He tries smoothing them over, but it's hopeless. Khafaji looks at his watch and sees that an hour has already gone by.

At some point, the tea begins to catch up with Khafaji. He crosses his legs, then uncrosses them. He looks at his watch. He looks around the room again. Nothing has changed. A thousand waiters, a thousand cups of tea. The same old men sitting with each other. Telling the same old jokes and stories. Playing the same old games. The same old waiting.

Khafaji's bladder begins to make him squirm, but he does not move from his corner. He notices one of his hands is resting awkwardly on the box below his knees. He sits up and stretches his arms. He looks at his watch again and crosses his legs. His mind begins to wander. Away from his body. Away from crowded cafés filled with unemployed men. Away from the fact that a man Khafaji does not know may or may not come to help him.

By the time the shoeshine reappears, Khafaji is nearly pissing in his pants. Khafaji surprises himself by saying yes before the man even asks to shine his shoes. The man happily agrees to watch Khafaji's stuff first while he goes to the bathroom. When the poor man smiles, a row of missing teeth shine. "Of course. Take your time. I'll be right here. Where else would I go?"

The bathroom floor is wet and sticky. Khafaji breathes through his mouth to avoid having to whiff the stench of urine coming up from the cracked orange and brown porcelain. Khafaji studies the water as it drips into the basin. As he pisses, an old poem comes to mind:

> They put us in the press hoping to squeeze out petrol
> Cheers, my friends, drink it up!
> The only pollution you suffer is that of your mortal flesh
> One man sells everything
> And supports every cause in the world
> Only to flee from the fight in front of him.
> Pissing on him makes me drunk.

Khafaji's loins wring themselves out, and a warm feeling begins to tingle in his belly and chest. Like he just pissed out gallons of black bile. *You are not going to leave your daughter. You're not going to leave this place. This is your city and you're not going to surrender it.* Khafaji goes to wash his hands. When he finds that the sink is broken, he is neither surprised nor upset. By the time he wipes his hands on his pants, he has made up his mind.

The man is standing patiently by the table and smiles when Khafaji returns. Khafaji stretches sock-clad feet out on the cardboard the man sets on the ground. Khafaji orders two more teas, one for himself and one for the man shining his shoes.

By the time Karl arrives, Khafaji is no longer in a hurry. Somehow, time has slowed down. The two men smile and shake hands.

"Thanks for coming. Let me get you a cup of tea. I'm sorry about the other day. It's just that there's a mess right now."

Karl waves him off. "There's a war going on right now. I expect people to be late."

Karl talks about his family. About his pregnant daughter-in-law. About more grandchildren. Two cups of tea later, he stops long enough for Khafaji to speak. "I need your help in a getaway. It's not for me. It's for my wife's family. They need to get to Amman. They are already packed and ready to go. They're taking nothing, only what would fit in your car."

Karl laughs. "My car!"

"Today. You need to leave tonight. You'll be paid well."

"How much? It's not an easy drive these days."

"I can give you ten thousand dollars right now if you agree. Ten more when you deliver them."

Karl leans back. "I have to think about this."

Khafaji removes one bundle of bills from his pocket and hands it under the table to Karl. "Why don't you go into the bathroom and count these before making your decision?"

Khafaji pays the bill and tells the waiter to keep the change. Karl returns with a look on his face somewhere between ecstatic and terrified. He only says, "Yes. I can do it. Let's go."

Clutching his box again, Khafaji follows Karl to the battered old Peugeot station wagon. "Seats up to nine, if you put the suitcases on the roof." Khafaji puts the box on the floor in the back, and the two men drive across the river.

Khafaji says nothing to Karl until they get to Nidal and Maha's apartment building. They sit in the front seat and Khafaji wonders where to begin. He starts by taking out the other bundle of cash and showing it to Karl. "That's the other ten thousand dollars."

The look on Karl's face is dead serious, and somehow it comforts Khafaji. He hands the money to Karl. "Look, I trust you. Take it all. This is my family. They're in your hands – this is all we've got."

Karl grins. "Don't worry. We can go whenever they're ready. I just need to call my wife."

His smile disappears completely when he takes the money. As if the bills were contaminated. He opens a glove compartment and throws both bundles in. When he tries to slam the door shut, it falls open again. With one hand, he jams the money into the back of the compartment, and with his other, he slowly latches it shut again. By the time he's finished, he says, "Let's go see them." The tone in Karl's voice suggests that the hard part of the journey is already over.

Khafaji grabs his box. Karl helps him to carry it up the stairs. Children run up and down the stairwell calling out to each other. A young girl teases the men as they stop to catch their breath on the third floor.

Maha answers the door, kisses Khafaji's cheeks, and welcomes both men inside. Neighbors visiting from next door stand up to greet Khafaji and Karl. Everyone sits down, and Maha disappears into the kitchen to make coffee. When they hear Maha crying from the other room, one of the women goes to be with her. Khafaji turns to Nidal and asks to speak to him in the other room. They walk through a bedroom to a tiny balcony. Khafaji offers Nidal a cigarette, but he declines. Khafaji lights one for himself.

"Nidal, I want you to listen to what I say. And I want you to take my advice." For the first time, he sees how much Nidal has aged in the past week. It is not just that you lose, but that in losing, you lose even more.

Khafaji is halfway through his story when Nidal finally asks him for a cigarette. Maha delivers two small cups of coffee and stares at her husband. "Allah? You haven't smoked in years!" Nidal sends her off with a serious look.

"In the other room is a box. In the box is a bag full of money. Think of it as compensation for what you've lost. It won't bring Sawsan back. It won't bring back your old life. But there's enough there for you to start a new life. Take that bag into your bedroom, and pack the money into one of your suitcases. When we're finished, you are not going to tell anyone what we have done and you are going to leave immediately. All of you. The man I brought with me…"

"Who is he?"

"He is someone. A driver. I know him from a long time ago. His car is parked downstairs. He's ready to take you to the border. He's already been paid. He does not know what is in the box, and he does not want to know. Don't take anything but clothes. Anything else might attract attention."

Maha walks onto the balcony. She scowls at Khafaji, then attempts to smile. Nidal nods at her, and she goes back inside.

"When you get to Amman, open a bank account and deposit everything. Don't tell Maha anything until you have done all this. Understood? Then call me and let me know where you are."

Khafaji looks at his watch, and realizes he has to leave. The shock is etched on Nidal's face as he walks back into the salon with Khafaji. He picks up the box and carries it into the bedroom. At that point, Nidal and Khafaji work fast. Nidal empties an old suitcase and together they fold the money into bundles of clothes. Nidal looks at Khafaji from time to time, his eyes frozen in fear. As they close the suitcase, Nidal touches Khafaji's hand and says, "Muhsin, where is this really from?"

"Don't ask. Just take it."

Nidal takes Maha aside and they talk. She protests for a moment, then calls two teenage boys to come back into the apartment. Khafaji and Karl go into the kitchen. Khafaji hands him the revolver and says, "You have enough money to pay anyone who gets in your way. And if you don't, you also have this." Karl puts the gun in his pocket and laughs.

"I'll wait a couple days and call to make sure you got home safe."

Karl bends the fingers of his other hand into a gun shape and makes a clicking noise. "Bang."

Khafaji says his goodbyes to the family. The boys are out of breath from playing soccer outside, and they huff and puff as they shake Khafaji's hand. Maha cries as she kisses Khafaji.

"I'm so sorry, Maha. I will join you in Amman just as soon as I can."

Maha says nothing, but bursts into tears again. Nidal offers to walk downstairs, but Khafaji stops him. "You've got enough to do today. I'll see you in Amman," he promises, even though he's not sure it's true.

The sun is low, and the children playing on the street begin to run home. Khafaji is still carrying the box as he walks by Karl's car, only now it's not so heavy. He notices that the doors are unlocked and windows wide open. The glove compartment is wide open. Khafaji reaches in and feels the money right where Karl left it. He closes the compartment door twice before it sticks shut. Khafaji smiles, sure that he found the right man for the job.

Saturday Evening
6 December 2003

By the time Khafaji arrives at his building, the sun is low in the sky. The guards in the foyer are sipping their tea as he walks in. They smile and half-stand as Khafaji goes by. "No, men, don't get up," Khafaji calls out and waves to them. The electricity comes back when he is halfway up the stairs.

It doesn't take long for Khafaji to gather his things. For the last week, he knew he was leaving. Only today did he learn the destination. He takes the uniform out of the box, and realizes that the files are missing. He packs two changes of clothes – underwear, socks, undershirts, dress shirts, trousers, a sweater, a jacket. After that, there's no room for anything else. He looks around, wondering what else to take. He finds an old photo album. Later on he will regret that it only contains pictures of Suheir and Uday and Mrouj, but none of his parents or sisters or brother. He walks over to the bookshelf and agonizes over what to take. One book of poetry, but he can't decide which. His fingers finally pull al-Maarri from the shelf. *Making the Unnecessary Necessary.*

Khafaji hears a man cough behind him and then a voice. "Brother Muhsin, Peace upon you."

He turns to see Ali, who is standing at the open door. "Upon you peace, Ali. What can I do for you?"

"I hope I'm not bothering you, Brother Muhsin."

"Not at all." Khafaji looks at his watch and waves him into the room. Ali takes two steps forward. Khafaji asks, "Have you come for the keys?"

Ali shakes his head, but says nothing. Khafaji looks at him again and adds, "You'll find them over there next to the door. On the table, right there." Khafaji points, but Ali ignores him.

Khafaji goes back to looking through the books on the shelf. Without turning around he calls out, "I hope you don't mind, but I can't offer you anything. I'm in a hurry. I'm leaving in a few minutes."

"That's what I wanted to talk to you about, Muhsin. You're not leaving."

"Pardon?"

"Muhsin, I mean, we've reconsidered."

Khafaji sits down, and puts his head in his hands. He stares at the floor and says nothing.

"Look, you do not have to leave. I hope this is good news. But I can understand if you're not in a mood to thank me. In any case, I hope this makes things right. We can't force you to stay, but I hope you do."

Without a word, Khafaji gets up, walks back into the bedroom and picks up the suitcase. He drags it down the hall and past the living room. He sets it down next to the front door. Only then does he come back and extend a hand in Ali's direction.

"Thanks for telling me, Ali. And yes, it is good news to hear that I'll be allowed to stay in my own home. Should I bother asking why you changed your mind?"

"Brother Muhsin, let me know if there's anything else I can do. We are neighbors."

Khafaji looks at him. He stares behind Ali at the bookcases.

He sees the empty bookshelf, then says, "There is one thing you can do for me, Ali. I don't care about the couch. I don't care about the chairs or the pots or the pans. You can have them. But I want my poetry back. All of it. If you can do that, then you can be my neighbor."

Ali nods and puts his fingers together.

"Oh. And another thing. I'm going to be gone for a little while, but I am coming back. Can I count on you to keep an eye on my place while I'm gone?"

Ali smiles. "Sure," he says as he gently takes the suitcase from Khafaji's hand, and then carries it downstairs. In the foyer, the two men shake hands. Ali tells one of the guards to help Khafaji with the suitcase. The man carries it all the way to Abu Nuwas Street.

RED ZONE

And lightning burst across the sky, like a lily of fire,
Opening above Babylon, lighting the valley.
A spark shot through our land,
Laying bare its seed and root and its dead.
And clouds poured down rain upon rain. Were it not for
    the city walls, the waters would have quenched our thirst.
In the eternity between one thunderbolt and the next,
We heard not the rustle of wet wind through the palms,
But the clamor of hands and feet,
A murmur, the sigh of a girl seizing a moth-like moon,
    or a star, in her hand.
Seizing the tremor of water, of a raindrop in which
    whispered the breeze
To tell us that the sins of Babylon will be washed clean.

BADR SHAKIR AL-SAYYAB

Sunday–Thursday
7–11 December 2003

The helicopter takes off vertically into the night, then widens
into flat zigzags out of the city. Two long rows of men, strapped
to the ribs of the aircraft, each looking at the man facing
him. The man opposite Khafaji goes to sleep as soon as he
sits down and doesn't wake up until they land in Kirkuk.

Fifteen years since Khafaji rode in a helicopter. Fifteen
years and a lifetime since he was in the north. Khafaji closes
his eyes but is wide awake throughout. The vibrations of the
machine shake his bones. *For the first time in months, you are
where you are because you chose to be. Fate dealt you a good hand
this time. One so good you made Nidal take it and leave the game.
Deal yourself a new hand and play again.*

It is early morning when they arrive. Everyone but Khafaji
carries a large green backpack. Khafaji walks behind them,
dragging his old suitcase across the tarmac. There is nothing beyond the wide fields of cracked concrete. Only now
does it dawn on him that "Kirkuk" means a base somewhere
nowhere. Olds taps his shoulder and he turns to see a black
Suburban pulling up. They drive to a cluster of white trailers.

"Welcome to Chooville, folks." An officer comes out to
greet them in the middle of the night.

Olds looks over at Khafaji and explains. "Customized Housing Units."

"That's right, CHUs. We choose only the best when it comes to our guests. I'll show you yours."

The man takes them to one end of a trailer, opens the flimsy plastic door and turns on the light. Khafaji looks at the plastic floor tiles.

"Well, not so lucky, yours don't come with toilets. Gents, you'll find your cans over there," he says as he points behind another trailer. Olds claims one bed, and Khafaji throws his suitcase on the other and begins to unpack. He hangs his suit up in the closet, then his shirts and his ridiculous uniform. When he finishes, he realizes that he must have forgotten to put al-Maarri's diwan into the suitcase. He goes outside and eventually finds the latrine. He washes his face in icy water. He walks back to the room, breathing night air so cold and dry it burns. Khafaji looks up and sees a canopy of stars he hasn't seen in years. Stars stretching out forever. He begins to name his favorites. Yedelgeuse, the hand of Gemini. The Warrior. Rigel. Saiph. Nairalsaiph. Alnitak. Alnizam. Mantaka. Almisan. He looks at the Bull, at Aldebaran. Althuraya. The brightest part of the sky. The hunter's arrow that never flies and never strikes its target. And the enemy that only ever appears on the opposite horizon.

Khafaji says goodnight to Olds and climbs into a skinny bed. He turns out the small reading light on the nightstand and tries to wrap the blankets around him. He gets out of bed a few minutes later to search for more blankets. When he can't find any, he puts on a second pair of socks, then pulls the covers over himself again.

He wakes up in the early morning to find that the blankets have fallen onto the floor. He pulls them over his body again, but cannot go back to sleep. He looks at the glass of water on the nightstand. He stares at the metal lamp one foot from his pillow. He looks at his wristwatch and listens to the ticking. Outside the blankets, the air feels like ice. It almost hurts to breathe. He stares at the condensation around the window. Olds turns over, his mouth-breathing a roar. Khafaji is now wide awake, his thoughts like lines connecting dots, making constellations out of the dark sky. He lies thinking about Sawsan, then Nidal. Then Citrone, then Zubeida. He tries to steer the lines back to Suheir, but they do not go in that direction. Each time he tries to imagine Suheir, her eyes, her lips fade into Zubeida. Even though they look nothing alike. The more Khafaji thinks, the hazier Suheir's silhouette becomes, the clearer Zubeida's becomes. Khafaji tries to think about anything else. About Mrouj, and then about Uday, but always he arrives back at the villa in the cane fields.

And then it gets worse. Suddenly, he is in Kirkuk. Then in Sulaimaniya. Then empty mountain villages. Empty green hills. Greener than anything Khafaji ever knew. He dreams of thick carpets of wildflowers. And fields of freshly-turned dirt. So much dirt. The dirt of trenches dug by engineers. The dirt of graves turned in the night. Of flowers and grass, and dull roots stirring with the late rains. Cruel spring bred from a forgetful winter. The ground churning with hunger.

Khafaji opens his eyes and tries to think of poetry. To remember anything. Another word. A phrase. An image. A sound. An association. One line that might open up the flood. Poetry to bury memory. Poetry to soften the past. Poetry to turn corpses into fields of flowers.

Nothing comes. Not a line. Not a phrase. Khafaji's mind feels like a long trench of dirt packed cold and hard. Barren earth, with no flowers, no roots. Hours go by as Khafaji stares at his water glass and reading lamp and wristwatch. He falls asleep again only after dawn begins to crawl out of the bloody eastern hills.

They spend the morning in meetings. As Khafaji walks into the meeting room, a man with a thin moustache hands him a small folder filled with pamphlets, and a small envelope. When Khafaji opens it later in his room, he finds crisp hundred dollar bills.

Besides Khafaji, there are three other Iraqis, one from Basra, one from Hilla, and one from Karbala. Their fatigues are as ill-fitting as Khafaji's. The British and American liaison officers in the room make a show of how eager they are to meet their Iraqi counterparts. Khafaji doesn't catch their names. A contingent of Kurdish officers sit on the opposite side of the table, all dressed in other uniforms.

"I will be candid with you. We are facing setbacks and challenges across the country," one British officer begins in English. "CPA leadership has decided to regroup and focus our efforts on establishing the police force in Kirkuk. So we have brought you from around the country for a workshop, a summit if you will." As he speaks, the words become slower, more deliberate. Khafaji notices a young man frantically scribbling notes. More than once, he leans forward as if to interrupt the speaker.

"Out of this, we hope to create a nationwide network of working relationships and, more importantly, the sense of trust and confidence that comes from knowing that you are not alone, but part of a team. Look around you – this is your team. We are your team." When he finishes, he looks at the young man and nods. The young man takes a deep breath and begins to translate, mixing formal Arabic and colloquial Baghdadi. His eyes never leave the page of notes he holds in his hands.

The British officer continues talking, and as he does, he makes a point of looking in each man's eyes for a moment before pausing and moving to the next. The interpreter comes in again, and hurries again through his notes. Next, Olds stands up and begins to talk about the need to identify problems, create solutions and set realizable goals. Each time the interpreter comes to the word "benchmark" he stumbles. At first he translates it as "the sign of the bench", then "trace of the long seat", then "imprint of the work table", and so on. Other words like "synergy" and "entrepreneurism" wreak even more havoc. Olds talks for a half hour, and when he finishes, his audience is thoroughly confused. Olds hands out a work schedule, and for the first time Khafaji learns that he'll be staying in Kirkuk for a month. His heart sinks. He'd told Mrouj he'd only be away for a few days.

Besides ten British and American officials, the Iraq Police Reconstruction Working Group includes eight Iraqis, none from Kirkuk. "Paradoxically, this will be an asset to our work in Kirkuk," a British officer tells the group. "Because neither you nor we are from here, we will all be more objective. We will be in a better position to see the reality of Kirkuk than a policeman who comes from here or an official who is too caught up in details to see the bigger picture. Any questions so far?"

No one asks a question.

During breaks, Khafaji talks with one of the Kurdish policemen, Salah. They vaguely recognize each other from the academy. Was it really forty years ago? They share cigarettes, and ask about others from their class. Salah remembers names and faces Khafaji forgot long ago. As he goes through the list, Khafaji is struck by the fact that so many are gone.

For the most part, the other Kurdish officers keep to themselves. They are friendlier with the foreign liaison officers, as if they already knew each other.

In theory, they attend sessions designed to brainstorm. That word also poses problems for the interpreter. When he tries "tempest of the mind", two people laugh out loud and the first British officer asks what is so funny. At some point, everyone switches to using English phrases.

Sunday and Monday are spent in meetings like this. In one morning session, a Ukrainian police chief lectures on civilian administration. After the coffee break, a British naval officer uses slides and graphs to discuss asymmetrical force. After lunch, there is more of the same. The interpreter begins to slip more and more. He starts cutting and editing out material, prompting one of the Kurds to interrupt constantly and ask for the deleted material to be added back in. "Not for my sake," he insists. "But for those in the audience who might not speak English so well."

Khafaji listens to it all and is struck by the fact that it makes no real difference if the interpreter adds or subtracts from the lectures. The message is always the same: *things have to get better.*

Each presentation unloads large amounts of data. Each presenter seems to have an enormous capacity for collecting and commanding data. One American MP cites census records from the Mandate Period. He occasionally uses Arabic phrases, and calls the Basran *"habibi"*. There is nothing to do but smile. Another presenter refers to figures indicating rising levels of primary education. Among girls. In the Kurdish region. For the period 1991–2002. Everyone smiles again. After the first day, the group is taken around the base to meet various officials. The Americans drink coffee. The British drink tea. The Iraqis drink the tea and wish it were stronger. Conversation is light, polite and positive. Everyone practices their English. Everyone practices their Arabic. Khafaji keeps his mouth shut, except when someone asks him a direct question.

On Tuesday morning, without notice or explanation, the foreign liaison officers do not come to the morning meetings. Nor do the Kurdish participants, and the Basran says he saw them leave early in the morning. After the first session passes, someone shows up to say that the Americans and British were called back to Baghdad temporarily. The man from Hilla puts a motley pile of newspapers on the table, and the workshop transforms into a tea-fueled reading session. *Al-Bashira. Al-Dawa. Al-Hawza. Al-Mutamar. Al-Sabaah. Azzaman. Sawtaliraq. Tareeq al-Shaab.* The Basran calls the group "The Central Coordination Committee for Information Gathering, Processing, and Recapitulation" and the name sticks. Everyone laughs at the acronym, the CCCIGPR, even though it's not that funny.

On the first day, Khafaji doesn't read a word of print. He paces down the corridors and smokes his Rothmans until they run out. When he rejoins the others in the conference room, he leans back and thinks. But on the second day, he relents. For the first time since 1968, Khafaji looks at a local newspaper. He looks at stacks of newspapers. He enters the world of print and begins to read the local opinions, as well as those appointed in Tehran and Washington and Riyadh. Each morning, the Basran gets a fresh stack from someone who got them in the city. An hour after breakfast, he comes in with a fat pile of the day's papers.

Khafaji is astounded by what he reads. Everybody – from the Communists to the Wahhabis – has a daily now. There are newspapers and magazines from all over the Arab world. Some have today's news. Some yesterday's. Some are a week old or older. The editorials are no more sincere than the ones that used to appear in *Babel*. After skimming the opinion pages for a day, Khafaji gives up on them and reads only news items. As he reads, it is easy to imagine that they all have something to do with him. Every day, the Resistance reports, more heroes are martyred. They report that another imperialist agent has died. Every day more puppet policemen are killed or kidnapped. Every day more disappear. Every day is one day closer to the end of the occupation.

Khafaji reads that a Resistance fighter sacrificed his life when he drove a car into the gates of the US barracks in Tala'far, thirty miles west of Mosul. The blast injured fifty-nine American occupiers and six Iraqi agents. He reads that the attack occurred at 4.45 a.m. and that guards at the gate opened fire on the vehicle, which exploded instantly. He reads that an American military spokesman claimed that the injuries were not serious. Other sources said that there were many severe injuries, and that the foreign oppressors were forced to transport casualties out of the country for more serious medical attention. He reads the next item. It describes how, at 2.30 p.m., surface-to-air rockets brought down an OH-58 Kiowa surveillance helicopter.

In another newspaper, Khafaji reads that hundreds of Shiites demonstrated in Baghdad yesterday. They were protesting the death of a cleric at the hands of the Americans on Friday. The demonstrators gathered in front of the Palestine Hotel and waved black flags. They carried pictures of the Imam Shaykh Abd al-Razzaq al-Lami and pictures of the wreckage of a car. Khafaji learns that the sixty-four-year-old cleric was inside when it was crushed under an American tank. He reads that on the same day in al-Khalidiyah, west of Falluja, three hundred people demonstrated against crusader provocations. They were demanding the release of their neighbors and relatives who had been taken into custody by the crusader army. Demonstrators marched from al-Khalidiyah mosque, waving Iraqi flags. Some carried placards denouncing the local municipal council as collaborators. They also demanded that the council be ousted. Demonstrators stopped at the crossroads leading to al-Habbaniyah airbase. Khafaji reads that the demonstrators sent a five-man delegation there that presented a petition of demands. These included the release of citizens held without charge, and a halt to American provocations. Khafaji reads a small item about the downing of an American military transport plane at Baghdad airport.

The next day, Khafaji keeps drinking tea and keeps reading. He reads that imperialist Department of Defense officials acknowledged a major disappointment on Wednesday in their plans to set up a puppet army in Iraq. He reads that Pentagon officials admitted that one-third of Iraqi trainees have quit the puppet army. "We are aware that a third have apparently resigned and we are looking into that in order to ensure that we can recruit and retain high-quality people for a new Iraqi army," said Lieutenant Colonel James Cassella, a Pentagon spokesman. In the same report Khafaji reads that this battalion was highly celebrated when the newly retrained soldiers, marching to the beat of a US Army band, completed a nine-week basic training course in early October, and passed in review before America's Proconsul in occupied Iraq, L. Paul Bremer. He reads that officials worked for weeks to speed up the training of Iraqi puppet soldiers and police in the face of the accelerating pace of Resistance attacks. He reads that the private American defense contractor Vinnell Corporation had done most of the training, using "civilian instructors", mostly ex-US military. He reads about the Titan Corporation and another called CACI, and their ties to the corrupt puppet regime.

In a Jordanian newspaper from a few days ago, Khafaji reads about how the American army had delivered seven unidentified bodies to the puppet police of Fallujah. He reads that an American military spokesman in Baghdad promised to investigate the matter. He reads that Ahmad Alwan, a police officer in Fallujah, is quoted as saying, "The American forces contacted us and told us to pick up seven bodies left outside their base in Fallujah." Khafaji reads that the corpses were wrapped in the plastic body bags regularly used by American forces. Khafaji reads that there was no explanation regarding the circumstances of the deaths of these persons, nor any information on their identity. He reads about Ali Khamis Sirhàn, a physician in Fallujah Hospital where the bodies were taken, who explained that many residents of the city, including relatives of missing persons, have been prevented from identifying the bodies.

Khafaji puts the paper down and stops reading. He walks outside and wishes he had a cigarette.

These are the benchmarks Khafaji and his colleagues hit on Tuesday and then again on Wednesday. They spend the day together in the conference room, but say little to one another. They are friendly together. They eat together. Those who have cigarettes share them with the others. But they are not together.

When they talk it is only about news items. One man

finishes a newspaper, and folds it. The next man picks it up and reads it. When they discuss and argue, it is as if it were about fantastical stories from a distant planet. No one speaks of themselves. No one speaks of families. Or pasts. Khafaji does not wonder why.

The only break in the routine comes when an American officer enters the room on Tuesday and asks for Khafaji. He hands Khafaji a note: "Break in case. Need to talk re Zubeida Rashid. Call ASAP. Parodi." It takes Khafaji some time to find a phone, and even more to dial the number, and then to be redirected, God willing, to the right extension. It rings and rings. No one answers. Khafaji waits by the phone, wondering what to do. He pulls out Karl Abdelghaffar's phone number and tries it. A young man answers in an anxious tone.

When Khafaji asks for Karl, he demands, "Who is this?"

"This is his friend Muhsin."

"My father just got back from a trip, and he's very tired."

"Did he say…?"

"Who's calling?"

"My name is Muhsin. I'm the one who hired him to —"

"He said to tell you everyone is safe."

"Great. Thank you. Please thank your father for me. I'm away right now, but will call him when I get back to town."

Khafaji tries to reach Parodi again. Once, he is redirected to another office in the American zone. The other times, the phone rings but no one answers. He dials Karl's number again, but hangs up before it begins to ring. Then he rings Ibn Sina Hospital. The nurse at the fourth floor reception promises to transfer his call, and he begins to lose hope. When Mrouj comes on the line, Khafaji apologizes. "I must have woken you up, Mrouji. I'm sorry."

"Not at all, Baba. How are you?"

"It's you I'm worried about. How are you doing?"

"I'm sleeping a lot."

"What do the doctors say?"

"They say I should sleep a lot, so I guess I'm doing something right."

"Any improvement?"

"They changed the treatment a couple days ago. Since then the pain is less."

"That's good."

"Baba, do we have to talk about my kidneys all the time?"

"What else do you want to talk about?"

"How about those files you gave me?"

"I didn't give you…" Khafaji pauses. "I didn't mean to leave them there."

Mrouj doesn't say anything.

"Did you read them?"

"What else am I going to do? You give me a bunch of files about brothels, of course I'm going to read them."

Khafaji doesn't say anything.

"Baba, you still there?"

"Yes, I am."

"Don't you want to know what I think?"

"I'm not sure, Mrouj." Khafaji listens to the crackle on the phone line before he surrenders. "Fine. Tell me what you think, Mrouj."

"It isn't about sex, Baba."

"What are you saying?!" Khafaji cannot help shouting at the phone.

"Calm down and tell me who this woman is."

"Which woman?"

"Zubeida Rashid. Why didn't you tell me about her before?"

Khafaji feels his cheeks begin to burn. He says nothing.

"Is she pretty?"

"That's irrelevant," Khafaji says before he realizes his mistake.

"So she is pretty, Baba?"

Khafaji doesn't answer the question. "Let's talk about something else before we hang up, Mrouj."

"OK. Here's a line for you then, Baba: *As we prepare sword and spike, death slays us without a fight / Tethering our steeds at hand but still, they cannot rescue us from…*"

Khafaji thinks for a moment, but says nothing.

"I stumped you? My God, that's a first!"

"No, you didn't, Mrouj. I'm just tired. Go to sleep, I'll call you again as soon as I can."

On Tuesday and again on Wednesday everyone in the group decides to go to bed early. They also decide to sleep late. Khafaji sleeps so deeply, he does not even dream. He closes his eyes and then nothing. When each day comes to an end, it is over. It does not bleed into the next. Like a newspaper, he folds up each day and puts it aside for good. For the first time in weeks, Khafaji begins to rest. His breath becomes slow and measured and deep. On the third morning, he looks in the mirror and decides not to shave his upper lip.

On Thursday, Khafaji wakes up expecting another day of newspapers. When he sees the Kurds outside the conference room, he realizes the program has changed again. He steps inside and sees Olds and the other liaison officers have also come back. The meeting starts as if there had been no interruption. Khafaji sees the same look of surprise on the others as they come in late. During a coffee break, the Basran asks for the working group to be provided with newspapers every day. The chief liaison officer asks for a list of titles, and hands them to an assistant. By the afternoon break, a stack of newspapers awaits each Iraqi.

The presentations today are different because now there is a concrete topic. Now there is a concrete task. They are told that tomorrow they will be attending the induction of new cadets in downtown Kirkuk. For the first time there are two police officers from Kirkuk in the room. They begin to lecture on the rule of law. As they speak, they look over at the British liaison officer sitting next to them. Even though they look like college students, they somehow hold the rank of superintendents. When they finish, the British officer shakes their hands and congratulates them. Then he begins to talk about the decapitation of the insurgent leadership and how legal modes of authority always triumph. He concludes by saying, "Among the most vexing aspects of counter-insurgency are the paradoxes involved in conducting war that is simultaneously political and military." At lunch, this same officer tells Khafaji about his adventures trekking across Afghanistan the previous year. "Brilliant place. Generous people. Have you been?" In his smile, Khafaji begins to recognize that the man's confidence is ingenuously distilled from fear.

At one point Olds asks Khafaji if he's had a chance to speak to Parodi. Khafaji says, "I've tried calling, but..."

Olds doesn't say anything. The smokers step outside for a cigarette and Khafaji notices the front page of a newspaper on the table. What catches his attention is a picture of the Mosuli exile standing next to Abd al-Aziz al-Hakim. He picks up the paper and reads the caption: "Interim Governing Council Establishes War Crimes Tribunal". The others walk ahead while he goes in the opposite direction, newspaper in hand. He begins to read: "Today is an important historic event in the history of Iraq." The article relates that the tribunal will begin by focusing on the murders of the Barzani clan in 1983. Then it will concentrate the prosecutions on Halabja. Then on the southern massacres after Kuwait.

Khafaji folds up the paper and looks around. At the opposite end of the building, he sees the others huddled together against the cold wind. Their clean uniforms stand out against the fading white concrete. He continues reading. *The tribunal will have the authority to investigate crimes against humanity, war crimes and charges of genocide committed in the country between 14 July 1968 and 1 May 2003. 38 of the 55 most wanted leaders of the old regime have already been caught and will soon be facing this tribunal. In addition to these numbers, CPA authorities acknowledge the arrests of over 5,500 people, though not all for war crimes.* Khafaji skims the next article. "Since May, investigators have discovered more than 200 mass graves throughout the country. In Kirkuk, Kurdish officials reported the discovery of a grave containing 2,000 bodies. In the village of Muhammad Sakran, more than a thousand bodies have been unearthed. In al-Mahawil, investigators suspect they will have uncovered in excess of 15,000 bodies when they are done."

Khafaji feels his head start to spin and he walks back to his room. He lies down and stares at the ceiling. But nothing happens. No sleep. No poetry. No memories.

The sun goes down and the room goes dark. Outside, phosphorous lamps cast long streaks and shadows through the window. Khafaji covers himself with a blanket, but it is not enough.

Sometime after dinner, Olds comes back to the room. The Basran is with him. Olds shakes Khafaji's shoulder. As Khafaji rubs his eyes, Olds apologizes in English. The other man, in his warm southern accent, invites Khafaji to come out with them. Then they turn on the light and insist: Khafaji must come along. Reluctantly, Khafaji gets out of bed, shivering. He puts on an extra undershirt and two pairs of socks when he dresses. In the parking lot, they find one Suburban still waiting for them. Everyone else already left in the other car. In minutes they are flying down an empty stretch of highway. Khafaji cracks the window open and the wind wakes him up. The dry desert seems to suck the air out of his lungs. He looks out the window and sees nothing for miles. As they speed by, a corral filled with horses suddenly appears under a bright floodlight. Huge, wild horses. The kind that belong in a poem. Khafaji looks again, and they are gone.

When they come to the city, the driver tells them they are heading into the Almas district. Khafaji does not recognize the neighborhood at all. Even when he thinks he sees something familiar, he knows it's only his mind playing tricks on him. They stop at a three-story building where a group of Peshmerga stands at the entrance. The other SUV is already there, parked opposite. The gunmen salute without saying a word. Khafaji notices they carry the same weapons as the men at his building.

A young boy opens the front door. Light and smoke and noise spill across the dark, silent street. Once Khafaji's eyes adjust, he sees men bunched like thick knots around tables. The red curtains and ornate glass chandeliers look garish, then soften. Strains of plucked ouds crash over the room from stereo speakers. Older waiters, dressed like refugees from the Ottoman court, flit around the tables, delivering bottles of clear liquor, replacing full ashtrays with empty ones. They make elaborate, clanking sounds as they work, to show

how attentive they are. Khafaji scans the room, hoping to glimpse others from the group, but sees no one. An elegant older woman floats across the floor. She is wearing enough embroidered fabric to upholster the whole room. She greets them, one by one. "Welcome, welcome, gentlemen. Please come back this way. Your party is in the back."

Khafaji walks through the room, watching men playing cards so intensely they never look up or notice the table next to them, let alone anyone walking through. Down a corridor, lit by red lights covered in satin, a hand draws back a curtain of smoke. Raucous laughter pours out from behind another door. The Kurds from the group stand up to welcome the arrivals, taking each by the hand and walking them to empty chairs at the tables. "Tonight," says one of the officers from Kirkuk, "you are our guests. Make yourselves welcome."

Two waiters are dedicated to the party. One comes over quickly. "What would you like to drink, sir?"

Khafaji looks around and sees only bottles of arak and vodka on the table. "How about whisky?"

"No whisky, unfortunately. May I bring you a bottle of what the others are having?"

Like all who order vodka, Khafaji understands it is a compromise. He reads the label on the bottle slowly. Letter by letter, sounding out the Russian name. But before he can finish, someone grabs the bottle out of his hands and pours a shot. Soon everyone is raising a glass. Small speeches are made. After each, they swallow a small shot of liquid fire. At one point, Salah gets up and clears his throat. By way of introduction he simply says, "Hardi." Then he begins to recite a long poem. The Kurdish sounds are foreign, but not. Most of the words are foreign, but not. Poetry is a country, Khafaji thinks. When Salah finishes, everyone applauds, and someone demands a translation. Salah hesitates, then tries to translate:

We are the defenders of lowly peasants,
We are the flag of unity hoisted high,
We are the swords in the hands of the broken,
We have risen against tyranny.

The Basran demands to hear the rest, but Salah insists it's too long and too local. The Kurds grin. Someone raises another toast, to the National Police Force. One of the Kurds shouts, "And to Hardi! *The flag of unity hoisted high!*" Released by alcohol, the tongues in the room finally embark on their journeys. Someone begins to sing, and many in the group stop talking and join in on the chorus. Eyes, clear and sober for days on end, begin to soften and fade into pinker tones. The room is warm. Khafaji looks around at his colleagues. *The rebuilders of free Iraq.* Somehow it comes out as a question.

Soon, the men at both tables start playing cards. Every now and then, the door opens a crack, and the old lady peers in. Sometimes she comes over and rubs the shoulder of one of the loud-mouthed Kurds at the other table. Sometimes she says nothing but leaves the door slightly open and goes off. At Khafaji's table, they begin playing whist. Then someone suggests poker and takes out a stack of hundred-dollar bills. The game is friendly enough, and Khafaji is drunk enough that he antes up with the others. Someone puts a carton of Marlboros on the table next to the bottle. Everyone has been smoking since they sat down. While lighting one, Khafaji notices two young women looking in at the door. The door shuts. At some point, one of the Kurds, Sherko, suggests a game he learned in the US. "Texas Hold 'Em," he shouts as he begins to deal and explain the rules. Everyone regurgitates the name with slight variations, until it finally becomes *tiguss kholdoon* – "snip Kholdoon". They raise a glass to Kholdoon and his circumcision, and laugh hysterically. Khafaji plays a few games, loses a lot of money, and then asks a waiter where the toilets are.

When he stands up, the room starts to spin. The floor catches itself and stops moving. On wobbly legs, he tries walking. A place to wash his face in cold water until he can see straight again. He wants to breathe fresh air. Cold desert air. He holds onto the walls as he walks down the corridor back the way they came in. The front room is now mostly empty. Without the crowds of men the décor seems ridiculous. Twangy mountain music plays somewhere, and while Khafaji can't understand the lyrics, he knows that somewhere a poet has lost his beloved. Khafaji looks around for signs of a washroom. He hears laughter and turns to find a flight of stairs. Another party upstairs, another card game upstairs. He grabs onto the handrail and begins to climb. At the top of the stairs, he finally finds a bathroom. He goes inside, locks the door and runs the tap.

With each handful of water he splashes on his face, he imagines he is waking up from another layer of dream. His cheeks begin to lose their heat, and his head begins to clear. He looks at his face in the mirror, then goes to the toilet. Just as he is flushing, there's a knock on the door. Khafaji mutters, "Just a second," and washes his face one more time.

Khafaji opens the door and finds himself staring into the face of a girl he recognizes. A girl he has never met. He stares at her and stares again, so startled that she pushes by him before he realizes what has happened.

When he finally gets his bearings, he calls out, "Zahra? Zahra Boustani? I need to talk to you."

He begins to knock, and calls out her name again. "Zahra? Please come out. I need to talk to you."

There is no reply. Khafaji knocks again, hesitating, and pleading in a gentle voice. Then he is no longer hesitating. His voice is no longer gentle. Soon he is slamming his fists into the door and shouting. Then he is leaning into the door, trying to force it open. This goes on until he feels thick hands twisting his arms behind his back. Khafaji struggles, but the pain is too intense. He goes limp and falls face-down on the carpet. When he looks up next, he sees the old lady's slippered foot. And the boots of a younger bouncer. As she escorts Khafaji downstairs, the hostess tries to calm him down. "It's going to be fine."

"I just want to talk to Zahra."

"You can't talk to her, *habibi*."

"I need to speak with that girl."

"Zahra's not yours to speak to. Your party is downstairs, *habibi*."

The bouncer's hands are still clutching Khafaji's arm. When Khafaji agrees, the hands let go. He returns to the others, and slumps into his chair. The game has gone on without him. Just as if he never left.

Someone pulls out a new deck and deals. Khafaji picks up his cards and looks at them before realizing what they are. A shit hand. Ten of Clubs: Latif Nusayyif Jasim. Four of Hearts: Humam Abdal-Khaliq Abd. Khafaji looks at the five cards face-up on the table, hoping to build something. The guy to his left picks up one of the cards and starts to laugh out loud. He pokes the next person and hands him the card. Soon the whole table is in on the joke. When they finally show Khafaji the card, he already knows what it is: Three of Diamonds.

Khafaji laughs as much as the others, but inside he's already folded this hand. His thoughts drift upstairs. Toward a closed room where Zahra Boustani sits with another group of men. *Was it her? Does it matter? And even if it was her, what could she tell you that you didn't already know? What do you know?* Suddenly, it's not Zahra he is thinking of, but Zubeida.

Khafaji rubs his eyes and decides to get back into the game. He wins a hand. He loses two hands. No one at his table is taking the game very seriously. But at the other table, the play is serious. At some point, Khafaji's group decides to stop playing and they turn to watch the other game. One of the Kirkukis changes the game to Seven Card Draw. Within a couple of hands, the contest becomes lopsided. Before, the Basran had been on a winning streak. Now he begins to lose hand after hand, and the pile of bills in front of him is redistributed. The dealer is grim. He never smiles, even when he wins two hands in a row. His face makes it all look like business. After thirty minutes of losing, the Basran throws his cards on the table and shouts, "OK! We've played your game long enough. Now let's play another one. Here's an American game."

"What's it called?"

"52-Card Pick-up. It's easy to play. You play it once, you never forget the rules."

The others decide to humor the Basran.

"Go ahead and deal!" the Kirkuki mumbles as he passes the deck across the table.

The Basran leans forward and shuffles. Then he asks, "Are you ready?"

"Yes!" the whole table says.

He has a huge stupid smile on his face as he turns to the Kirkuki. "Ready?"

"Just deal."

At that the Basran shuffles the cards again, then flips them across the table into the other man's face and lap.

Silence reigns.

The Basran points and howls, "Good game!" Then switching into English, he exclaims, "That's 52. Now pick them up!"

The Kirkuki lunges across the table. Other men have to jump in to keep them apart. Even so, fists are thrown and faces bruised. By the time tempers have cooled again, the party is over. The old lady walks the party out. When Khafaji tries to speak to her, the bouncer appears and takes him by the arm.

Driving back to the base, Khafaji presses his face into the window. Outside, it is absolutely black. He looks for horses, but sees only tiny glimmers of light in the distance. Flickers scattered across the wilderness. The black Suburban speeds through the black desert night, slips through emptiness. The only thing that can stop such travel is the fear of one's own thoughts. Khafaji cracks the window, and breathes in the thin air. He looks at the stars, searching for Orion, but it has already set. He looks toward the other horizon, and sees Scorpio beginning to rise. He imagines there is nothing between him and the horizon. Then the horizon melts away and Khafaji imagines he is flying across the heavens. The air is so sweet and cold it hurts. Like inhaling shards of glass. He rolls up the window and closes his eyes, knowing that he will sleep fast. His sleep will be as dreamless as it has been every night since he left Baghdad.

Friday
12 December 2003

Between the frigid morning air and his throbbing head, Khafaji stays in bed. Olds calls to him as he goes out, but Khafaji waves him away and pulls the sheets over his head. Eventually he gets up to go to the bathroom. He showers and shaves his chin and cheeks. Only then does he wonder what time it is. More than an hour after he was supposed to be at the parking lot, Khafaji leaves the room.

By holding the induction ceremony on a Friday morning, the chief liaison officer pointed out, they would be assured of no disruptions. The streets would be empty until noon. By prayer time, the ceremony would be done. When the Basran asked about risks, the Kirkuki smiled. "You're in the north now. We don't have the problems you have."

"The city deserves to see these young men honored properly," the British MP said. "They deserve to witness each step the country takes on the path to reconstruction."

Khafaji wanders through the conference rooms until he comes across another straggler, a Ukrainian police chief. They share a cigarette as they walk over to the parking lot. Together they climb into the Humvee that will take them to the ceremony.

Looking out toward the north, Khafaji sees the weather

changing. High thick clouds roll in from the west. The air feels damp now, heavy. The first rains. In the distance, Khafaji hears a low rumble, like thunder.

As they drive, Khafaji sees that that the desert he imagined empty is actually full of life. This was no wilderness. Windbreaks of pine and eucalyptus line the route. Railroad tracks and electric lines periodically cross the road at oblique angles, then vanish in the distance. Lines of cars and trucks. For miles, they find themselves trapped behind a long articulated lorry with Turkish plates. Thick black clouds of exhaust pour out from the truck and envelop their car. Khafaji stares at the tiny baby's shoe that dangles from the rear bumper. Off in the tan and brown fields, Khafaji sees a shanty town of black barrels and tents. A woman in a bright orange and green dress removes laundry hanging on the line. The radio crackles on and off. The driver plugs in headphones and concentrates on the road.

A few kilometers away, in the city center, a black cloud rises into the sky. The driver speaks slowly to the wire in his ear. A mile later, he talks over his shoulder. "Massive bomb. Multiple casualties." They pass through one checkpoint, then another. Two more Humvees fall in behind them. No one talks.

They park blocks away from the station. Khafaji and the Ukrainian walk beside an MP waving a pistol. Plumes of burning petrol blot out the sun. The hot clouds begin to rain soot and ash down on everything. Firemen run down a side street, dragging long hoses behind them. Khafaji ties a handkerchief around his face, and runs toward the wreckage.

A shallow crater tells them where it happened. Sections of the station's courtyard wall are gone. So is much of the façade of the main building. The fronts of buildings across the street are also missing. Empty windows. The broken glass is like a sparkling carpet.

On a side street, a line of bloodied men lie on their backs. Some try to sit up. Some hold bandages to their limbs. Others are tended by people who have rushed to help. Every few minutes another stretcher arrives. Every few minutes someone is taken off. Khafaji looks around at the crowds. The men running. He stares at the charred remains of cars, and wonders which frames are set to explode next. *When streets are bombs...* he begins, but can't complete the thought. He notices the Basran lying on the sidewalk, a bandage on his forehead. His eyes are closed.

Khafaji comes over and gently touches his arm. "Can I help?" The man opens his eyes, points to his bleeding ears. Then he shakes his head, and shouts, "I can't hear." He begins to cry. Khafaji goes to a grocer and takes as many bottles of water as he can carry. He goes back to get more water and boxes of tissue paper. He begins to clean the man's head. Despite the blood, the head wounds are not deep. Khafaji tries to talk to him, but the man keeps his eyes closed. The blood from his ears will not stop, and he winces when Khafaji stuffs them with tissues. Khafaji gets up and wanders into the courtyard.

The bodies of young men lie scattered in the debris. The lucky ones were crushed under the wall. Khafaji joins a group of firemen heaving bricks and concrete slabs from the pile. With a medic, he picks up a body in a uniform that matches his own. When they set it down alongside the others, Khafaji covers Salah's head with a jacket. As the line of bodies grows longer, Khafaji recognizes two others. He counts fifteen policemen in uniform. There are also six others in civilian clothes. One of the British liaison officers asks Khafaji if he has seen Olds. Khafaji shakes his head.

Later, after Khafaji has watched them as they loaded bodies for the morgue, someone comes over and tells him to come inside the station. Khafaji goes to the toilet and washes in an old bathroom sink. Then he walks through halls filled with glass and dust until he finds the rest of the group. In the room, everyone is eating from platters of kebab and kofta. There are salads and fresh flat bread. Only then does Khafaji realize how hungry he is.

When Khafaji sits down to join the others, no one seems to remember he wasn't there. He doesn't correct them. The group sits and eats in silence. Then they sit and listen to the British liaison officer talking at them.

"Here is what we know at this stage. Shortly before the induction ceremony commenced…" The man clears his throat and begins again. "A four-wheel-drive car drove into the gate. Our men managed to shoot the tires. Otherwise, we might not be here talking to one another right now. Luckily, the driver did not manage to penetrate inside the courtyard."

He then starts giving details of another incident and it takes Khafaji a moment to understand that it has to do with the two young officers from Kirkuk. "This is to confirm what you heard earlier this morning, gentlemen," he says in a hushed voice. "Our two colleagues were murdered, along with five others, as they reported for duty this morning at Nnnnn…" He stumbles for a moment. "At Nahiyat Hammam station. We can confirm now that the men who murdered them were dressed as policemen. Intelligence suggests that it may have been an inside job. I apologize in advance for what I have to say next, but I do hope you will understand why it is necessary. All you lot are ordered back to the base immediately. You will stay there until we complete our investigation into this breach. We will need your cooperation now more than ever if we are to close the breach. You will have the opportunity to contact your families once you get there."

The sound of boots outside the door interrupts the officer, and everyone in the room turns to look at the door. A group of US MPs enters the door, then spreads out to each corner.

The liaison officer continues. "Do not think you are under investigation because we think you are guilty of aiding and abetting the enemy. We know that the vast majority of you are here because you want the right side in this fight to prevail. Personally, I doubt very much that we have been infiltrated, and I hope that my belief will be vindicated. But nonetheless, until we get to the bottom of this, we need to clean up this mess together. We can't let these incidents undermine the progress we're making. We cannot let the terrorists win."

He pauses and looks around the room. Then he adds, "If you have a weapon, please remove it from your holster and place it under the chair you are sitting on as you stand up and move to this side of the room. These MPs will escort you back to the base. You have my word that we will do everything to make this ordeal as comfortable as we can. The sooner you help us, the sooner it is over."

Khafaji looks around the room. At bleary-eyed men, tired and now angry. The expressions on their faces waver between anger and disbelief. Khafaji puts a piece of cold meat in his mouth and chews. One of the local recruits shouts out, "What are you saying? We are killers?"

The British officer puts his hands up in the air, then lowers them slowly. "You need to remain calm. You are not criminals, no one has said that. But for the safety of everyone here, for your safety and the safety of your colleagues —"

"They are the terrorists! Not we. Fuck you!" the young

man shouts as he stands up. One of the MPs walks slowly over, baton in hand.

Other recruits begin to stand up, shouting and waving their fists. The MPs move in quickly, forming a cordon around the group. Khafaji sees his chance and drops to the ground. He crawls among kicking feet until he gets to the door. Then he stands up so slowly that no one sees any movement at all. As fights break out across the room, Khafaji walks, then runs down the hall and downstairs.

Khafaji runs too far and ends up in the basement. In a grungy dressing room, he begins trying the doors on lockers. Most are locked or empty. But in one he finds what he needs, though it's not what he expected. The clothes look like they will fit better than the uniform he has on. He finds a changing stall and empties his pockets. He takes off his uniform. The concrete floor feels like ice on his bare feet. In another locker, he finds a towel and goes over to an old metal sink. He splashes cold water on his face, then does it again and again. His eyes are red. They look like they belong to a stranger staring at someone else's mirror. He washes the grime and dirt from his hands and under his fingernails. He removes his undershirt and splashes his chest with more water. He runs the soap over his torso, then rinses off and does it again. He looks at his body in the mirror. Then stares at his face. His eyes are still bloodshot and tired. His moustache is now filling out. He begins to shiver. Standing in a puddle of icy water, his feet begin to feel hot.

Khafaji rolls up his uniform into a ball and throws it into an empty locker. He puts on the vest. The fabric is soft and worn. Khafaji fills the pockets with his wallet and papers. He slips the old white *dishdasha* over his head. The sandals are too large, but the leather is smooth and comfortable.

He takes the *kuffiyyeh* and wraps it around his shoulders and neck. He puts on an overcoat that was hanging in another locker. It's too tight to button, but better than nothing.

Then he walks up a flight of steps and out the side door. Outside the station, Khafaji walks beside a row of trucks, their engines blasting diesel exhaust. Then Khafaji almost walks right into her. She is standing in a small shop, speaking on a cellphone. He almost doesn't recognize her because of her headscarf and heavy overcoat. He almost doesn't recognize her because she looks like a woman you're not supposed to stare at. But there is something about how still she is standing, like she was just about to leap, or just about to flee. After studying her picture for a week, Khafaji is not caught off guard. He would recognize Zahra Boustani anywhere. And after this morning's slaughter, he knows exactly what to do.

Khafaji starts to run as fast as he can, wondering if there was anyone else watching him. Blocks away, Khafaji squeezes into a crowded market street and walks, before turning between a juice stall and a kiosk. He stops to buys a pack of Royales and smokes while watching the street behind him. Finally, he turns to ask about the bus station. The man stares at Khafaji. In that moment, Khafaji feels like he's naked. But the man points and mumbles a few words, and Khafaji heads off in that direction. More than once, Khafaji thinks he hears thunder somewhere far away. His feet walk faster and faster as he goes.

He gets to the station just as the rain starts. Inside, he buys bags of dried chickpeas and sunflower seeds. At a newsstand, he looks for a book of poetry. When he can't find any, he buys as many newspapers as he can. He finds the next bus for Baghdad, and waits for an hour before the seats fill up. He imagines that the policemen in the station can see straight through his costume, then wonders what they would say if they saw his ID.

He tries to read the papers, but when a policeman boards the bus, he puts them down and pretends to be asleep. The policeman walks up the aisle, checking everyone's IDs. But when the driver starts the engine, the policeman turns around and jumps off the bus. Only as they leave the station does Khafaji look up again. And even then, he cannot relax. He imagines other possibilities. Other men with guns stopping the bus, searching for puppets, for terrorists, or for men who aren't who they say they are. Khafaji stares out the window. The last thing he sees before the sunlight dies is three men racing each other on horseback. The rust-colored speckles on the lead horse look like splatters of blood.

It gives Khafaji no comfort to imagine that the desert could be a place of escape, because he knows it too is home to animals and men and guns. When the lights come on inside the bus, Khafaji finds himself staring at his own reflection. He remembers the lines of poetry Mrouj recited: *As we prepare sword and spike, death slays us without a fight / Tethering our steeds at hand but still, they cannot rescue us from…* It is frustrating, because he knows the poem. An elegy of Mutanabbi's. Fright? No. It's not the rhyme, it's also the meter.

Khafaji gives up. He looks at the newspapers in his hand, and throws them on the floor. He leans his head against the window and falls asleep. At some point, he wakes up shouting and flailing in his seat. The man next to him glares as if he had gone mad.

Saturday Morning
13 December 2003

When the bus arrives, Baghdad is wide awake. Clouds cover
the sky. The air is cold and heavy. A wind kicks up, then dies
as it rolls down the wide boulevard. Khafaji walks through
the crowded bus station and crosses the street to a busy café.
He drinks one cup of tea and then another. A boy comes
by hawking newspapers, and Khafaji shoos him away. A few
minutes later, another comes selling magazines. Khafaji gives
him some dinars and tells him to fetch a pack of cigarettes,
Iraqi cigarettes. The boy comes running back with Royales,
and Khafaji lets him keep the change.

He pays for the tea and gets up. He lights a cigarette and
walks down Rashid Street. A plan begins to form in his mind.
A plan to rescue Mrouj. To resign. Or to disappear without
a word. A plan to go home and stay there. At a busy corner,
he stops to light another cigarette. He stands there, looking
at the motion around him. The chaotic, frenetic movement
of men and women and children walking and driving and
riding and going. The dance of the city, its messy pulse. Its
life. Its life despite everything.

Khafaji watches a boy herding a flock of fat sheep across
the intersection. Against the signal. The first cars swerve.

The next ones stop. The ones stuck behind begin to honk their horns. The boy is a study of focus and grace. He hits the shanks of the animals calmly, but ignores everyone else. He could be in the village right now.

Khafaji watches the herd complete its journey across the boulevard, then steps off the curb. He collides with a young woman. In that accident, he feels for one moment the girl's body. The warmth of her body, and its solidity. As they both stumble, Khafaji is aware that the contact doesn't so much arouse him as remind him of his own body. He holds out an arm to help the girl get up, but she just glares at him and rushes away. Khafaji starts to apologize, but too late.

He looks around and suddenly the street is full of women. Women wearing hijabs, and not. Women wearing tight pants. Women wearing loose skirts and thick black robes. Women who look at men when their eyes meet. Women who turn away. Young women who are beautiful only because they're young. Older women who are beautiful because they are beautiful. A street of women, it suddenly seems. *They cannot rescue us from the sweet wanderings of night.* Khafaji stands there taking it in, and finally remembers the line: *As we prepare sword and spike, death slays us without a fight / Tethering our steeds at hand but still, they cannot rescue us from the sweet wanderings of night.*

The line Mrouj stumped him with. The words tell him to go to see his daughter, but the meaning tells him something else. Who better than Zubeida to ask about wanderings in the night?

Khafaji decides to go straight to her. He stops a taxi and gets in. As soon as Khafaji says "Madain", the driver declines and pulls over to let Khafaji out. He gets the same response from the second and third taxis as well. He walks past a stall selling kitchen supplies. He looks through the knives, and buys the biggest one he can find. The seller turns to find newspaper to wrap the blade, but Khafaji is already walking back to the curb.

When the driver of the fourth taxi refuses at the word "Madain", Khafaji surprises him by taking out the knife. The man begins to stammer and then cries. Khafaji doesn't stop him when he opens the door and gets out. Khafaji slides over into the driver's seat, kicks off his sandals, and accelerates before the man can return.

He speeds out of the city. At the fourth checkpoint a soldier asks for his ID, then disappears behind a thick concrete wall. Khafaji smokes a cigarette before they signal for him to step out of the car. Khafaji stands there listening to the radio snap and spit as someone makes a call. One and a half cigarettes later, a Humvee shows up and an interpreter gets out wearing an oversize bulletproof vest and helmet. She and two other soldiers walk over to Khafaji. She orders him to follow them behind the wall.

"This says you work for the CPA," she says. Her accent is educated. She looks at him skeptically through small eyeholes. And Khafaji suddenly sees himself. No man in his family ever wore a *dishdasha* before.

"Are you on official business?" Her voice is soft and young. Through the mask, her eyes seem pretty. Khafaji wonders why he is thinking about that.

"I'm meeting colleagues in Madain," he says.

She looks at his ID again, but says nothing. She walks over to the US soldiers. A few minutes later, a young soldier returns and hands Khafaji his ID. "They'll radio ahead. Have a good day."

As Khafaji drives away, he wonders why they didn't ask what he was doing driving a taxi.

At each checkpoint, Khafaji slows up and rolls down his window, but the men wave him through. It's difficult to spot the interpreters. They're either well hidden, or these units have been left without them. Soon Khafaji is sailing over seas of sugar cane. He goes so fast that he misses the side road. He turns around and goes back. As he turns down the road, he watches a flock of pigeons flying up in a widening circle about the cane fields. They soar up, then suddenly dive down. He drives through the gate but doesn't notice it, his eyes mesmerized by the flock. He almost runs into the row of black Suburbans parked at the end of the gravel. Khafaji brakes. The tires make a loud churning sound on the gravel. Dust starts to rise. When it clears, he looks more closely at the cars. He rolls down the window, reaches for his cigarettes, and thinks. It takes another moment to recognize the insignia: Meteoric Tactical Solutions. Outside, Khafaji hears nothing but the rustle of the wind in the cane. Faintly, he hears the whisper of the flock as it plunges, then catches itself, then rushes off again on its wobbly loops. Khafaji inhales and watches the pigeons as they struggle to climb.

When they come, he doesn't see them. It's their footsteps on the gravel he hears first.

Two large young men holding assault rifles are walking down the driveway. Khafaji smiles and waves to them. But this only makes them point their weapons. One of the men shouts something. They fan out, one to Khafaji's left, the other to the right, and their pace becomes very slow and deliberate. When two other men appear behind them, Khafaji puts the car into gear and begins to roll. Khafaji smiles and waves. He knows how hard it is to shoot a man when he's looking right at you, and so he never takes his eyes off theirs. The other men begin to jog toward Khafaji. He accelerates, then slams the wheels to the left, putting the car between his body and their guns. He hears the first bullets hitting the passenger door and the trunk of the car, pushes his foot down as far as it will go and crouches down. Head beneath the dashboard, he speeds down the narrow lane as bullets rip apart the trunk and smash out the back window. Khafaji flies blind down the narrow lane until at last the sound of hot popping metal comes to an end. By the time he sits up and looks in the rear-view mirror, there's nothing to see but dust. He takes a last drag from the cigarette on his lips, and flicks it out into the cane.

Khafaji's hand is fumbling in his vest for another cigarette when a figure leaps out into the highway. A man whose face is wrapped in a *kuffiyyeh* points an AK-47 at Khafaji. And this time Khafaji stops. The man walks up to the passenger side and opens the door. He looks at Khafaji, then exclaims, "Mr Muhsin. Thank God!"

Even without unwrapping his mask, Khafaji recognizes Zubeida's driver.

The man disappears into the cane field. A moment later he comes back, a woman hanging over his shoulder. Khafaji leaps out and helps carry her to the car. Khafaji holds Zubeida in his arms while Omar brushes off the back seat. The two men then lay her down. Khafaji looks at Zubeida. She opens her eyes, closes them again. Khafaji feels for her hand and is surprised by how hot it is.

Khafaji gets back into the front seat, and they race along the highway toward Baghdad, Khafaji's hands gripping the steering wheel, Omar's fingers clutching the gun on his lap, Zubeida's hand falling limp onto the floor. She coughs and coughs. Khafaji adjusts the mirror and looks at her face. But she doesn't move. As they come up to the first checkpoint, Omar shouts, "Turn right."

Khafaji smiles and ignores him. He slows down and waves at the soldiers. When he sees one soldier behind them pulling traffic spikes across the road, he realizes he's made a mistake. Khafaji pulls over. Smiling, waving and maintaining eye contact, as always. The soldier walks up to the car. He looks at the damage. When he asks Khafaji and Omar to put their hands above their heads, Khafaji punches the gas pedal, knocking him over the hood of the car. The body makes a sickening thud as it rolls across the windshield and slides off. Without warning, a storm of bullets hits the car, but not before Khafaji has put distance between them. In the rear-view mirror, Khafaji sees a Humvee in pursuit. The vehicle gains, but then disappears when the highway takes a bend through the cane. Omar shouts at Khafaji again and this time he does not hesitate to turn off the highway. For a few kilometers, they zig left toward the river, following a dirt road that crosses one irrigation ditch and then another. Then they zag right, crossing the highway again and entering a vast date orchard. In the faint shade of the trees, they pass men climbing barefoot up tall ladders. Other men on the ground carry thatch baskets. One peasant, buried up to his knees in earth and mud, watches them go by. Low in the sky behind them, an Apache helicopter swoops low and fast along the highway. Then another right behind it.

Khafaji slows down to avoid ruts and ditches. A few people watch them, but no one stares.

Eventually Omar wakes up. He looks at his watch and then at the road. He accepts a cigarette from Khafaji and smokes. After a few minutes he says, "Stay to the left up here. We'll be at the hospital soon." He looks at Khafaji and shakes his head. "Why did you come?"

"I should be asking you the questions. What happened back there?"

Omar looks at the road as he answers. "The Americans came to the institute this week. They took everything. It didn't take long for them to find the house. They weren't coming to arrest anybody. They were shooting before they showed up."

Omar turns around and looks at Zubeida. He looks so long, Khafaji has to ask, "Who is she? I mean to you?"

"She is my aunt. My mother's sister. She took me in when my parents died." He looks at Khafaji and adds, "I'm not the only one. There are a lot of us who depend on her."

A minute later, the date trees end, and the road spills into the town of Madain itself. Omar directs Khafaji through crowded streets until they arrive at a hospital. Two medics come out to the car and greet Omar by name. Khafaji gets out and inspects the car. The only unscathed part is the tires. A streak of blood runs along the passenger side. Only then does Khafaji notice his *dishdasha* looks no better.

The nurses rush Zubeida inside. Khafaji walks alongside, holding her hand, watching her face. Her eyes never open, but her hand holds his tight. When they take her into an operating room, Khafaji finally lets go. Omar walks up and murmurs, "We've got to get out of here. Now." Khafaji watches Omar walk down the corridor. Then he turns and walks in the opposite direction.

In the corner of a crowded waiting room, Khafaji sits, thinking. He takes his coat off, then turns it inside out. It looks ridiculous, but better than horrible. He walks out of the front door and crosses the street to a taxi station. He pays the driver the fare to downtown. They manage to enter the city without passing any checkpoints. Khafaji tells the driver to go to Checkpoint Three.

The man is silent for a minute before he admits, "I don't know what that is." Khafaji directs him through downtown and then across the river. Stuck in a traffic jam on the bridge, Khafaji offers the man a cigarette. He takes two. He lights one immediately and sticks the other one behind his ear.

Saturday Evening
13 December 2003

When you visit the American zone, leave your *dishdasha* at home. Wear clean clothes. Wear pants. Iron your shirt. Better yet, wear a jacket and a tie. And while you're at it, wash the blood off before you get to the gates.

They should post this advice at every barricade and every checkpoint. Maybe it's so obvious that they don't need to. And on any other day, Khafaji would have laughed at the idiot who needed this advice. If Khafaji had thought about it for a minute, he would have simply gone home. But Khafaji wasn't thinking. If there were any thoughts in his head at all, they were about his daughter.

People begin to stare as soon as Khafaji steps into the crowd. They don't even wait for his turn to come; they step up, weapons drawn, and order him to take off the overcoat. When they see the blood, they push him to the ground. A boot pins his shoulder blade while they pat down his body. Khafaji protests. The words are like pebbles spilling out of his mouth and across the sidewalk. Then they zip-tie his hands behind his back and pull him inside the gates. Which means that someone has looked at his papers. Khafaji shouts, "Call Mr John. Mr John Parodi. He wants me there. Call Mr John Parodi, he knows who I am." It is unclear whether anyone can understand.

Khafaji waits for an hour. He starts to shiver, then closes his eyes and rests. Eventually, he hears a voice, "Yeah, that's him. You can release him. I'll take him." Khafaji turns and sees a black man whose face he doesn't recognize. The man is holding his ID and wallet.

"Khafaji. Rawls. We met last week. Parodi sent me. You're in trouble. Come on."

Rawls whistles as he hands Khafaji his wallet and papers. The man holds onto Khafaji's gun for an extra moment. Rawls intervenes. "I'll take that."

Khafaji feels around in his jacket pocket. "Where are my cigarettes?"

He regrets it immediately. The man at the gate shakes his head and says, "Sorry, man. You can get some at the Hajji shop." Khafaji looks around and notices a crumpled pack on the ground. He picks out a couple that are smokeable. He puts one in his vest pocket and the other in his mouth. His fingers look for his lighter. When he doesn't find it, he gives up.

Rawls and Khafaji walk over to the palace. They do not talk. When they pass someone smoking, Khafaji asks for a light. His appearance terrifies the man and he surrenders the lighter anyway.

When he walks into the building, Khafaji realizes it's come down to this. *You'll go to Parodi. You will talk with him. Then you will quit. You will set it down on paper. You will write a letter spelling it out. There should be at least one record of someone telling the Americans how dangerous it is to work for them.*

When Parodi sees Khafaji walk in, he blinks. He stares in disbelief, then mutters, "I can't fucking believe this shit. Straight out of camel-jockey central casting!"

He shakes his head, then yells, "Go clean yourself up and then come back, Khafaji!" He turns to a soldier typing on a computer. "Get him something decent to wear. Go down to the commissary if you have to."

Rawls takes Khafaji down the hall to a private bathroom. Khafaji locks the door and strips down to his underwear. He turns on the water and waits for it to get hot. He washes the blood and dirt from his face. He sticks his head under the faucet and lets the water run over his scalp. Then he turns the cold water on, and washes his face and head all over again. By the time he has done this twice, he is wide awake.

He is drying off with paper towels when a man arrives with a pair of oversize khaki pants and a plain white under-shirt. The pants are too big. Khafaji folds the waist over and then again and tucks in the undershirt. It looks odd, but he doesn't care. He puts on the sandals and looks into the mirror again. *Eyes tired. Chin covered in gray stubble. Cheeks hollow.* His fingers rub the whiskers of his new moustaches. *Everything comes back, doesn't it?*

Rawls is waiting outside the door when Khafaji opens it. They walk back to the office. Parodi doesn't get up when Khafaji comes in. He doesn't even look up from the papers on his desk.

"What the hell's going on, Khafaji? You're supposed to be in Kirkuk."

Khafaji sees that the conversation isn't going the way he imagined. "Sir, I got the message. I tried to call so many times. I thought it was an emergency. Olds told me to come fast."

Parodi finally looks up. He squints for a moment, then asks, "Olds told you to come back here?"

"Yes, sir."

"That's bullshit. Olds didn't say that."

"Sir?"

Parodi shakes his head in exasperation. "That's a load of shit. You scared? A bomb goes off and you come running home?"

Khafaji decides not to correct him. He stares at his feet. Parodi continues, "You're AWOL and you're in trouble. You want to tell us what really happened?"

"Sir?"

"We're going to need you to tell us how you pulled that stunt in Kirkuk."

"I did not pull any stunt, sir."

"Well, you need to tell us what you did."

Khafaji stares at the ground for a minute, then finally meets Parodi's gaze. "I was scared, sir."

"You like desk work, huh?" He laughs and Rawls joins in. "All right then. We'll put you back to work at the desk – we've got a lot of paper to get through. And we need to get through it fast. Rawls – want to fill him in?"

Rawls turns toward Khafaji, but his eyes never leave the ceiling. "Citrone was off the reservation. You probably know that by now. Seems he kept a girl. Seems he had something going with the girl's boss too."

"Pardon?"

"Did he ever talk to you about Zubeida Rashid?"

"Sir?"

"Woman by the name of Zubeida Rashid. Citrone was up to his neck with her. And deep in bed too. She runs a prostitution ring and some other angles as well. We visited her office, and found a treasure trove."

Parodi interrupts. "Normally, we'd hand this stuff over to the linguists. But in this case there's a problem."

Rawls continues, "Since you like desk work so much, you're going to go through what we found. It's all there next door.

It's a rush job. We need this stuff gone over yesterday. Get some coffee and get to work."

"I don't drink coffee," Khafaji objects.

"What?"

"Nothing."

Khafaji follows Rawls into the other office. There are rows of boxes in the corner. Most are full of files in Arabic. Some in English or French. "The entire contents of her office. We got her." Khafaji clears off a desk and begins to open the first box. Rawls sits down at the desk next to the door.

Khafaji's mind begins to wander as he opens the first files. More than once he imagines her holding the pen that touched the paper. Each file is a piece of her.

Most of the files are lecture notes. Irrelevant. At the university, she taught courses on organizational structure. That was her specialization. He looks over an old lecture on complex decision trees. Khafaji finds her dissertation and spends an hour trying to read it. The questions Zubeida asks are original. According to her, it was not ideology that shaped the Party's organization, but organizational shape that dictated its ideology.

In some old files, Khafaji finds transparencies of graphs depicting the development of networks, from simple vertical hierarchies and top-down chains of command into more horizontal ones with multiple nodes of decision-making. In the last transparencies of one lecture, Zubeida illustrates how even the most developed organizations can be undone by their own rigidity, by their own desire for control. She shows how most unexpected situations are the direct result of networks whose real linkages only become visible to planners after the fact.

In another box, he finds drafts of old conference papers

where Zubeida argued for hybrid models. Organizational structures where many actors could collaborate with one another in ways no single actor was ever conscious of. At the end of the paper, she concludes, "Organization is not structure. It is activity."

In the margins are remarks made by a stranger's hand. Notes urging the author not to pursue this argument. In the other boxes, which contain more recent material, these claims disappear. In the manuscript for a book entitled *The Administrative Vision and Method of the Leader* the arguments are the reverse of what she wrote earlier.

The first unusual document Khafaji finds is tucked deep inside a first-year course on statistics. He nearly passed over it. He looks at a memorandum dated July 2003. He looks at the smudged emblem of the General Command and blinks. He sits up in his chair and looks over at Rawls, who is right where he was two hours ago.

The memo is a response to an inquiry regarding logistics. At the bottom, in the hand Khafaji now recognizes as Zubeida's, he sees a familiar list: 126 Salhia, 44 Sheikh Maarouf, 19 Shawaka, 77 Fatih. Those addresses again. Khafaji skims through other boxes – more lecture notes and forms and reports submitted to the university administration. There is a lot of repetition and duplication. Everything is in perfect order; no one could claim the author was disorganized. And then, in another file for another statistics course, he comes across another communication between Zubeida and Party leadership, this one even more recent.

At this point, Khafaji goes through the remaining boxes, removing the statistics files set among the other course files. Eventually, he is sitting in front of a stack of dossiers, communiqués, memoranda, private letters, and notes. It is not clear what they all are, only that they would be damning if they landed in the Americans' hands.

Khafaji leans back in his chair. Only then does he notice that Rawls has left the room. Khafaji begins stuffing the correspondence into Manila envelopes. He puts those inside plastic binders and hides them in a desk drawer. Carefully, he puts the other materials back into the boxes they came from. He stacks the boxes and looks down the hall. He peers into Parodi's office. Empty. He walks down the hall to see the old office, but no one is there either. Only then does Khafaji look at his watch and see how late it is. Past 10 p.m. He walks back to the new office and takes the binders out of the drawer. He reconsiders the idea of leaving without saying anything, and decides to write a letter. After five minutes and five attempts at the first sentence, he gives up. *Just leave.* Khafaji sees a wool jacket hanging next to the door and borrows it.

Only when he hears the cheering downstairs does he realize that no one else is on the second floor. As he walks down the stairs, a man rushes by, shouting, "We got 'im, we got 'im!"

Khafaji walks through the cafeteria, and is surprised to see it packed to capacity. Some stare slack-jawed at the television sets. Others hug each other or slap each other's hands and dance. From the corner of the room, Jabbouri runs over to greet Khafaji. "Congratulations! It's unbelievable, isn't it?"

Khafaji stops and joins the others. At some point, he sets the binders on a chair next to him. They are watching a televised press conference. A man wearing combat fatigues reads a statement: *At approximately 8.26 p.m. local time, elements of the Fourth Infantry Division and Special Operating Forces raided a farm compound about fifteen kilometers south of Tikrit, capturing former Iraqi President Saddam Hussein. At least 600 troops were* *involved in the raid, which resulted in the capture of Hussein and two men, armed with AK-47s. Hussein was found hiding in a six-by-eight-foot crawl space below an outbuilding, armed with a pistol and carrying $750,000. Saddam Hussein was then transported by helicopter en route to a secure, undisclosed location without incident.*

Khafaji feels a slap on his back and turns around to see Louis Ford. They shake hands, even though Khafaji is not sure why. Everyone is congratulating each other, and Khafaji shakes dozens of hands before he is able to leave the room.

Khafaji reaches the front steps of Ibn Sina and takes out his last cigarette. Without a lighter, he puts it back. There is no one at the reception desk when he signs in. He looks down the corridor and into an empty room, then notices a crowd of nurses gathered around a television set. He is walking down the hall toward Mrouj's room when a nurse calls out, "It's after…" Then she smiles and says, "She's been moved!" She comes over and leads Khafaji down another hallway.

Mrouj is fast asleep when Khafaji walks in. He sets down the binders next to the bed, pulls up a chair, and waits. Every now and then, he strokes Mrouj's hair and touches her hand. It is quiet. Only when he looks around does he notice there's only one monitor. The only personal object is the poetry primer sitting on the nightstand. He looks for the other files he left, but they are gone.

An hour goes by. Khafaji sits there, aware that Mrouj is asleep for the night. He gets up and leaves quietly, but not before stacking the files on the nightstand. As he walks out, he asks the nurse, "Why have they moved her?"

The woman nods and smiles. "Her condition has finally started to improve. When you see the doctor, he can tell you about it. She's responding very well to the new medication."

He shakes her hand and says, "Thank you, you are a good person."

Khafaji pulls the borrowed jacket around him to keep the cold out. He reaches for his cigarettes, then walks as fast as he can toward the gates. Two American soldiers insist on slapping his hand and congratulating him before he can leave.

Sunday
14 December 2003

Khafaji sleeps deep and dreamlessly. He gets out of bed once in the early morning, then goes back to sleep. Each time he begins to wake up, he closes his eyes again. Eventually his stomach pushes him out from under the covers. He shuffles to the kitchen and goes to make tea. The water's off. He looks around for bottles of water, but can't find any. He finds a tin cup and holds it under the bathtub tap. A small stream spills out, enough to fill the cup. Khafaji feels the stubble on his cheeks and looks at himself in the mirror, then decides to give up and go out.

As he puts on his shoes, he notices a small stack of books sitting on the rug next to his reading chair. He looks at the titles. Nazik al-Malaika's diwan sits on top.

Khafaji smiles as he passes the guard on the second-floor landing. The young man stands and salutes as Khafaji walks by. The guards downstairs offer Khafaji tea, and for once he accepts. One man puts down his gun and puts three cubes of sugar in a small glass on the tray. He pours the tea and stirs. The clink of the spoon in the glass echoes up and down the stairwell. The man hands the tray to Khafaji. He takes the glass and sips. When he finishes that, they pour a second glass and then a third. For the next few minutes, they drink their tea together in silence.

When Khafaji finally sets down the glass, he thanks them. On the curb, he looks down the street. It's quiet. Some pedestrians walk past, their heads bowed, their eyes on the ground as they thread through the debris. Khafaji walks over to Abu Nuwas Street. He looks up at the thick black clouds gathering to the north of the city. The air feels cold and pregnant.

When he signs in at the reception desk, a new nurse smiles at Khafaji. He walks down the old corridor and only realizes his mistake after walking into Mrouj's old room, now occupied by a frightened old man. When he gets to her new room, Mrouj isn't there. Stacks of folders are strewn all over her bed, the nightstand, the chair and the windowsill. Khafaji starts to straighten the papers when he hears a clicking sound behind him. He turns to see a frail Mrouj standing in the doorway. Her hands grip the metal walker so hard her knuckles are white.

"Baba!"

Khafaji holds his daughter and begins to sob. They stand clutching each other in the middle of the room. Khafaji strokes her hair. Mrouj tries to soothe her father. When her legs begin to give out, Khafaji realizes that she is helping him to stand. She sits down on the bed and pulls the covers over her lap. She looks around, searching for something but not finding it.

"Thank God you're back safe," Mrouj says.

"The doctor says you're improving."

"I am." She reaches for a folder, flips through pages. "Let's talk about these."

She looks around some more, then shakes her head. "Baba, did you move the stuff on my bed? It was just here."

"I was tidying up," Khafaji protests. "I put it over there."

"I had them all organized. Let me see if I can put them back in order."

She shuffles the papers for a minute, then says, "OK. I found it. You know what they say?"

"Of course."

Mrouj calls his bluff. "So what do they say?"

"You were right, Mrouj. It wasn't about the sex."

She throws a Manila envelope onto the bed. "The girls weren't interpreters. This tells of a plot to overrun the Green Zone."

Khafaji nods. "Good."

Mrouj holds her finger in the air and spends another minute sorting through the folders before she finally says, "My notes. These are what I was looking for."

She scans them and begins, "Not surprisingly, it's mostly about your friend."

"She's not my friend."

"Fine. This woman who was running a ring. Only it wasn't a sex ring."

"It was something else. She's into organizational structure."

"Yeah, but not just in a theoretical way. For her, organization is everything."

"It's the means to every end."

"Right. Listen to this. It's from her paper, 'The Static and the Dynamic'. Here it is: 'Loose ends turn structure into network'."

"What does that mean?"

Mrouj laughs. "I don't know, but it does seem like a comment on the plot she was hatching."

"She's a loose end."

"No, this woman of yours is a gatherer of loose ends. That's what she is."

"She's not my woman," Khafaji protests, but Mrouj changes the subject.

"Baba, it's your turn to listen. The first memos here outline the main goal of the organization during the first months. To befriend and collect information on senior officials and CPA staff. But things changed when Citrone came into the picture."

"You mean when they fell in love?"

"Baba, just listen! Citrone's money was key. It helped them immensely. But what was more important was that he offered security. The houses were safe. Unbreachable. Untouchable. There was no safer place to be than in those houses."

"And it worked —"

"It worked as long as he bought a story. Zubeida tells him the girls need protection. She tells him this is a conservative Muslim society and we don't have sex and we don't talk about sex and we kill girls who have sex and so on."

"So, her houses are protected, thanks to Citrone."

"Doubly protected. The US Army keeps the Iraqis away. And the CPA keeps the Army away."

"You could use these safe houses for anything, then…"

"You could. And so could the Resistance. And they were."

"As long as no one finds out —"

"Baba!" Mrouj says. "This is my story to tell, so let me tell it. Someone does find out, only too late – but that comes afterwards. They start using these houses to move fighters in and out of the city. That was back in September. By then, they had dozens of legit CPA IDs for the girl interpreters. Who knows, maybe a few men were even dressing up in *abayas* and started posing as translators? In any case, by October, they are moving through checkpoints with ease. At least that's what your Professor is reporting."

"So who's she reporting to?"

Mrouj says nothing for a moment, then answers, "We don't know, do we?"

"We're lucky she's doing everything the old-fashioned way. Duplicate and saving a copy. Or triplicate."

"So we have no way of knowing whether these reports arrived? Or whether they were being read, and by whom."

"No, we know there is an ongoing conversation."

"An argument. Some just want to keep them as safe houses. Others are thinking about how to use them as forward bases. Launch attacks from the inside. They realize they'd better do it soon, since it looks like the wall is going to close up.

"That was proposed by the missing girl, Zahra Boustani. Here, you should read the last communiqué. It's signed by her." She hands the document to Khafaji. The language is telegraphic: *General Command. Inside American compound. Key offices and personnel (see memorandum, 10/07/03). Sizeable team, including explosives unit, sniper units. Probable martyrdom. Successful attack = American withdrawal.*

"Ridiculous, but plausible," Khafaji admits.

"There's more, Baba. But this is what I managed to put together."

"I didn't expect you to do all this."

"Maybe if you'd brought me something better to read I wouldn't have." She grins. For the first time in months, her smile suggests strength.

"Speaking of which, I found Nazik."

"So why didn't you bring it?"

"Tomorrow. I promise."

*

The sunset disappears behind dark clouds as Khafaji leaves the hospital. He lights a cigarette. He wraps his scarf tight around his neck and walks with his hands in his pockets. He looks over at the CPA palace, then turns and walks toward the front gate. As he leaves the Green Zone, he lights another cigarette and takes a deep breath.

By the time Khafaji walks up to the gate on his street, night has fallen. He enters the foyer and it's pitch black. He strikes a match to light the way. The electricity turns on just as he arrives on the first floor. Abu Ali opens the door and looks over the railing. He sees Khafaji, smiles and waits for him at the top of the stairs. When Khafaji finishes his climb, Abu Ali invites him in for tea. Khafaji accepts, mostly because he's too exhausted to say no. The first thing he hears when he walks in is the sound of the television. Then Umm Ali's sobs. She wipes her eyes and stands when she sees Khafaji. "God's grace! How are you? How is Mrouj? Are you fine? We were so worried."

"We're fine. It was all a case of mistaken..." Khafaji starts to explain, but realizes they don't care. They never cared. They're just neighbors. Abu Ali is already flipping through the channels. One shows US officers presenting details of the capture. Blueprints of the house. Images of helicopters hovering over palm orchards. The picture of a table of evidence: piles of guns, grenades, explosives, money. An American officer points at each item with a small wooden stick. Khafaji almost laughs when he notices the familiar red duffel bags behind the table.

Eventually they watch the clip of a bearded man being pulled from a small hole in the ground. The third time they see him, he looks more animal than man. He is half-asleep or drugged. Umm Ali leans forward and starts yelling at the screen, "What kind of man are you?"

She shouts and tears roll down her cheeks. "Goddamn you, Saddam! You couldn't even defend yourself! Look what you put us through!" She falls back on the couch and sobs. Khafaji drinks his tea in silence. The footage repeats over and over in loops. They continue sipping tea and watching as Abu Ali flips through the channels. In another clip, an American doctor in latex gloves inspects Saddam's thick mat of hair, then prods his mouth with a small stick. Umm Ali leans forward and yells at the screen again. "You couldn't even stand up and fight, could you?"

Khafaji finally turns away and puts down his tea. He puts his hands on his knees as if to leave, but the screen won't let him go. They watch different channels as if this were something happening somewhere else to other people. They watch it some more. Each time Jaafar pours more tea, and each time Khafaji sips it. Each time Saddam Hussein is pulled out of his hole for the cameras, Umm Ali curses him. Each time he sticks out his tongue for the doctor, she curses him louder. Then she goes back to wailing and sobbing on the couch. Today is the end of something. Khafaji decides to leave before he starts crying too.

Khafaji says, "Thank you for the tea. Goodnight." Abu Ali only manages to wave to him. Ali walks in as Khafaji leaves. He greets Khafaji then whispers, "I need to speak to you in private."

"Sure. Come over, I was just leaving."

"I'll be right there. I just have to get something to show you."

Khafaji opens the door to his apartment and smiles when he sees the books sitting there in a pile. He goes to the kitchen to get a knife. When he cuts the string, the books tumble across the floor.

Ali knocks on the door, and Khafaji calls out, "Come in,

it's open." Ali walks in, his face blank. He looks at Khafaji and says nothing. After a long pause he waves some pages of paper in the air, then drops them onto the table.

Khafaji gets up. He looks at Ali, picks up the pages. They are printouts of pictures. Photographs. It takes a while for him to understand what they mean.

Khafaji is looking at an image of Checkpoint Three. He sees a crowd of people waiting at the gates. Khafaji sees an American soldier pointing at the lens. In the bottom right corner, he reads the date and time of the photograph.

Khafaji looks up at Ali, puzzled. Then worried. In the next image, Khafaji sees the weeping woman. Then he sees his own face clear as the day the photo was taken. In the next photograph, there he is again. Each has its own time-date stamp. Khafaji begins to shake, and throws them on the ground.

"What is it you do for them?" Ali's voice is rough. He clears his throat and waits. Khafaji says nothing.

"Pictures mean nothing, Brother Muhsin. And in any case, I don't take you for a collaborator." Khafaji looks at the carpet and says nothing.

Khafaji breaks the silence. "What do you want?"

"Patience."

"I don't understand."

"Just be patient, that's all, until we understand the situation better. We have no problem with you working for the Americans. On the contrary, we might welcome the idea."

"I've resigned."

"I think you should stay on."

"I said I resigned."

"Don't rush. Like I said, be patient. We'll give you time before we let you know what we have decided." Ali turns toward the door.

As he reaches the hallway, he adds, "I'm glad to see you found your books again."

Then he walks out.

Khafaji ignores the hours as they go by. He ignores the darkness and the solitude, and they ignore him. Outside, a burst of gunfire tries to interrupt the silence, but dies too quickly.

A book lies open in Khafaji's lap. Nazik al-Malaika's diwan. He only had to touch the cover before the lines came back to him. *That voice, your voice, will return. To my life, to the years' audition. Haggard with the scent of a sad evening... It will return with a strange lyrical echo. Filling night and streams with lullaby sounds.* He recites the lines to himself. The words fill the empty apartment and come back to him like someone else's voice. Mrouj's voice. Zubeida's voice. Suheir's voice. And other voices too.

It is early morning when the electricity jolts on again. The explosion of light kills the soft halo that Nazik's language had cast around Khafaji as he sat in the dark. He puts the book down. Water begins to hiss in the pipes, and he runs to the bathroom to fill the tub. In the kitchen he fills the kettle. Then he fills bottle after bottle from the tap. When he finishes with that, he finds a small Turkish coffee cup and walks to the cabinet in the dining room. He removes the bottle from its hiding place and pours himself a shot of Black Label. Two more bottles. Two more weeks.

Khafaji walks through the apartment turning off light switches one by one. First the bedroom. Then the bathroom. Then the kitchen and dining room. He sits down in his reading chair and sets the whisky beside him. He takes a sip and feels the heat flowing down his throat, then spreading through his veins and across his chest. *Once, the tongues of fire licked at our house and spread and spread, chewing at the door, setting fire to the tassels on the curtains. It consumed our cheeks, our lips, our fingertips...* Outside, a small clicking noise begins to sound. Tick. Tick. Tick. Soft, imperceptible at first, then growing louder and louder. Tick. Tick. Tick. Ssss. Unmistakable. The sound of rain falling from the sky. Drops hitting every surface under the skies. The balconies, the windowsills, water tanks on the roofs, cars, men, and the thirsty streets and the dusty heaps of garbage. Slowly at first, the parched surfaces crack and spit like drum skins. Then louder, more violently, with the slapping, tossing sound of creeks and rivers. The skies open up and a cold torrent drops onto Baghdad. Washing away the dust from the trees and buildings, washing the dirt from the concrete and roads. Below, Khafaji hears men shouting as they rush indoors. Across the city, thunder begins to crash and rumble. Lightning flashes against the window, then vanishes back across the night.

Khafaji picks up Nazik al-Malaika's diwan and places it on his lap. He takes a deep breath and opens it to the last page. Only then, after he turns off the lamp, does he begin to read again. And only then do the lines begin to pour again into his ears. Only then do they wash across the dry shores of his mind.

> *That voice will return*
> *To my life, to the audition of the evening.*
> *I will hear your voice when I am*
> *Amidst Nature's commotion, in moments of madness,*
> *When echoes of thunder evoke*
> *Stories sung by Scheherazade*
> *To that mad king*
> *On winter nights.*

I will hear your voice every evening
When light dozes off and worries take refuge in dreams.
When desires and passions slumber, when ambition sleeps
When life sleeps, and time remains awake, sleepless
Like your voice.

Acknowledgements

There are many places where poetry plays a key public role. But perhaps it is only in Iraq that the public repertoire of poetry includes modernist, often experimental verse. Statues of poets are urban landmarks in Baghdad, Basra and Najaf, giving names to prominent public squares and the neighborhoods around them. In contemporary Iraq, Shiite religious parties routinely sponsor poetry performances just as the Baathist regime once did, and before them the Communist Party and the Hashemite court. Even when composed as lines on the page, Iraqi poetry is never silent. Entire poems are memorized and debated, individual lines are relished and used in everyday speech. To educated Iraqis, none of the poets in Khafaji's mind would be unknown. In fact, many of them are household names. *Baghdad Central* offers a fleeting glimpse of this rich corpus of Iraqi poetry. In the attempt to render these poets into English, I was fortunate to rely on the work of the literary translators credited below:

Extracts of 'Myths' and 'To Poetry' by Nazik al-Malaika, translated by Ferial Jabouri Ghazoul. © *Modern Poetry in Translation* 2002, reproduced with permission.

Extracts of 'The River God' by Nazik al-Malaika, translated by Ibtisam Barakat. © *Modern Poetry in Translation* 2002, reproduced with permission.

Extracts of 'The Hijra to God' by Nazik al-Malaika, translated by Saleh Alyafai and Jenna Abdul Rahman. © *Modern Poetry in Translation* 2002, reproduced with permission.

Extract of 'Bridge of Old Wonders' by Muzaffar al-Nawwab, translated by Saadi Simawe and Carol Bardenstein. © *Modern Poetry in Translation* 2002, reproduced with permission.

Extract of 'God's Freedom Lovers' by Ahmed Hardi, translated by Muhamad Tawfiq Ali. © *Modern Poetry in Translation* 2002, reproduced with permission.

Extracts of 'Sleepers, Wake!' by Ma'ruf al-Rusafi, translated by A. J. Arberry. © Cambridge University Press 1965, reproduced with permission.

Other translations from Arabic mine.

Thanks to the following writers, journalists and scholars for educating me on modern Iraq and American counter-insurgency: Nadje Sadig Al-Ali, Sinan Antoon, Fadhil al-Azzawi, Shimon Ballas, Orit Bashkin, Hanna Batatu, Hassan Blasim, Sargon Boulus, Rajiv Chandrasekaran, Terri DeYoung, Joy Gordon, Lisa Hajjar, Jabra Ibrahim Jabra, Hussein N. Kadhim, Laleh Khalili, Dina Rizk Khoury, Joseph Sassoon, Anthony Shadid, Samuel Shimon, Saadi Simawe, Ali al-Wardi, and Saadi Youssef. Thanks also to the many Iraqis who showed me what steadfastness means and also how to make *shakirlamma*. Thanks to family and friends and everyone else who told me the other stories that found their way into this book.